WHISTLE-BLOWERS

a KATE ADAMS novel

HOLLY A. BELL

ISBN: 0692073027
ISBN-13: 978-0-692-07302-5

DEDICATION

To Robert, Maria, Cody, and Ian

ACKNOWLEDGMENTS

Writing by its very nature is a solitary pursuit, but it wouldn't be possible without the encouragement and inspiration of others. While many of those individuals prefer to remain anonymous, there are two I wish to thank publically. First, my editor Joanie Chevalier, who was sensitive to my characters' voices while at the same time keeping my prose lucid. And last, but certainly not least, my husband Eldon, who has learned to embrace my writing habit and other assorted flaws.

1
LONDON

The hotel was intentionally difficult to find, identifiable only by its red awning and bronze plaque, *The Harborage, Private*. It was an upscale British boutique affair with a discreet doorman who lurked behind the blackened glass façade until his services were required. A cab drew to a stop at the curb and a young man stumbled out into the bright sunlight without tipping the driver. Tipping rarely occurred to him and his tendency for wearing cheap, artistically torn blue jeans with a simple red t-shirt seldom caused anyone to expect one. *Damn that sun*, was the only thought occupying his mind.

Even in the dark wrap-around sunglasses the sunlight caused the young man's eyes to sting. He stretched his sleeve downward as far as he could to cover his nearly transparent skin, its pallor a symptom of his propensity to break out in hives and itchy blisters every time he spent more than a few minutes in the sun.

The anxiety caused by his social awkwardness welled up in him as he approached the hotel's desk clerk.

"Um, hullo," he choked out, "I'm here to check into my room."

"Your name, please?" the clerk's cheeks dimpled as a broad customer service smile lit her face.

"Liam Tremblay."

The desk clerk's eyes grew wide at the sight of Mr. Tremblay's room reservation and prompted her to discretely signal the bellman in case the young man had any immediate needs that required attending to. Fearing she had misjudged the man standing across the counter from her, she immediately revised her impression from dim-witted commoner to merely eccentric.

"I've found your reservation Mr. Tremblay, may I see your passport please."

"Yes, of course." Liam fumbled with his messenger bag before handing over the Canadian passport he'd been given.

"Thank you Mr. Tremblay, you're all set. Follow the hallway on your left to the elevator and be sure to swipe your room key in the slot provided before pressing Floor P for the Presidential Suite. Will you be needing any help with your luggage?"

Not having any luggage beyond his messenger bag, the young man was befuddled. After an uncomfortably long pause he managed, "Um, no thanks. My, um, luggage will be arriving by courier later." He snatched the key from the desk clerk's hand too quickly and scurried for the elevator.

The Presidential Suite welcomed Liam with a wall

of windows overlooking London. But what caused him to abandon his messenger bag in the entryway was the Steinway grand piano sitting atop a circular rug in the salon. He sat at the bench and tested a few keys for tunefulness.

Bowing his head over the keyboard, Liam began to play Chopin's tragic Polonaise in C Minor, Opus 40, Number 2 with the intensity of a concert pianist. He played with his entire body, the muscles in his jaw flexing as his shoulder-length hair fell in front of his closed eyes. It wasn't until the second sharp knock on the door that his concentration was interrupted.

Through the peephole he could see two men standing in the hallway next to a luggage cart stacked with boxes. He opened the door and ushered them in.

"I can see why you wanted a space with a piano, you're very good."

Liam shrugged off the complement.

After the luggage cart was parked inside the door, the three men walked to the grouping of sofas and chairs beside the piano. Liam chose a seat that allowed him a view of London and the security of the piano at his periphery.

"You come with a good reference," Liam began as a calming sensation washed over him. "I've been working with our mutual acquaintances for nearly two years now. They've been good to me."

"And we understand you've been good to them as well," the balding, heavier set of the pair responded as the second man remained a silent, shifty-eyed observer. "We've been looking for a good, reputable hacker for quite a while."

Liam winced, "I'm not a hacker gentlemen. Hackers do what they do for kicks; I'm a businessman. What you've been looking for is a cyber mercenary like myself who is willing to do the things for businesses and countries that they can't do for themselves. After all gentlemen, survival is highly competitive." Liam added a contrived grin. Meeting with clients was the only setting in which he felt in complete control of the people around him. He set the terms. He made the demands. Being in a position to say *take it or leave it* gave him momentary confidence and put him at ease. The process was a well-rehearsed dance and Liam was leading.

"I assume our mutual friend has told you which of your services we are looking for?"

"Yes, and I assume he has told you how I expect to be compensated?"

"He did, but we are still trying to secure asylum for you once the job is finished."

"I see. Is it going to be a problem?"

"We don't anticipate so. Especially once your results begin to become public."

"Excellent." Liam clapped his hands together and stood, "Let's see what you've brought."

The three of them proceeded to cut packing tape and open boxes.

"We've brought all the computer equipment you asked for. You can work out of this suite until we find a more permanent location for you."

"It's all here, shall we begin?"

The balding, heavyset man tapped some keys on his phone, "I think you'll will find the money is in your account and the documents in your inbox."

Liam clicked around his phone, "I see that they are. Stop by any time gentleman."

"We'll be seeing you regularly."

Liam escorted the men out before putting out the do not disturb sign and throwing the locks. He returned to the piano bench and picked up the Polonaise precisely where he had left off.

2
PALMER, ALASKA

Professor Kate Adams gasped and opened her eyes wide as the pain unhurriedly seeped from her shoulder through her arm and into her fingers before dripping steadily away onto the carpet near where her golden retriever Zoe napped fitfully beside her chair.

"Are you all right?" a woman roaming the nearby stacks asked with mechanical obligation.

"I'm fine," Kate responded, forcing her grimace into a smile, "I'm sorry if I alarmed you. It's just an old football injury that flares up every once in a while."

The woman offered a nod and expression of relief that society's norms no longer obligated her to additional action or conversation. Kate was always grateful when questions about her recurring pain were deflected. The actual events surrounding her injury were best reflected on privately.

Zoe rolled over onto her back begging a belly rub.

Kate obliged. The dog had recently completed emotional support animal training and had the vest to prove it, but sometimes the vest made her itchy. Kate reached under it and scratched Zoe's belly as the dog emitted a humming sigh.

Kate told herself the primary emotion Zoe would be supporting was her own guilt about leaving the dog at home all day while she worked, but deep down she knew otherwise. Zoe also provided "fur therapy" on campus for students who needed a break from their day. It was her dog's popularity that had driven Kate to flee her office and seek refuge in an isolated corner on the library's second floor near a window that looked out on a snow-covered Pioneer Peak. The winter break was approaching and Kate needed freedom from distractions to finish her grading. It had been nearly a year and a half since she had been kidnapped and left to die, but Kate's ability to concentrate remained impaired.

At the next table a local syndicated cartoonist who journeyed regularly to the campus library in search of solace and inspiration had sketched a comical moose and polar bear holding ice-filled beverages in their anthropomorphic hands. Thought bubbles devoid of text loomed vacantly above their heads. The artist shook his head and mumbled something to himself before flipping to the next page of his sketchpad.

The creative process should never be watched, Kate thought to herself. *It destroys the illusion of brilliance one gets from viewing the finished product.*

The cartoonist must have felt the heat of Kate's gaze because he lifted his head to smile at her. Kate blushed as she quickly looked away.

"Busted," she whispered to Zoe who looked up in anticipation of a command or possibly a treat. Kate pulled a small doggie biscuit from her pocket and bestowed it upon Zoe to reward her attentiveness. Zoe seemed pleased with herself as she ground up the biscuit. Kate patted her soft head and cooed 'good dog' sounds near her ear.

Perking her ears abruptly, Zoe stopped chewing and looked alertly toward the stairs at the far end of the room, her tail thumping rhythmically on the floor. Kate turned her head in the direction of Zoe's stare in time to see her friend Joe and another man appear at the top of the stairs. Joe was a CIA psychologist with whom Kate had spent nearly a year living in a remote Alaska cabin where she unwittingly helped the CIA solve a case, forever altering the course of her life.

Joe knew much about Kate, but she knew little about him. Their previous assignment had not allowed her to know his last name, where he had lived, or if he had a wife and children. Kate was happy with the arrangement, preferring to keep Joe at arms' length. They had remained friends, but Kate knew Joe was perpetually an Agency employee first. That meant part of his job might be analyzing the state of Kate's post-kidnapping emotional health, making their relationship indistinct at times between doctor/patient and friends.

Kate stood and hugged Joe when he arrived at the table. Zoe was also standing and Joe made a point of scratching her head and telling her he had missed her too. His companion was introduced as Mr. Elliot Poe of the National Security Agency.

Looking around Joe asked, "Is there somewhere

more private we could talk?"

"If you don't mind broom closets, we can use my office."

The cartoonist watched them quizzically as they walked away. Kate hoped they had provided the inspiration he was looking for.

Kate fetched an additional chair from the classroom adjacent to her office so Mr. Poe would have a place to sit. The trio sat in a triangle nearly touching elbows. A shoehorn would have been required to wedge in a fourth person.

"To what do I owe the pleasure of your and Mr. Poe's visit?" Kate nodded toward Mr. Poe.

"It was my idea. I asked Joe to introduce me to you Dr. Adams," Mr. Poe pleaded with apology in his voice, "I need your help."

"Slow down a minute Elliot. We need to give Kate a little background information first."

"That would be great," Kate sunk back into her chair and intertwined her fingers as she rested her hands in her lap.

"Before I say anything, please remember that whatever we say here is classified and cannot leave this room," Joe raised his eyebrows in request of agreement.

Kate nodded. "I'm officially an Agency contractor now, so the room is secured. We can speak freely and privately here."

"Kate, Elliot and I have been working together, as part of a team on a rather unique national security situation. You have probably heard the news reports about the person who claims to have stolen large amounts of classified information off NSA computers and is slowly releasing it onto the dark web."

"Of course, 'The Executive' I believe they call him. Because he has such high level information."

"Yes, that's the one. There has been concern and speculation that an executive-level employee at NSA or some other intelligence branch is leaking the information to whomever is posting it to the dark web. But that premise is a bit problematic for me for a couple of reasons."

"How so?"

"The psychological profile of past agency employees who have gone rogue is fairly consistent. They're usually smart, but lazy, believing their superior intellect entitles them to privilege rather than an expectation of hard work. While they may think their intelligence should be self-evident, their lack of demonstrable results means they don't get promoted as quickly as their peers. They feel overlooked and left behind so they become frustrated with the system and turn on it."

"If it were an inside person stealing and revealing secrets they would have to be at a very high level within the Agency to have access to all the information they've released. However, that is not consistent with the psychological profile because the leaker should never have been promoted to an executive level. Of course, it could be someone who provides support to an executive and has access to information. Like one of their tech people or even an administrative assistant, but we haven't been able to come up with any viable suspects. There are also reasons to believe it is not someone on the inside."

Joe squeezed open the metal clasp on a manila envelope and handed Kate one of the papers inside.

"What you have in your hand is the list of the twenty-five pieces of alleged classified information The Executive has released about the U.S. government so far. You'll notice about a third of them are highlighted in yellow." Kate nodded. "The ones highlighted are not true."

Kate knitted her brows and leaned forward in her chair, "So what are you thinking? Is this person a foreign propagandist set on swaying public opinion about the U.S. government?"

"Bingo, but it's not just the U.S. government." Joe handed Kate the remaining papers, "The information he is spreading covers many countries. While our allies are not telling us where the fact versus fiction line is drawn, they have confirmed some of the information being spread is false. Yet, The Executive claims all the information has come from U.S. and foreign intelligence databases. Based on the information we actually do have about foreign governments, we've been able to confirm or deny some things, but there are others we are unable to know if its true or not."

"That's what I'm hoping you can help with Dr. Adams," Mr. Poe added.

"Please, call me Kate. What is it exactly you think I can do for you?"

3

WASHINGTON, DC

Harrison Steyn was having one of those days. He had
served as Chief Aide to the Principle Deputy Director of
National Intelligence for more than a year. Yet, today it
was as though he had entered NSA Headquarters for the
first time and was struggling to simply find where the
men's room was located. As a career intelligence
bureaucrat, he was a man who knew how to get things
done, but today his edge of experience was dull. The
Executive case had become a hot potato that no one
wanted to touch. A certain level of paranoia had set in
within the building. Being asked to help with an aspect
of the case had begun to be interpreted as a sign that
someone within the division or office might be under
investigation. He had never seen anything like it in his
eighteen years in the intelligence community.

The fact that there were no solid suspects made
the problem even more perplexing. The oddly delusion

air that had descended upon the place made him wonder how many staff members had guilty consciences. Perhaps they were wondering if that slight slip of the tongue at a cocktail party or a secure system password written on a Post-It Note and stuck inside a desk drawer might have contributed to The Executive's information.

"I don't give a flying flip about the details, just find it and secure the consarn thing!" Principal Deputy Director of National Intelligence, Marc Lanser slammed the handset down and looked up as Harrison stepped into his office. "Cheese and rice! We've had a major infiltration into the National Security Agency's computers and all I get from the technology bozos is that they can't find any evidence of a breach. There has to be an access point. For the love of dog, someone has the information and is putting it on the dark web!"

PDD Lanser slapped his hand on a stack of files atop his desk and bolted straight up out of his chair before realizing he had nowhere to go, no action he could take to solve the problem that required him to leave his desk. He flopped heavily back into his ergonomically optimized chair and frowned.

Harrison suppressed a smile. He was always amused by how Deputy Director Lanser's Midwestern Catholic school values prohibited him from swearing even when his face was red with rage. The punishment delivered by the nuns at St. Peter's for uttering obscenities must have been swift and harsh.

"I want you to oversee this investigation personally," PDD Lanser barked as he poked a finger in Harrison's direction, "and report back to me daily with updates. I don't trust that weasel Faulkner in

13

technology."

Harrison wondered why Lanser always called Faulkner a weasel, he seemed quite competent and straightforward to him. He guessed it was because Lanser didn't fully comprehend what Faulkner or any of the other techs ever told him. Technological proficiency was not his strength. The Luddite still banged out correspondence on an electric typewriter he kept in his office near the window and had documents delivered by hand whenever possible. An extra administrative assistant had to be hired to scan his correspondence for archiving before they were sent out, still creating the dreaded electronic copy PDD Lanser feared.

"This is why I don't trust technology," Lanser bellowed, "makes it too easy to steal information. The 'cloud' is the worst thing to happen in the history of the intelligence community. We didn't have nearly as many data breaches when we typed and hand delivered messages. I'd trust one of our couriers over email any day of the week. Always best to have eyes on the intelligence, who knows where those bits and bytes go out there in the ether."

"Well, I suspect Faulkner does," Harrison replied, anxious to diffuse his boss's heated, yet non-profane rant. "I'll work with him and report back."

As the NSA's Director of Cyber Security, Faulkner wasn't good at putting technical information into sentences non-technical people like PDD Lanser could understand. Creating those sentences would be Harrison's job.

Harrison left PDD Lanser muttering to himself and descended into the third level basement of the building where he shuddered slightly as he stepped off the elevator. Looking around at the dim space, he saw a room full of programmers and data analysts huddled around computer screens in pods of four or five.

The weather down here is always florescent, Harrison muttered to himself. He tried to suppress the shock he felt from suddenly being immersed into a grim, windowless space sprinkled with asymmetrically flickering computer screens. *I really hate it down here.*

He grabbed the arm of the next man who walked by, "I'm looking for Faulkner. You know where I can find him?"

"Private office, back right corner. You might wanna call him first, he doesn't answer the door unless he's expecting someone. You'll need to use the phone on the wall next to the elevator, cell phones don't work down here in the Salt Mine."

Harrison called and Faulkner met him halfway to his office, "Hey, man," Faulkner said as stuck his hand out to shake Harrison's, "welcome to the Salt Mine. I'm really sorry you had to come down here though. I still don't have anything new to report."

"That's okay," Harrison said as Faulkner laid his hand onto the biometric scanner that unlocked his office door, "you can start by telling me what you told PDD Lanser."

The pair sat at Faulkner's small office table stacked high with reams of computer printouts. Faulkner pushed aside one of the stacks creating enough room to lay the yellow pad containing his notes on the table. Harrison was forced to balance his own notepad in his lap.

Faulkner removed a dull pencil from behind his ear and used it to point at the first note on his pad.

"There are several clues we look for when trying to determine if we've been infiltrated by a hacker. The problem in this case is we haven't found any. No one's password has been changed without his or her knowledge and we've found no cases of anyone being locked out of any programs. We've found no evidence of malware or spyware, no signs of malicious popup messages or emails that were detected and scrubbed. There are no internal or external data downloads, no down time in our security software, and no indication of infiltration from other more classified means of investigating that I can't talk about specifically. The bottom line," Faulkner shrugged, "is I have no reason to believe anyone from outside the agency has hacked into our computer system or that anyone inside the agency downloaded the materials that have been released. As far as we can tell, they didn't get the information from our systems."

"I hate to ask this, but if there is no evidence of a computer breach, have you thoroughly checked out my boss? I've always been a little concerned that his paper memos are flying around out there in the breeze somewhere."

"We did consider that, but no, he's not a viable suspect. While some of his typed memos are included in the publicly released materials, most of the materials didn't originate on paper or with the PDD's office. Several of the released correspondence would never have even crossed his desk and we don't have any evidence that he or anyone on his staff ever accessed them electronically. By the way, that takes you off our radar too, which is the only reason we're having this conversation."

"Well, I was pretty sure it wasn't me, but I'm glad you concur," Harrison smiled as Faulkner offered a nervous chuckle.

"I'm in an uncomfortable position here. Everyone is looking at me and my team to figure this one out, but I don't think I'm going to have any good answers on this from an IT perspective. My best guess is that we have a mole who was able to get ahold of these documents internally. But again, with security protocols being what they are, I don't know how that could happen. All offices are secured and any documents need to be placed into a safe or closed on a computer screen before anyone else is allowed to enter the room. Yet, I'd be looking at our people including contractors, mail clerks, and the lot and not hackers on this one. I'd also recommend trying to find who is posting this stuff publicly on the dark web. It may be our thief or another person involved. We may have another Julian Assange on our hands."

"And an Edward Snowden." Harrison raised his eyebrows and looked around the room, "I don't know Faulkner, you seem to have a lot of documents sitting around unsecured in this office so it wouldn't surprise me if others do too."

Faulkner emitted his nervous laugh again, "You would be seriously disappointed in the intelligence value of these printouts. In fact, I took them out of the safe specifically for your visit. These are all the negative results of our search for a hacker or mole so far. I just wanted to illustrate to you how much we've done and inform you they are all at your disposal should you want them."

Harrison looked around the room again, "That's a lot of documentation, but it couldn't hurt to have one more set of eyes look at it, could it?"

"No, not at all. If you'd like I can have them copied, categorized and sent to your office by the end of the week."

"Yes, I think I'd like that."

Faulkner returned to PDD Marc Lanser's office and shared what he had learned from Faulkner in language Lanser might be able to understand.

"I'm having him send over the reports and database printouts in case we need them as part of our investigation. I expect there will be 10 to 15 boxes of information delivered next week. In the meantime, we really need to do as Faulkner suggests and start looking at people on the inside."

"Well, monkey trumpets, that's not the answer I was looking for at all! There has got to be more he can do to find the hacker."

Harrison uncharacteristically raised his voice, "Dammit Marc, what the hell? Have you not heard a word I've said?"

Lanser bolted out of his chair, "Hey, don't use that language and tone of voice with me!"

"In the name of all that is secular and non-vulgar, you don't have a hacker, you might have a mole Marc. A mole!"

4
LONDON

Liam played a computer's keyboard even more adroitly than the piano, accomplishing much in his first day at the task. Mere minutes after the first of the documents had spilled onto Liam's website, the balding, heavyset man returned with another man Liam had never met. Only this time there was no dialogue about deals. They had returned as overseers, closely controlling Liam's access to his beloved keyboard.

"Only the task at hand," they had told him. There would be no outside communication, no surfing the web, no leaving the suite.

It was on the second day that a third man appeared. He stood stiffly upright and entered the suite with a deliberant gait, his footfalls pronounced on the parquet floor. The right corner of his mouth was turned upward in the self-satisfied smirk of a man in control of all things he desired to influence. He looked around the room with the bearing of a conqueror, his hands resting on his hips. This was his territory now and Liam's contrived bravado seeped away, reducing him to his defensive, awkward core. Not only had the dance music changed, Liam instinctively knew this man intended to tango with his date. Liam scratched at his abdomen where a cluster of hives was surfacing as he stood up on his gangly legs to confront his subduer.

"You have no right to hold me here against my will. You have implemented parameters I never agreed to. I can't work under such conditions, it's outside the bounds of our movement."

"Your movement?" the man threw his head back in a fit of feigned cachinnation. "You mean your beloved commune. What do you think this is, the 1960s? Communes are for hippies and flower-power and all that shit."

"You really don't understand us, do you? The hippies of the 60's thought they could change the world with peace, love, organic food, and the occasional bombing of a Federal Building, an ironic twist on their peace value I might add. Idiots. What a screwed-up movement. No man, we're not hippies. Do we want to change the world? Sure, but we do it by creating our own world, with pure freedom and no government. We have skills the hippies only dreamed of. We've created the dark web with its own communications networks, currency, businesses, and culture. Hell, we've become so mainstream even lit net businesses are taking Bitcoin as payment. We have the skills to make change and bring down the government; we're no hippies sticking flowers in the barrels of guns. We represent the new world and anything I do for you, I do for the *movement* first. And in our world we don't hold anyone against their will, all people are free."

"We're not holding you, Mr. Tremblay, we're protecting you. I don't think you realize how many people are already looking for you. It's not safe for you to return to the commune, the online community, or any other place yet. Besides, I want to expand the scope of your work and it will require us to be in constant communication. Don't worry, we'll be taking you someplace soon where you'll be able to move around a bit, do some grocery shopping and other normal everyday stuff. By the way, the Americans and the press are calling you 'The Executive.'"

"A classic American corporate title. I'm offended. I'll never feel like my life is normal as long as you're 'protecting' me. I feel imprisoned here. You say you're protecting me and giving me a safe place to live, but there is a price and I pay it every day by doing your bidding. That's not the world I wish to live in. I agreed to a specific contract, I don't wish to do anything else for you. I'm beginning to realize you have other goals, I don't support."

"I think you'll find we're willing to make your life a whole lot easier than if the American intelligence community gets ahold of you."

"Hell, man. Other than the people in this room, no one even knows who I am. I've been dark for a long time now. I provide my own security."

"And do you really trust those of us in the room not to expose you?" Liam remained quiet. "To show our benevolence and make your stay a little more comfortable, we've asked your girlfriend Lana if she'd like to come stay with you. She has agreed."

"Hey, she's not *my* girlfriend, I don't own her, Lana does what she wants. I'm happy to hear she's coming though. Sometimes being with her helps me focus better and remember what I'm fighting for. Can I get back to writing the new encryption program now? I need to make sure the Bitcoin you're paying me is untraceable. Ha! There I go, creating my own security again." The sarcasm in The Executive's remark intensified as his forced grin melted into a clenched-tooth grimace while he glared at his protector.

5
BERLIN

Perhaps thinking about returning to the field would have been more difficult than just leaping back in, but Kate couldn't help but feel things had moved too quickly. One day she was grading papers, the next she was on a small government jet enroute to Germany, fully immersed in the mission. Throughout her struggle with trauma, Kate always knew intuitively she needed to get back to the field before she could fully heal. This just wasn't how she envisioned it happening.

Don't think about it. Work on the task at hand. But it was too late. Kate felt like a teetering glass of liquid, wobbling to and fro, walking closer to the edge of the table threatening to throw itself over and spill its contents onto the floor. Standing abruptly, Kate made her way to the lavatory where the tension welled up inside as her breathing became shallow. She struggled, gasping audibly before her ability to draw a complete breath returned. Her mind reached out to steady the glass.

Just a few more deep breaths, she coaxed as the tingling in her hands began to fade away and the muscles in her face and between her shoulder blades began to release their grip. This was not a convenient time for a full-blown panic attack; it would have to wait until later. Kate splashed water on her face before exiting the lavatory and returning to her seat at the plane's table.

"The session you need to attend is by a group called Programmers for Peace and Freedom," Joe slid the dense Global Programming Conference brochure toward Kate and tapped his finger where he wanted her to look, "here, this session, tomorrow at 3pm."

"Developing a Culture of Independence Online," Kate read from the brochure just as the jet hit turbulence causing Kate to grip the arms of her seat.

"It's as good a place as any to start and with your academic credentials you're a natural attendee at this conference. Just poke around the Programmers for Peace and Freedom group and see what you can find out. If you can actually infiltrate the group that would be preferable, but if not, make some contacts."

"It will be fun to play the radical for a while. I think you'll enjoy the paper I'm presenting during the conference's early morning session on how to use Bitcoin as the new Swiss bank account."

Elliot chimed in, "Just find out what you can and make some connections. We're hoping that somewhere within Programmers for Peace and Freedom lies a person with six or fewer degrees of separation from whoever is releasing the classified information onto the dark web. Maybe one of the members was their professor or a mentor or somebody's brother-in-law, who knows? The group is known to support whistleblowers like the person or people releasing the documents we're dealing with now. Last year they brought in Edward Snowden via Skype as their conference speaker. One thing is certain, if someone within PPF has a connection to The Executive they will be proud of it. But first, they'll have to trust you and believe you're on their side. That may take some time."

Kate continued to page through the conference brochure. All the other sessions appeared to be boilerplate academic conference fare on topics like programming effective risk management algorithms for financial markets and using the Python programming language for operations research. The conference was large and the Programmers for Peace and Freedom were hosting only a single session. A virtual blip in the program that would go unnoticed by most who would remain unaware of their radical, anti-government leanings.

The air they were flying through had smoothed. Elliot sipped coffee. Joe starred out the window with his chin in his hand. Kate tapped the eraser of her pencil against the edge of the table as uneasy thoughts moved through her head. The cockpit door opened and the captain, a tall, slim man with sandy blond hair emerged. Kate sat up a little straighter as he walked toward the small table the trio was gathered around.

"Dr. Adams," he extended his hand, "I'm Spenser Voss, and on behalf of myself and First Officer Eleanor Collins, I just wanted to say it's been a pleasure having you onboard."

"The pleasure is all mine Captain Voss," Kate said as she shook his hand, "but please, call me Kate."

"And I'm Spenser," he said. "We should be landing in about forty-five minutes so if you would all please wrap up what you're working on and buckle into your seats for landing I would appreciate it."

The lone flight attendant hustled over and began clearing their coffee cups and Joe dashed for the lavatory as Kate and Elliot buckled in. Forty-five minutes later they were on the ground in Berlin and in separate taxis, ready to work their way toward the hotel.

From this moment forward, the three of them would act like individual conference attendees, although adjoining rooms at the conference center's Crowne Plaza had been arranged. Kate arrived first. As she walked away from the check-in counter with her key, Elliot was approaching the counter to check in. They passed each other and Kate said, "Good morning," and Elliot returned her pleasantry. Joe wouldn't be arriving for at least another hour.

It was 8 am and Kate was exhausted. She had tried to begin transitioning time zones while still in Alaska, but had been unsuccessful. At home, it was ten o'clock at night and time to go to bed. After eating a room service breakfast, Kate peeled off her clothes and climbed under the covers to sleep until noon.

What seemed like only moments later, Kate heard a sound in the distance and as she began to gain consciousness, realized it was her alarm.

"Oh shit," Kate groaned as she sat on the edge of the bed and silenced her alarm. Simultaneously there was a sharp knock on the adjoining door.

"Just a minute!" Kate stumbled to the closet and pulled on the hotel robe before placing her ear against the door, "Who is it?"

"Candy-gram," the answer came in Joe's voice and Kate opened the door. "Pardon me, but you look like shit," Joe was quite matter-of-fact about this.

"I feel like I have a hangover, but didn't have any of the fun of drinking," Kate held her head, "I have a splitting headache."

Kate's room was in the middle and Joe let Elliot in through the other adjoining door as Kate opened a bottle of Tylenol.

"What's the matter with you?" Elliot asked as he entered.

"The empathy in this group is overwhelming. Are the two of you not horribly jetlagged?" Kate popped two of the pills into her mouth.

"Not really," Elliot said.

"Years of training," Joe added.

"Well a fuck you to both of you and what do you want?"

"We missed your smiling face," Joe said and both men laughed.

Kate picked up a pillow and threw it at Joe. "You better have a good reason for being here or the lamp is headed your way next."

"Wow, I lived with you for the better part of a year and I never saw you quite this cranky."

"I'm tired, I have a headache, and our previous adventure together sharpened my edges." Kate was startled by the tone of her own voice and became aware of the tension returning to her muscles. She ran into the bathroom and closed the door. A full-fledged panic attack was sweeping over her and she gasped for breath as she clutched her chest and turned on the water faucet. She splashed cold water onto her face before burying it into a towel, struggling for control. The decision to leave Zoe at home with the house sitter now seemed like a shortsighted one.

It all came flooding back. The murder of her husband Max. Her kidnapping. The torture. The betrayal. Kate hadn't first worked for The Agency willingly. She had been unwittingly thrust into a world of spies and organized crime, an unconscious pawn in a game of international espionage. It had left her deeply scarred. And then there was Brad. Had he really been duplicitous, or had he really just been trying to help her? Kate's entire body shook as her crying began with a wheeze.

Joe wrapped lightly on the bathroom door as he opened it. "I sent Elliot away. Go ahead let it out."

Kate slowly slid down the wall to the floor with the towel still over her face. The crying built to a moaning sob as Joe sat down beside her and let her cry, his hand on her shoulder. As her agony escalated, he wrapped his arms around her and began rhythmically rocking her.

After a few minutes the sobbing began to subside and Kate began breathing more deeply.

"Oh, Kate," Joe whispered into her ear, "I hope we haven't pulled you back into the field too soon."

"I'll be all right, I just can't allow myself to get too fatigued. I don't cope well when I'm fatigued."

"I know you can do this Kate, there is no woman stronger than you. I've seen every sign that you're ready and I'm going to help you through this." Joe squeezed her tightly.

"I'm feeling better now. I think I need to take a shower and clean myself up."

"I'll wait for you."

Fifteen minutes later, Kate emerged from the bathroom refreshed. The grip of the headache had surrendered and she managed a weak smile when Joe looked up from the book he was reading in the room's overstuffed chair.

"Are you ready to meet with Elliot to go over the plans for tomorrow one more time? You can also rehearse your paper presentation if you want. I've ordered lunch."

"Sounds great, why don't we meet in Elliot's room?"

"Elliot's room it is."

They ate and fine-tuned Kate's presentation. That evening, Kate was warming some leftovers from lunch in her room's microwave when Joe came through the adjoining door.

"Can we talk?"

"Of course," Kate sat on the edge of the bed and began moving her food around with a clear plastic fork to cool it.

"I've never done this before with you, at least not overtly, but I'm going to put on my psychologist hat a bit on this trip and offer some counseling. You can take it or leave it, but I think I probably understand you better than most having shared your previous field experience. I might have some insight into how to help you now."

"I appreciate your candor Joe, I'm always willing to listen to what you have to say...well...unless I'm fatigued," Kate turned up one corner of her mouth in a smirking grin.

Joe's face remained sober and his voice emitted a soothing tone. "When you worked with us on the financial markets case, you were unaware that you were working for us on that front. The operation was so covert, even you, as an active participant, didn't know what was going on. You also didn't know that you were in danger, Brad kept that information from everyone in his effort to protect you. I think that was unfair."

Kate gave a single nod of agreement.

Joe continued, "You need to understand that while so much was out of your control when you last worked for us in the field, you will never be in the dark or out of control again. You are now and always will be an active participant in any operation you engage in. Information will not be withheld and if you are in danger you will know it and have backup. If you ever feel the danger is too great, you can walk away. This is your show, not Brad's, or mine, or Elliot's and you can pull the plug at any time. We came to you for help, you are the principle, we are the support."

"I appreciate that, Joe. The best way for me to get stronger is to work. But I think you're correct, I struggle for control in more ways than one. I never want to be used as a pawn again and I want to make my own mission decisions. I genuinely like serving my country even in covert ways no one will ever know about, but I also struggle with some internal mental control. I can't tell you how many times I have played my kidnapping over and over again in my mind searching for the thing I did wrong that made me so vulnerable. I need to get control of those thoughts. Feeling vulnerable is just not an option for me anymore. Sometimes I wish I could just stop feeling at all and be more mechanical about things."

"Kate, feeling is what gives you your great instincts. I know it's been difficult for you to deal with your husband's death and the way in which you were thrust into this business, but it will get easier, trust me. You have better skills and training than you had last time and I know you're ready to handle yourself in any situation that comes your way. You've had to build some walls around yourself, I get it, but don't forget to put in a few windows so you can see beyond them and a door so you can step outside once in a while."

Kate nodded her head in silent contemplation as she stared at her food. Joe squeezed her shoulder and left her alone with her dinner. An international news station played at a low volume in the background.

Pressure is building in Washington, D.C. today to implement significant strategic changes in the global war on terror after documents released today by The Executive indicate that a joint Intelligence Committee and Department of Defense study found that the U.S.'s current efforts in the Middle East are not significant enough to win the conflict.

When asked about the report, The Chair of the Joint Chiefs of Staff, General Dutton replied, 'We are aware of the report and have already taken decisive action to correct the situation'. Asked specifically how

U.S. strategy had changed, General Dutton refused to answer. He did, however, say that he was very concerned about the security breach that had allowed the documents to be made public, but that they fortunately contained outdated information that wasn't representative of the current situation in the Middle East.

Up next on BBC World News...

6
BERLIN

Kate had slept well. A blueberry scone taken together with a tall cup of English breakfast tea infused with notes of cinnamon and orange completed her transition from merely awake to fully functional. In the light of day she had come to realize that today's conference presentation skirted ethical boundaries and could be professionally risky. Her apprehension faded after reminding herself she would never again see most of the people attending today and that the purpose was to gain the attention of the more radical programmers at the conference. It was a risk worth taking.

A group of about twenty people had gathered to hear her presentation, but about midway through her discussion Kate noticed the group had dwindled by half. The remaining crowd was dominated by whiskered academic-looking men in a sea of slim jeans, button-down shirts, and pointed toed dress shoes, their brows furrowed in curiosity about whether Kate was actually going to suggest people commit a crime. A faint aroma of pipe tobacco wafted in Kate's direction from one such man in the front row. By the time Kate began explaining how to move money off-shore without the government knowing about it, the room was nearly empty.

"Once you've set up your bitcoin wallet and run your bitcoins through a tumbler, no one will know that you own them, except you. What makes the wallet I've built unique is that it doesn't contain your bitcoin balance; it only shows if your account is 'empty' or 'full'. 'Full' just means you have some amount in the wallet, not how much. I keep the number of bitcoins remaining in my account written on a scrap of paper hidden inside my house. Just a number, nothing else to identify it."

At this point the conference goers who remained in the room began shifting uncomfortably in their chairs.

"While holding bitcoins is not new or particularly like a Swiss bank account, what I've written about in my paper is how it is now possible to trade bitcoins for U.S. dollars at some Caribbean and Central American banks. You'll need $25,000 in cash to establish an account, but then the banks will convert your bitcoin into U.S. dollars and establish a separate account under the name of a shell company. That money can be invested tax-free because as far as the government knows, you're just holding bitcoins."

A lanky, squeamish-looking man sitting sideways in his chair with his knees pulled so close to his body that he was approaching the fetal position asked, "Isn't that illegal?"

"Technically no. The company resides in a foreign country and is not subject to U.S. taxes. As long as you pay taxes on the bitcoin, a U.S. asset, you shouldn't attract any attention. Besides, I'm just saying it's theoretically possible, I'm not suggesting you do it. "

"That still sounds fraudulent to me," the man responded as he pushed himself up from the chair, grabbed his briefcase, and hurriedly exited the room as if just hearing about such a thing would get him arrested. He was right of course, doing what Kate suggested was technically illegal, but she wasn't looking to align with the law-abiding element of this conference.

Only five people remained in the room when a dark-haired man standing against a sidewall asked, "Is this bitcoin wallet, tumbler thing available anywhere?"

"Not yet. I've built the wallet, but I'm still looking for someone who has a tumbler with the right encryption."

The man thanked Kate as he and the remaining people filtered out of the room. The next presenter offered a weak smile as he sidestepped nervously around Kate to begin setting up his PowerPoint slides.

Well, that was fun, Kate said to herself as she packed up her things.

At noon lunch was served in the main ballroom. A panel of nominees for the conference's major award for research looked down upon the attendees from their head table perched on a platform about four feet above the floor.

A pinch-faced Frenchman sitting to Kate's right leaned over and in a nasally French accent observed, "Having these people sitting at a special table above everyone else in the room would never happen in France. It's not very modern."

Who was Kate to disagree, she hadn't been to France in fifteen years. The French have had entire revolutions in less time. Certainly a Head Table Revolt could be resolved within days with a sympathetic sanitation workers strike. Kate was just grateful the French kept croquembouche in fashion.

The seat to Kate's left was empty and she was leaning over it discussing South American politics with a Chilean man sitting in the next chair when she heard a familiar voice behind her, "Kate Adams, is that you? I haven't seen you in ages!"

Kate turned to find their pilot, Spenser, approaching. The sight of him in this place and the words he was saying baffled her. Spenser took advantage of her momentary discomposure to reach over and heartily shake the Chilean man's hand.

"Hi, I'm Ernie Green, I didn't mean to interrupt your conversation, but Kate here and I used to be colleagues in Alaska and I'm just so surprised to see her. My gosh, what's it been, five years?"

Catching on Kate replied, "At least. It's really good to see you Ernie! Sit down next to me so we can get caught up. Will you excuse me?" she asked looking at the Chilean man. He waved her off and made sounds about how old friends should get reacquainted as he winked in Ernie's direction implying a deeper friendship than Ernie had expressed.

Disgusting, Kate thought.

Spenser leaned in close and said softly, "You sure know how to clear a room with your radical talk of illegal activity."

"Yeah, they scattered pretty quickly, but I didn't see you there. How did you know people left?"

"I can assure you surveillance here is excellent. I just wanted you to know that others and I are here watching your back. So, tell me, how did you enjoy the 10 am session you attended?"

"I attended a fascinating panel discussion on programming software for space missions and debugging code when the programmer is billions of miles away from the program. But, if surveillance is as good as you say, you already know that."

Spenser touched the side of his nose to indicate she was correct.

Kate added, "I enjoyed it very much and learned a lot."

They leaned back in their seats as lunch was served. "So, you probably don't know, but Bev and I divorced last summer," Spenser said louder than necessary. The Chilean man made a staccato grunt that sounded suspiciously like *I told you so*.

"I'm sorry to hear that Ernie, but I'm not surprised. Bev is a great person, but the two of you seemed ill-suited for one another." Kate threw 'Ernie' a mischievous grin and began cutting the rubbery chicken drenched in cream sauce she'd been served, "Are you seeing anyone special?"

"Not really, but it is pretty special seeing you today." The Chilean man turned to the person on his left and whispered something as he jerked a thumb in Spenser and Kate's direction.

"It's nice seeing you as well Ernie, it's been too

long between visits."

"Well, since we're both here for a couple of days, how about drinks later and maybe some dinner?"

"Sounds wonderful. Shall I meet you in the bar around 5:00 for happy hour?"

"It's a date." Spenser said before poking the Chilean man with his elbow and asking, "How'd I do?"

The Chilean man responded with a "Meh" and motioned *so-so* with his hand.

7
WASHINGTON, DC

Like nails on the blackboard of Harrison's psyche, life at NSA headquarters continued. Jurisdictional squabbles had erupted within the Joint Interagency Task Force working on The Executive case and finger pointing had commenced. The FBI was blaming CIA counterintelligence of cyber-incompetence, while the CIA accused the FBI of being unwilling to look internally. The FBI had put a CIA man, Robert Howard, at the top of their list of potential hacker suspects and were subjecting Mr. Howard to execution by committee as they turned his life upside down. The CIA was closing ranks around Howard and became reluctant to share any information with the task force.

Meanwhile, outside the official task force, NSA Director Admiral Reynolds insisted Harrison should manage a quiet investigation of his own through PDD Lanser's office. The hushed nature of the inquiry meant

Harrison had a great deal of responsibility, but no real authority outside being the aide to PDD Lanser. With apprehension amongst the department heads still running high, asking for information without cause was a challenge.

Even though Harrison's investigation had failed to unearth a hacker, internal conflict with his superiors over the possibility of a mole somewhere within the intelligence community continued to be a frustration.

"Horsefeathers! That's codswallop they're feeding you over there. How can we have a mole when it doesn't appear that anyone has accessed all the documents that have been released? Plus, a bunch of the stuff they're putting out there isn't even true. Who would do that and why? Sounds like twaddle to me."

Harrison took a deep breath and replied, "Look, I admit it might sound like bullshit on the surface, but a deeper analysis reveals some possibilities."

PDD Lanser made a huffing noise and crossed his arms over his chest. Harrison knew moving his boss off his hacker theory would be challenging.

An administrative assistant opened PDD Lanser's office door and announced, "Sir, Admiral Reynolds is here." The NSA Director walked in with the discipline of a career Naval officer.

"Good afternoon gentlemen, are you ready to brief me on your progress?"

"Yes, sir", Harrison said as PDD Lanser stepped out from behind his desk to greet the Director in the firm handshake, back-slapping manner prevalent between men of power. They moved their conversation to the secured conference room attached to PDD Lanser's office and went through a formal security protocol before beginning their discussion.

Harrison opened up a PowerPoint presentation and began describing the means taken by the Cyber Security Group to find an entry point a hacker may have used. Even though they hadn't found one, they had deployed methods to frustrate any hacker who might gain access.

"That leaves us with a few theories," Harrison explained, "First, we might have a hacker using a new technique we don't have the knowledge or means to detect. If that were the case, we would also have no means of either counter-hacking or preventing their penetration. However, we view this probability as low." The two men in attendance nodded politely.

"A second possibility is that we have a mole. We don't have any suspects yet because there's no trail indicating that a single person accessed every piece of the released information, plus it doesn't really explain the fabricated portions of the release. Yet, in my conversations with our tech people we see this as the higher probability case. But frankly we have no evidence for or against either. We're just working on instinct at the moment."

The Director made a noise that indicated he was thinking and then looked back and forth between Harrison and Lanser. "I don't like this, any of it. The mole scenario doesn't make any sense. How would they get access to both high level U.S. intelligence as well as foreign intel? Hell, even I hadn't seen every memo they released!"

"That's what I've been trying to tell him," PDD

Lanser said with a look of satisfaction. He again crossed his arms signaling he wasn't changing his mind no matter what Harrison said.

"I admit it's a stretch, but I feel pretty good about what the tech folks have done down there and I think it would be difficult to find a method we haven't considered. Of course, there's another option. It could be that a third party gained access to the information in a non-technical manner we haven't discovered yet. In that case some or all of the untrue reports might have been part of a foreign counterintelligence operation. If the releasing party has all the information, he or she may be unable to separate truth from fiction so released it all."

"True, true something like that could potentially happen. What are we doing on that front?" the Director asked.

"We have a covert team in the field trying to establish if we have a third party who either hacked us or got information in some other way."

"And what have they found out?"

"We don't know yet. We are limiting communications significantly since we don't know the degree of penetration The Executive has."

"I think that's the best course of action for now, but keep looking at all possibilities. Lanser, I need to send a quick note to the President on this and will be in meetings most of the day, may I send a quick email from here?"

"Of course," PDD Lanser said, "you may use my office." And with that the meeting was over.

Faulkner rubbed his throbbing eyes. He was not so much regretting his decision to become the NSA's Director of Cyber Security, but there was a sense of loathing coursing through him at the moment. He hadn't left the Salt Mine in three days and kept checking and rechecking the work of his analysts trying to find what they might have missed. Short naps on the sofa in his office were all he seemed to be able to manage. The desire for sleep or food eluded him.

The phone on his desk made a short, loud buzzing noise that caused Faulkner's heart to rise in his chest. Faulkner made his way to the phone and hit the intercom button before managing a gruff, "What?"

"Sir, it's Mary, I need to see you, it's urgent."

"Okay, I'll open the door." By the time he did, Mary, one of his Senior Analysts, was standing outside quivering with excitement.

She came in as Faulkner collapsed into his desk chair while scratching the three days worth of whiskers on his face. "Hurry up, I think I need to lay down before I pass out."

"It's the Brits sir," Mary announced with the nervous excitement of big news in her voice, "they found a penetration."

"A what?" Faulkner sat up in his chair, renewed by what he thought he might have heard.

"They found evidence of a breach into their system. It's a hacker's footprint; they found evidence of an infiltration. We're planning a conference call with them for a briefing in 12 hours."

"Thank goodness," Faulkner said with all the enthusiasm he could muster. "Have someone wake me an hour before the call." The next ten hours of his life were lost in a series of dreams.

8
AN UNKNOWN LOCATION

"It was wonderful of you to come Lana. You're the only one here who understands me and our movement," The Executive was stroking Lana's arm as they lay together, their lovemaking complete.

"I was so afraid." Lana's voice had a child-like quality, "I didn't know what had happened to you. I thought you had been kidnapped, arrested, or killed. Or, worse yet, that you didn't care about me anymore and had just moved on. It was eating away at me."

"I'm sorry, it was a great opportunity, but I had to drop out for a while. I sent for you the minute I could."

"It's all over the news. People are looking for you around the world."

"Yes, but they don't know who I am and never will. I think I lost the UK access today. They found my entry point, but don't worry, we have enough

45

information to keep the money flowing from both directions."

"Who are these people who are hiding you?"

"Government officials with their own plan to bend the world in their own direction."

"We're never leaving this place, are we?"

"No baby, I'm beginning to suspect we aren't, but as long as I'm willing to do some work for them, we'll be safe."

"But what about the commune and our life there?"

"Honey, we can build our own world anywhere. Besides, we'll eventually be virtually connected to them. Think of it as opening a new branch, to grow the movement a bit. There'll be a new commune here."

"I'm so glad I get to be here with you."

"Me too, darling, me too."

9
BERLIN

After lunch Kate browsed the vendor booths in the exhibition hall and took a short walk around outside the conference center. Across the street, next to a Dunkin' Donuts, she found a Baskin Robbins and went in for a cone. She hoped Berlin's suburbs weren't littered with strip malls full of Banana Republic, Abercrombie & Fitch, and Eddie Bauer. It wasn't the manner in which she wanted America to contribute to German society. The Metropolitan Opera Company, Mark Twain, Sylvia Plath, and even Disney would be much more substantial offerings. Kate realized, reluctantly, that she might be reaching the curmudgeonly stage of her life.

Can you believe these kids with their blue and purple hair, torn jeans, and lack of work ethic, she laughed at herself and looked around for someone she could instruct to 'sit up straight' or 'pick that up'. Alas, no opportunity presented itself.

As 3 o'clock approached, Kate made her way to the Leipzig Room where the Programmers for Peace and Freedom were holding their presentation. The room was not large, but the space was three-quarters full. At the head table sat three individuals she knew from her briefing as the President, Vice President, and Secretary/Treasurer of the organization. A fourth person who looked vaguely familiar to Kate joined the executive team. Kate thumbed through the conference program for clues to the identity of the man, but found none. To avoid the critical eye of conference organizers, PPF rarely published the name of their featured speaker.

A smartly dressed elderly woman with gray hair snuggly tucked into a low bun with two decorative sticks running through it greeted Kate and asked if she was a member of the organization.

"No, I'm not, but you always have such interesting programs I thought I would pop in. I hope that's all right?"

"Of course dear, and you're always welcome to join PPF if you'd like. You'll find we have great meetings and programs all over the world. We're always recruiting new members." The woman handed Kate a tri-fold pamphlet that had a membership form and an envelope to mail it tucked inside.

"Thank you," Kate said as she made her way to her seat. Looking around the room Kate could see why a membership drive might be in order. The average age of the majority of attendees appeared to be approaching 70, though an anomalous smattering of twenty-somethings thinly dotted the room.

Kate had learned in her briefing that the parent

organization of PPF was called People for a Better World. It was founded by academics in the fields of political science, economics, and natural science who were vocal communist sympathizers in the early 1960s after McCarthyism began to subside. Many of them had even been invited to live for extended periods of time in the Soviet Union and China in hopes they would take the movement of communism back to the United States. This fact was conspicuously absent from the brochure Kate had been given, but it did mention that PPF was formed in the mid-1980s as a sub-section of People for a Better World. According to the handout their mission is to 'Build a better world through communication, open-mindedness, and cooperation'. The entire pamphlet was comprised of insipid platitudes designed to mask the ideological makeup of its membership. It was a lesson in Propaganda 101 and as wafer-thin as the paper it was printed on, although to an outsider who knew nothing about the organization, it would seem ideal. After all, who doesn't want people to be more open-minded, peaceful, and free?

Kate found herself already mildly irritated with the people around her, but forced herself to let it go by reminiscing about Spenser's over-the-top Ernie Green persona. She wondered who the real Spenser was. Was his genuine personality that of the professional pilot, the gregarious Ernie Green, or somewhere in between? The problem with this business was, she'd never know.

The President of PPF took the podium and welcomed the assembled guests.

"We have a fantastic program for you today. As our members are aware, this organization as well as our parent, People for a Better World, is committed to creating a world in which the people hold governments accountable. A government should be willing to share both information and wealth with their people and we should be able to rely on their honesty when they tell us they are fighting for the greater good. Yet, all too often citizens discover after the fact that our government lied to us and engaged in unjust wars. Our speaker today is a man who has devoted much of his life to holding government accountable. He served ten years of a life sentence for treason before it was revealed that the government had fabricated evidence against him and his charges were dismissed. While he never denied what he was accused of, the State always lacked concrete evidence against him."

He looked sternly around the room, daring anyone to disagree.

"During the Persian Gulf War, our guest today served bravely in the Marine Corp to liberate Kuwait. He was awarded the Silver Star for his efforts to protect Kuwaiti citizen soldiers who had come under heavy fire. His efforts that day also earned him a Purple Heart. While he admits he only suffered a flesh wound, he has neither confirmed nor denied that it was on his backside."

The collective offered polite laughter.

"But seriously, our guest is someone I respect very much. He did what was right by exposing the unjust way our government was treating both locals and prisoners of war during that time. His only crime being that he stole the report that documented the abuse and made it public. He did so only because the government had been lying to the American people for years.

"At the time of the report's release, he had left the military and was working for a consulting firm that was contracted by the Department of Defense to conduct an investigation of the abuse. He, along with five colleagues, worked diligently for two years to conduct research for the report. When it was finished, he believed the evidence was so compelling that reforms would begin immediately. When the DoD appeared to take no action, he felt it was his duty as a citizen to release the classified report to the public so the people could hold their politicians accountable. Instead of receiving whistleblower protection, the government fabricated evidence and charged him with treason."

He shuffled his typed remarks to the next page.

"One psychiatrist who testified to treating our guest for depression and prescribing medication had never laid eyes on him until the day he testified in court during the trial. The injustices only compounded that day. But he was vindicated and today I am pleased to welcome former Marine Corp Captain Randy Tully!"

The room erupted into thunderous applause and several people leapt to their feet. This struck Kate as odd for someone she considered a traitor. Yet, in this room he was a hero, perhaps in part because a very sanitized version of his offences had been presented. Kate knew he wasn't just a whistleblower who exposed poor treatment of prisoners, he had also revealed the identity of twenty or more intelligence officers in the field and stalled the ability of the U.S. to collect intelligence in the region for years, possibly leading to 9/11. Evidence had also emerged that he may have helped enemy troops while a Marine Corp officer serving in theater by warning of planned attacks.

In preparing for the trial, the U.S. prosecution team had gotten sloppy. The psychiatrist the prosecution had called to testify was not the actual doctor who had treated Tully, but another psychiatrist in the practice. A filing error had been made and Tully's case notes had ended up in the wrong doctor's files at the psychiatrist's office. While the psychiatrist admitted he didn't specifically remember treating Tully, he was able to produce typed case notes from his files to which he testified. The mix-up was later discovered and reported to the defense attorney who used it to cast reasonable doubt on the prosecution's evidence as a whole and got Tully released.

"Thank you everyone, I appreciate the warm welcome." Tully's voice was raspy and thin, his face sunken and drearily ashen. "Let me begin by saying there is one thing my experience with prosecution by the Federal Government has taught me: never confirm or deny anything, especially the wounds of war."

There was more loud applause and whooping as Kate looked around the room to try to establish who Tully's most enthusiastic supporters were. Just about the time she was concluding 'all of them', she noticed a woman to her right and across the aisle with raised eyebrows and a look that said, *give me a break*. Although Kate had applauded with everyone else to avoid standing out, she regarded this woman as a kindred spirit and someone she should meet even if it didn't advance her mission.

Tully proceeded to justify his actions and

describe the outing of the intelligence officers as "collateral damage brought on by the government's inaction."

He went on, "If the Department of Defense desired to keep their identities secret, they should have implemented massive and immediate reforms. Their lack of action weighed on my conscience. Throughout the entire research process, I hated what I was doing and began to despise the government even more than I had before. I went to war to liberate Kuwait, but I ended up liberating the citizens of the United States from their corrupt government!" More thunderous applause as Kate's kindred spirit sat with her arms crossed.

The DoD had, in fact, made radical policy reforms to fix the problems identified in the report even before Tully had released it, but the DoD believed it was best to handle the issues internally rather than publicly. Tully, who expected to be part of the policy revision team, had been excluded due to increasingly erratic behavior at work. He was put on medical leave and having no first-hand knowledge of the DoD's response to the report, decided to release it to the media. When he had removed a copy of the report from his office in the secure facility was unclear.

Kate's kindred spirit raised her hand and when called upon asked, "It was obvious, even to you I think, that during the time you and your team were conducting your research, that you disapproved of the government rather broadly on a philosophical level regardless of the specific incident. The stress that this caused you was having a profound impact on your health." Tully nodded in the affirmative. "So why didn't you just quit and find another job or a different career field?"

"Mmmm…you are not the first person to ask me that question and the answer is really quite mundane. See, I was dating a girl…er… a woman, at the time. I liked her a lot and I was very much interested in having a long-term relationship with her. The woman was impressed by my important position and I needed a decent salary to date her in the way she expected. A transition to new employment would have been difficult at that point in my life. It's that simple."

And that's when you became a traitor, Kate thought.

"Of course once she broke off the relationship, the decision to release the report seemed very clear to me. That was my only option."

Kate was unimpressed. It seemed to her like a story that had played out over and over again. A man goes to work for the government with great expectations of saving the world and becomes disillusioned when he discovers the government is a large bureaucracy that moves slowly. He wants immediate action and becomes frustrated by his inability to get anything done. The man, or woman to be fair, grows increasingly erratic at work and in his personal life. A relationship with a woman or someone else close to him breaks down and the man, already unstable, acts out in a damaging and vindictive way. This is usually done out of desperation not only to expose the government but also to save the relationship. *Look, what I've been dealing with! This is why I behaved the way I did, you have no idea the stress I've been under!* Now, of course, he can talk about how exposing the report was the righteous thing to do. At the time he was reacting to his feeling that he had nothing left to lose.

Tully finished his speech with a call to action to stand by and help whistleblowers. "I have myself met with Edward Snowden and Chelsea Manning to council them and offer support. I've been fundraising for their defense and working with lawyers to ensure they eventually get fair trials and are exonerated for what should have been considered service to their country."

The meeting broke up and the woman sitting next to Kate stood, turned toward Kate and with her hand over her heart said, "Oh my goodness, wasn't he wonderful?"

Kate forced a smile and a "Yes, yes he was" as she excused herself and looked around the room for her kindred spirit.

She felt a tapping on her shoulder, "Excuse me, Dr. Kate Adams, right?"

Kate spun around, "Yes I am, oh, hello, you're the man who came to my presentation and asked about the availability of my bitcoin wallet. Please, call me Kate."

"Hi, I'm Eric Broudy," he said as they shook hands. Broudy was a dark-haired man who was in the younger minority of attendees with chiseled features and a light German accent. "I really enjoyed your presentation and you might find you have some things in common with members of this group."

"Perhaps," Kate said, "but the members appear to be either 70 or in their early 20s. I seem to be in an odd demographic here."

Broudy threw his head back and laughed, "The older people tend to come to presentations, they are the only ones who have the free time. The rest of us are too busy working." He had a pleasant smile, but his eyes had an intensity that gave Kate pause. "We're having an organizational dinner tonight, you should come as my guest. Most of the older people stay home for that and you'll get to meet some of the younger and more middle-aged members. We're honoring one of our founding members and he'll be speaking."

"I'd love to come."

And so it began.

10
BERLIN

When Kate arrived at the bar on the top floor of the hotel, she found Spenser sipping scotch at a back-corner table overlooking a cityscape aglitter with the red and orange hues of refracted late afternoon sunlight. Kate stopped at the bar and ordered a glass of chardonnay that arrived in a stemmed glass large enough to be a soup bowl. Using two hands to lift the glass to her face, Kate took a generous sip of her wine before returning her full attention to Spenser.

"I thought you were a pilot, what are you doing hanging around here as Ernie Green?"

"We're all operations officers, some of us just fly airplanes as part of our gig."

"Makes sense, I guess. So, what did you do all day?"

"Ah, I could tell you but then I'd have to kill you."

"I see you're not afraid to emit platitudes to tell me it's none of my damn business."

Kate was annoyed with Spenser's reminder that she would always be an asset and never an insider. There was a much larger operation going on around her and she hated that she would never be allowed to see the big picture. The fact that she was just a cog in the operation's wheel always made her feel like a circus animal being observed and evaluated for her performance. Did they applaud when she did something right?

Realizing she would always be the questioned and never the questioner in this relationship, Kate chillily changed the subject.

"So, lovely weather we're having."

"All right, I hear you, but let's see if we can find a happy medium on the conversation. Tell me how the Programmers for Peace and Security presentation went."

"Since I assume you either had people in the room or electronic surveillance, I will stick to my impressions rather than a recap of the presentation. Broadly, I believe Tully is still a traitor and the organization is loaded with his devotees. The demographic was skewed elderly, but I assume they are the aging communist sympathizers. There does, however, appear to be a replacement generation emerging, but I don't have any feel yet for what their ideological makeup is or what is steering them toward the organization. For all I know, they might be the true open-minded believers in peace and freedom the brochure pronounces. I met a man of around thirty who also attended my presentation. He invited me to attend

PPF's dinner tonight. He claims the younger and middle-aged members come out at night."

"Anything else? You've described the group as a whole, any impressions of individuals in the group?"

"The woman of about seventy who greeted me at the door was very friendly and seemed anxious to recruit new members. Oh, and there was one woman of middle age, either American or Canadian who, like me, didn't seem to be buying into the hoopla surrounding Tully. I tried to find her when his presentation ended, but I missed her."

"Interesting, she might be someone you want to get to know. Keep an eye open for her around the convention center. We will too."

"I need to get going," Kate said as she downed the last of her wine, "I have a cocktail hour and dinner to attend."

"Good luck, but before you go, will you do me a favor?"

"Perhaps," Kate said with squinty-eyed apprehension.

"You see that woman with the blonde hair sitting at the end of the bar?"

"Yes."

"Go over to return your glass to the bar and strike up a conversation with her. Before you walk away say, 'By the way, I know about the basketball game'. She's with us and there really was a basketball game. Trust me, it will be hilarious."

Confused, but seeing no harm, Kate did as he asked. When she turned to look behind her as she walked away, Kate saw the woman staring slack-jawed in her direction and Spenser rolling with laughter. *Always a pawn*, Kate thought.

11
BERLIN

The end of the day's formal conference proceedings had thinned the hordes of people moving through the sweeping hallways and transformed the conference rooms into spaces for small private dinners. Swarms of wait staff tended the banquets buzzing briskly between racks of plated and trayed food positioned in the hallways and the diners tucked in their cloistered rooms.

Upon arriving at her own dinner, Kate counted thirty or so people milling about balancing drinks and appetizer plates. The average age of the assembled was definitely younger, yet it was a small, silver-haired man who made his way quickly toward Kate as she entered the room.

"Hello, welcome, my name is Cecil," he said offering a weak handshake and a slight bow. His bearing was that of a self-important man punctuated with the flourish of a Persian accent.

"Pleased to meet you, I'm Kate."

"Will you join me for dinner?" he asked taking Kate by the arm and moving her toward a nearby round table for six. "We'll put you here, next to me." Cecil took the napkin from the place setting and draped it over the back of the chair to indicate the seat was taken. "Now, let me introduce you to some people."

Cecil never left Kate's side during the cocktail hour and introduced her to many of the people in the room, but Kate felt like her movements around the room were being closely controlled. The attendees were primarily academics and freelance programmers, but Cecil seemed to be directing her nearly exclusively toward her fellow academicians. At one point she made eye contact with Eric Broudy across the room and he smiled and shook his head at her.

While cocktail banter was primarily polite small talk, the conversation took a more ideological turn as they ate and the public veneer of the organization's brochure slowly began to peel away. Cecil had collected another elderly couple and two middle-aged men who appeared to be his devotees for his table.

"So how are things in Iran?" the middle-aged man named David asked.

"I think they are good," Cecil answered, his voice suddenly taking on the mechanical authority of a politician carefully choosing his words. "With sanctions easing, there is more food but traditions remain strong. The nuclear program seems to be going forward right under the noses of the West. The current agreement with the U.S. was a good deal for Iran."

David turned toward Kate, "You know, Cecil here played a big part in bringing down the Shah in the

1970s."

"Really," Kate said trying to sound surprised rather than shocked, "I thought the Shah was good for Iran, why didn't you like him?"

Cecil made some sort of humming noise as he pondered his response, "The Shah was okay..." his voice trailing off as he moved his fork in the air in a circular motion searching for the right words. "He did a lot for education, especially for women, but he moved the country away from the traditional culture and economy and toward Western democratic capitalism. Neither capitalism nor democracies are consistent with traditional Islamic culture and the spread of democratic capitalism throughout the world needed to be stopped. It's really just another form of American imperialism...capitalism I mean. So is progressivism for that matter. Mind you, I don't support radical Islamic rule either, but tradition calls for a more communist approach with a strong central government that can control the economy in a way that benefits all the people of Iran."

"Were you in Iran during the 1979 Revolution?"

"No, my dear, you must understand, the Iranian Revolution was organized and executed by people like me from within the U.S.." Cecil and David chuckled lightly as they gave each other a knowing glance.

"So how did you pull off a revolution in Iran from the United States?

"Revolutions are almost always executed outside the country. In this case, once Khomeini was expelled from Iran and sent to France it became relatively easy to put him back into power. His supporters in the West had relatively free access to him and we were able to utilize and, dare I say, manipulate Western media to move our objectives forward." Cecil raised an eyebrow to David and the men laughed at their inside joke.

"But how, specifically, did you accomplish that?"

"Ah, my dear, once you desire your own revolution, it will become clear. In fact, from what I hear, you may already be headed in that direction." Cecil flagged down the server, asked for coffee and redirected the conversation toward the benefits of sugar on brain function.

A short while later, the President of PPF introduced Dr. Richard Emory, one of the founding members of People for a Better World and tonight's honored guest. Dr. Emory looked to be in his 80s and had appeared quite feeble earlier in the evening when Kate first noticed him hobbling around with a cane. However, the opportunity to speak seemed to revive him and he set aside his cane and tottered unassisted to the lectern. He talked a lot about nuclear proliferation and how there were no winners in the Cold War.

"The U.S. was arrogant when the Cold War ended because they thought they had won something and could march into the former Soviet Union with an army of MBAs to convert them to Western-style capitalism. Well, that was the worst thing they could have done, because it wasn't what those countries wanted. The former Soviet countries needed to develop a system that worked for them. Russia, for example, would have been better off simply modifying Communism in a way that moved them toward a more market-based system like China has. There was no reason to make a one-hundred-

and-eighty-degree turn, when a simple nudge would have worked. Instead of prosperity, they ended up with an oligarchy that President Putin has been forced to break up."

When Dr. Emory finished speaking and photos were taken of the plaque presentation, the assembled were asked if they would like to ask any questions.

Kate's kindred spirit rose, "I was one member of that army of MBAs who went into Russia after the fall of the Berlin Wall and I found quite the opposite sentiment. The people were hungry for information about outside economies. No one knew how to have any sort of market-based system, be it market communism, socialism, or capitalism. I think we did a lot of good through our education of government officials and ordinary people. The problem Russia had was that the oligarchs already knew how to privatize the economy. How? Many of them were running the market-based black markets under the Communist system and had amassed small fortunes. They understood how markets worked and how to make profits. The reason they took over was because the learning curve for the rest of the country was too steep and they already had money to invest. Do you have any thoughts on that?"

"Yes I do. The oligarchs were criminals, black marketers who should have been thrown in jail even before the wall came down," he answered firmly before taking a few more questions.

As the evening came to an end, Eric Broudy intercepted Kate as she once again watched her kindred spirit cross the room and walk out the door. Eric noticed her watching the woman.

"Do you know that woman?" Kate asked him, jerking her head toward the door.

"No, I've never laid eyes on her before today. It's somewhat intriguing that she came to the dinner though."

"Indeed," Kate said still looking at the door the woman had gone through.

"I see your time was monopolized by Cecil tonight," Eric emitted a nearly imperceptible laugh meant primarily for himself. "He considers himself the godfather of the group, but he's part of the old guard. They're all still fighting some economic or political system, the 'capitalist scourge' they call it. They're too busy thinking about revolution rather than evolution, they're stuck in a world that existed forty years ago."

"So where is the new generation taking the group?"

"Well, we don't worry too much about nuclear proliferation I can tell you that. Let the world build nukes, with a few keystrokes we can prevent them from being launched. Problem solved."

"What I don't understand is what any of the stuff they're talking about has to do with programming. All I've heard is political dialogue."

"Ah, that's because most of these people don't even belong to the PPF section, they are simply members of People for a Better World and are seeking relevance and influence with the younger generation. PPF is really the only section that has seen much growth over the years, eventually I expect it will be a stand-alone organization and People for a Better World will no longer exist."

"Well, time does march on I suppose."

"Yes, it does. By the way, I meant to get your

business card earlier. I have some contacts who might be able to come up with a tumbler for you if you're willing to share your code so they can see if they can build some compatibility."

"Hmm, let me think about that. While I was planning to make the finished product publicly available, I'm not sure if I want to share the unfinished code with a stranger."

"I can assure you it will be in good hands. In fact, I might even have a way for you to make some money from it when it's finished. Think about it and if you're interested, get in touch." They exchanged business cards. Eric's card merely contained his calligraphically designed name and a handwritten email address at a private server.

12
WASHINGTON, DC

The temperature was rising in Washington both seasonally and politically. December was approaching the finish line pulling a stretch of warm, sunny days behind it. A steady stream of shirtless men in microfiber shorts and spandex clad women were running up and down the dusty trails surrounding the National Mall as political staffers in business attire clustered on the adjacent park benches, their elbows resting on the bench-backs.

Political pressure was growing to address the perceived government failures and intelligence tactics being exposed by The Executive. Throughout the mid-term elections bipartisan attempts to separate the truth from false information had largely failed and November's election results indicated the public was out for blood. The President had become keenly aware of the need for action on both the policy and security breach fronts. As staffers lounged in the sun, department heads met with the President to plan their strategy.

"Good afternoon lady and gentlemen," the President breezed into the Oval Office with the confident, casual air of a Harvard grad with the world at his fingertips. Waiting for him were Admiral Doug Reynolds, Director of the NSA; Nancy Wolf, the Director of CIA; Adam Alexander, FBI Director; and General Tom Dutton, the Chairman of the Joint Chiefs of Staff.

The assembled jumped to their feet, "Good afternoon, Mr. President," they chimed in relative unison.

"Sit down, sit down. So, what can you tell me about the security breech so far?"

Reynolds spoke first, "Well, sir, the Brits have found evidence of a hacker on their end that accessed about ten thousand documents. The released information so far is all contained within those files, however much of the stolen data has not yet been released, so we should expect additional disclosures."

"What about on our end, have we found a hacker?"

"No, sir. The method used in the British infiltration was a slight modification of a technique that has been widely used by other such predators. We've gone back and triple checked our systems and continue to find no evidence that a similar method of penetration exists on our side."

"Thank you Douglas. Tom, any thoughts on the military side from you?"

"I think we need to consider this an act of war, Mr. President. I also think…"

"Dammit Tom, will we ever be fighting enough

wars on enough fronts for you?" Admiral Reynolds slammed his fist on the table. "Who exactly are we going to point guns at on this one…a computer screen?"

"Taking up arms against computers was not exactly where I was going with this. I…"

"I don't want to hear it!" Admiral Reynold's face turned red and a vein popped out of his temple, "we don't need another Department of Defense intervention. What we need are some real policy changes and intelligence resources on this. The information that's been made public makes all of us in this administration look like idiots! It's time to change our Middle East policy, start bringing our troops home, and redirect those resources toward protecting the homeland. The U.S. is a virtual island and if you loosen up some of the restrictions on intelligence gathering and give me some more money, we should be able to adequately protect this island. I also think we should shut down the Guantanamo Bay Detention Center and send all those prisoners home. As long as you give me the resources to keep an eye on them, they're our best potential source of intelligence gathering. They'll lead us right to the people we need to eliminate in the region and we don't need to kill women and children in order to find them."

"We are not going to close GTMO, you arrogant prick!" General Tom Dutton shouted.

"Gentlemen, that's enough!" the President roared, "I agree, we need to change policy to save face, after all, we've already announced that our policies had changed before the documents were released. But no, we are not closing GTMO, Doug. So let's talk rational policy prescriptions."

Admiral Reynolds pulled a file out of his briefcase and opened it on the table in front of the President, "I have some specific tactical ideas about Syria..." he went on as General Dutton glared at him, his face fixed in a deep frown.

General Dutton remained quiet as Reynolds laid out his plan to save the world. The President listened intently before asking, "Tom, anything you'd like to add?"

"Here's my problem with this plan. Some of the information they're releasing is false, so why do we have to change all our strategies when we can deny our actions? The public doesn't know what's true or not."

The CIA director Nancy Wolf spoke up, "Since we've admitted some of the information is true, the public assumes everything is true and we're lying about it. I have several world leaders crawling up my ass right now because they believe we are listening in on and recording their personal cell phone calls, even though we're not actually doing so. I can't provide them with transcripts of calls we haven't even recorded. Frankly, our bigger problem is getting the public and world leaders to believe some of the information isn't true."

"I think you're correct, Nancy," the President added, "our relationship with our allies is strained right now over this. They don't know what to believe either. Maybe we need to make some policy and strategic changes, issue some denials where we don't want to change, and work on the public relations aspects of the false information."

"Mr. President," Reynolds interrupted, "might I recommend a more comprehensive approach to policy and strategic changes, I think we lose credibility otherwise. Let me explain…"

13
BERLIN

The PPF dinner complete, Kate trekked back to her room. Elliot looked up from his hand of cards and Joe continued sipping coffee as Kate entered.

"Joe, you're going to be up all night after drinking that coffee," Kate scolded.

"Hope so," Elliot said as he dramatically threw down his hand of cards indicating he was folding. Joe pulled the stack of peanuts they were playing for toward him. "You have no idea the amount of paperwork we have to do once you go to bed."

"Bureaucrats," Kate said kicking off her shoes, "let me get out of these clothes before we debrief. I think better without a bra."

Elliot appeared to blush as Kate closed the bathroom door and Joe yelled, "So do I!"

Kate joined the men in her plush hotel robe, hair clipped atop her head.

"Hot," Joe stated sarcastically. The comment made Elliot appear uncomfortable. He didn't understand that when you've lived with someone in the remote Alaska wilderness for a year, you develop a casual familiarity even if Agency policy discourages it.

"Relax," Kate playfully poked Elliot in the shoulder, "Joe and I moved past Agency formality long ago. He has my permission to engage in playful banter that may skirt the edges of Human Resource's harassment policy. Would you like that in writing?"

Elliot continued to look strained as he shook his head and smiled weakly, "Tell us about your evening Kate."

"Yeah toots, tell us about your evening," Joe smiled widely.

Kate slid him a sideways glance, "Don't push his buttons, Joe. Or mine for that matter."

Kate's tension was rolling back in, but was relieved by a couple of visibly deep breaths and the light touch of Joe's hand on her forearm, "Sorry, I crossed a line. Tell us about your impressions of this evening."

Kate proceeded to tell them about the old guard, Cecil and his claims of overthrowing the Shah, and Dr. Emory's speech. "The odd thing about Emory was that he kept referring to the U. S. as 'they' or 'them' as if he were disassociating himself with the events and errors he believed the U.S. made. To me this implied loyalty elsewhere."

She paused hoping Elliot or Joe would offer their thoughts, but the men just nodded their heads as a sign they were listening. "Go on," Joe said leaning in a little as though hanging on her every word.

"My kindred spirit was in the room too and challenged Emory on his claims that we made a mistake by sending an army of MBAs into the former Soviet Union."

"Your 'kindred spirit' as you call her, picked up an FBI tail as she left the room. We're treating her as an American until we know differently," Elliot offered matter-of-factly. "Continue."

"Eric Broudy stopped me before I could catch up with her and introduce myself. Broudy says he might have someone who could build a tumbler for my overseas transfer bitcoin strategy, but only if I'm willing to give them my code to review. Oh, wait, he gave me a card, let me get it."

Kate ran back into the bathroom to extract the card from her pocket and handed it to Joe. He looked it over and observed aloud, "Private server", as he handed it to Elliot.

Elliot studied the card, sat back in his chair, and stared at the ceiling as if the secrets of the universe were contained there. "Yeah, that might work." He leaned forward, "The Agency programmers are about two weeks away from completing their testing of the code and installing the backdoors anyway. That should give us enough time to get the permissions we need from the home office to turn the code over."

"I'd recommend it," Joe added, "I think it would go a long way toward building trust between Eric and Kate. And if he knows someone who can build that tumbler, I think we'd like to get to know that person even if they're not tied to our current case."

"I agree," Elliot stood up from his chair, "I'll get

the paperwork started."

The caffeine saturated men scattered to their rooms to work the night away. Kate found a pen and began filling out the Programmers for Peace and Freedom's membership form.

When she finally crawled into bed Kate could hear the faint hum of Joe's television seeping through the wall. She imagined him typing frantically on his keyboard until the early hours of the morning, the television's drone and flicker his only companion and comfort. For once Kate didn't mind being the pawn.

14
PALMER, ALASKA

The spring semester was well underway and it had been a little more than six weeks since Kate had sent the code to Eric. Several attempts to send follow-up emails had only resulted in 'failed to send' return messages. The code was in the wind.

The Agency team had built spyware into the code that allowed them to keep an eye on its location and shut it down at will. Kate had warned Eric about the safety feature and suggested he not modify it in any way without her permission.

"It's there to protect my code. Don't screw with it or I'll shut it down," Kate had warned him.

Currently the Bitcoin wallet code was residing unaltered on a server in Antiqua, but was being viewed from an untraceable location.

Meanwhile, Kate became more active in the Programmers for Peace and Freedom organization by co-editing their monthly newsletter, which gave her access to the membership roster including email addresses. She'd also been a regular attendee of the group's online seminars. The virtual nature of the organization's activities made it difficult to get to know people beyond their screen names and avatars, which were often pictures of pets or characters from graphic novels. So far the most she had learned was that PickleEater426 had a bulldog named Rosemary who would eat the kitchen sponge every chance it got and the flowers in Augger's avatar were White Knight roses. While not exactly great intelligence, Kate was able to establish White Knight roses only grew in zones 7 & 8. Not surprisingly, Augger mentioned at one point that he or she lived in Texas.

The FBI was trying to run background checks as best they could on the known U.S. members of PPF based on their screen names. The NSA was checking out the foreign members, while Kate was relegated to looking at avatars online with her head tipped to the side, resting in her hand. Unsatisfied by her pursuit, she began drumming her fingers on the desk before making a decision to head to the campus cafeteria in search of cookies.

Kate had finished one of the oatmeal raisin cookies by the time she returned to her office. An email notification was illuminated in red in the middle of her computer screen indicating there was a message from Eric Broudy in her inbox. The first thing Kate noticed was that it was from a different email address than the one she sent the code to.

Just checking to see if you're coming to the London

event next month, we can talk then.

    -- Eric Broudy

Kate picked up her secure phone and called Joe before booking her flight to London.

15

LONDON

The team's arrival in London was staggered over a week with Kate arriving on the fourth day giving her a couple of days before the conference to handle some preliminary business.

"Pleasant day," Kate remarked to the doorman as she exited the hotel, "I believe the decision to leave the umbrella in my room was a sound one."

"Indeed madam. The sun is expected to shine most of the day. It smells like spring too, first morning I've noticed."

"It smells quite wonderful after yesterday's rain. I think I'll try the upper deck on the tour bus today."

"Have a pleasant afternoon." The doorman tipped his hat in Kate's direction before turning to help a man capture his toddler who was making a break for the next block.

The short walk to the tour bus station left Kate with

plenty of time to browse through the Visitor Centre and gift shop before the next tour. She purchased a snow globe featuring Big Ben and the Houses of Parliament and a tea towel in the design of a union jack.

"There's an apron to match that tea towel if you'd like," the clerk offered as she carefully folded the tea towel into the bottom of the handled paper bag emblazoned with 'Keep Calm and Shop London Original' beneath a crown.

"No thank you, it's a gift for my house sitter and she'll never know that she missed out on a matching apron."

"No, I suppose she won't." The clerk offered a smile that unfortunately perpetuated stereotypes about British dental health and handed Kate her bag, "Here you are, enjoy your tour."

The early spring season made for thin crowds on the tour bus and Kate was the third person at this stop to ascend to the upper deck. A group of six South Korean tourists were huddled near the back of the bus. *One, two, three, four, five,* Kate counted the rows in her head before taking the interior seat on the starboard side of the bus. She placed her bag on the adjoining seat and sat back to enjoy the tour.

At each stop along the tour route, some people got on the bus and others got off. Near the Tower of London a doughy middle-aged woman in a bright yellow flannel coat with a headscarf knotted under her chin and burdened with a large tote and a shopping bag boarded the upper deck and approached Kate.

"Is that other seat taken by anything other than whatever that is?" she asked pointing to the shopping bag atop the outside seat.

"No, it's free."

"Would you mind removing your bag and moving over so I can share your row?" the woman said with forceful irritation even though there were plenty of other seats available.

Kate slid over and placed the shopping bag on the floor between the seats. As she did, she noticed the South Korean delegation huddled tightly together speaking with nervous excitement over Kate's public rebuke. It was difficult to tell if they were pleased or embarrassed.

Once seated the woman ignored Kate and exited the bus three stops later, but not before thumping a man on the head with her shopping bag as she passed his seat on her way to the stairs. The man turned toward Kate and shook his head in one of those 'I feel your pain' gestures and Kate shrugged an 'I know, but what are you going to do' back toward him.

Kate departed the bus on two occasions, the first to tour the Natural History Museum and the second to ride the London Eye, even though the wait time in the queue was fifty minutes longer than the actual ride. Returning to the hotel in time for dinner, Kate dashed to her room to change.

"Well hello, I'm glad you made it." Kate greeted Joe with a peck on the cheek as the door to her room slammed shut.

"Latch that," Joe said jerking his head toward the door as he relieved Kate of her shopping bag.

"I would never forget to latch the door and put out the 'Do Not Disturb' sign. I'm firmly ensconced in the culture and habits of the professional paranoid by now."

Joe narrowed his eyes and watched Kate huffily secure the door. "There's no need to be so flippant, Kate. I realize it may be a coping mechanism, but I'd suggest you check yourself."

Kate responded by crossing her arms angrily and shifting her weight to one side. Joe heard *"Don't even"* in her body language and decided to let it go.

"Great job today on the drop, we managed to pull it off on the first attempt."

"What's with the 'we' in that sentence? I believe it was the British Secret Intelligence Service and me that pulled it off. I still don't understand why I had to stand in line at the London Eye for over an hour when the exchange had already happened on the bus."

"Just trying to have you act like a natural tourist, that's all. Besides, you enjoyed the museum, didn't you?"

"Very much, but I did not enjoy the treatment by their agent on the bus. What a piece of work."

"Was she rude?"

"Yes, she was rude!"

"Most people become uncomfortable and look away when someone is being rude to someone else in public, it makes it easier to switch the bags without anyone noticing. It sounds like she practiced good tradecraft to me."

"I did enjoy when she whacked the guy in the head with her bag to indicate a successful drop though. He has no idea how lucky he was that I didn't buy the official cast iron Dr. Who Tardis Letterbox."

"If you had bought the letterbox The Circus might have made you carry it all over London until the final drop opportunity, you may be lucky yourself." Joe dumped the contents of the shopping bag the rude woman had switched with Kate's onto the bed. They sat down on opposite sides of the pile.

"Here's your cell phone," Joe said turning it on and leaning toward Kate. "They've duplicated all your apps, contacts, email, and such so it looks just like yours, except there are a few enhancements."

"This app that's been added to your first page called 'Cooking Everything' is your SOS button. If you open it, it looks just like a regular recipe app and anyone who opens it can click and scroll through the recipes. However, if you hold your finger on the home key, the fingerprint reader will send a help message to your exfiltration team. It will also trigger a window that simply says 'copies' with a text box next to it. If you want a stealth exfiltration, enter the number 1. If you're in serious danger and don't mind a large, very public response, enter 2 and the cavalry will roll in, guns blazing. Be very cautious about a level 2 response, because it will forever blow your cover." Kate nodded her understanding.

"Next, your maps app has some additional features. Open the map and select in the following order, Satellite, Terrain, Bike Paths, and then Explore." Joe demonstrated and a new map appeared with red and blue pins on it. "The red pins are safe places you can go and are labeled with code words. For example, this small, family-run hotel on the map labeled 'Aurora'. Simply go to the location and ask for the code name at the reception area. There are only a few of these locations and they are all available on the map at any time, but they do change frequently and will try to remain near your location."

"The blue pins are dead drop locations if we need to get something to you or if you need to drop something off for us. After you click on the pin, you'll be asked to enter your zip code. That code is 99586 and you'll need to verify with your thumbprint again. Once you've done that, a window will open and explain the exact drop location at the site and how to mark if it's been filled. If for any reason the package is too big, dead drop a note and we'll arrange for a pick up at one of the safe locations. Understand?" Joe looked at Kate with his eyebrows raised awaiting her response.

Kate sat with her eyes closed silently moving her lips before her eyes shot open, "99586, got it."

"All your usual contacts have been loaded, but we've added two. The first, Art Beldam, will connect you to our helpline and the second, Mary Fenn, will get you to our MI6 host's line. Your codename for the Brits is Peggy Albright, to whom we've also assigned a phone number in case your memory lapses under the stress of the moment."

Kate's eyes were closed again, but her mouth was frozen in an amused smirk as she archived the information into whatever files made sense within her mind palace. "You know I rarely forget anything, Joe," her face releasing itself to move through the full motions of her amusement at Joe's redundancies.

"I know, but there's a first time for everything. The rest of this stuff is fairly standard fare, but it's the Brits technology since we've agreed to let them have first dibs on the information and they'll copy us. The pendent in this necklace contains a small camera, but they tell us you'll have to have bright light to use it. It works like this." Joe demonstrated; Kate nodded silently. "If you can openly use your phone's camera, that would be preferable."

"There's also an earpiece that looks like a hearing aid, but since you've met Eric before and he may have noticed you don't wear one, we'll only have you wear it if we really need hands-free two-way communication and you can't use a cell phone. You turn it on here." More attentive nods emanated from Kate. "You know the mission, I'm going to have to discontinue any direct communications for a while after this meeting. Any questions before I go?"

"Nothing that I can think of."

"Then consider yourself in the wind. Now I'm going to go get some dinner and good luck at the conference tomorrow." Joe left without any additional fanfare.

That night as Kate tried to fall asleep a flurry of questions she wished she had asked Joe crowded her dreams and she woke in a sweat just before dawn.

16
WASHINGTON, DC

PDD Lanser walked the long-way back to the office. Moments of serenity were in short supply in this business and he wasn't quite ready to give up the moment yet. He was returning to his office after his briefing from Admiral Reynolds about the President's meeting. Lanser's division needed to move their efforts in a new direction and he was rolling over implementation details in his head as he walked. Harrison wasn't going to like it, he knew that much.

Harrison was looking at baby pictures with a member of PDD Lanser's administrative staff when he walked into the outer office and gestured for Harrison to follow him into his office. Once inside small talk was exchanged about the baby in the pictures before PDD Lanser informed Harrison of the change in operational direction.

"Admiral Reynolds wants us to write up our

report indicating what we've done including that we haven't located an outside infiltration. Afterwards, he wants us move on to the active policy reforms he's outlined and the President has approved. While he wants some IT resources to continue to work on trying to locate the hacker, our priorities in this office have changed. We're moving responsibility for the breach to the department level internally." Harrison took notes as PDD Lanser spoke.

"Well that doesn't make any sense. Shouldn't we work on both fronts since they're related issues and we need to put preventative measures in place? And what if we have a mole?"

"Doggone it Harrison, I don't give a diddley doot whether or not you think it makes sense. Besides, neither Admiral Reynolds nor I believe there's a mole. We've found no evidence of one. Plus, there's a chain of command in this organization and I'm closest to the south end of this northbound mule and if Admiral Reynolds instructs us to redirect, we redirect!"

"But what about the field team? I'd like to keep them out and working on this."

"Have they actually made any progress yet?"

"A little, but these operations take time."

"Harrison, we are out of time!"

"I really don't think we should call them in. A lot of goodwill has been expended with the Brits on this. I think we should leave them over there. We've been looking for ways to infiltrate this group anyway, so there may be other information about underground networks that come out of it that can only help us."

"If you leave that team in the field, I don't want

to know about it until they either find our hacker or discover a way to spontaneously achieve world peace." Lanser poked his pencil toward Harrison. "Your neck is solely on the line on this one, so make a good decision. Dismissed!"

Harrison went back to his office and pulled out his file box titled, "The Executive". He reviewed the material again, but just couldn't put his finger on what was nagging at him. After staring at his wall and rolling things around in his head for nearly an hour, he leapt to his feet in a state of decision. Moving briskly to the communication center he found a young woman he'd never met before occupying the desk.

"I need to send a message to the Aurora Team, please."

Arranging herself at the keyboard she responded, "Proceed with message."

"You're autonomous, period."

The woman waited, "Is that all, sir."

"Yes."

"Do you wish to wait for a response?"

"No." Harrison left the room with a slipknot tightening around his stomach.

17

LONDON

The London conference was a single day of lectures in a common large auditorium. Kate hadn't slept well and the darkened room flickering with PowerPoint slides reduced her to hibernation mode and the struggle to keep her eyes open was real. She had looked for Eric in the room and on breaks, but had not been able to find him. The emails she had sent asking where to meet him had been returned as undeliverable. She was giving up on Eric and giving in to the weight of her eyelids when her phone buzzed: *The coffee shop downstairs in 10 minutes?* Kate responded in the affirmative and abandoned her seat.

Kate arrived early to find Eric already sipping a mug of steaming liquid. "Hi Kate, have a seat." He signaled for a server. A woman with a perky ponytail that bounced excessively when she walked arrived to take Kate's order of green tea.

"I tried to send you some emails, but they were all returned. I was starting to think you might have taken my code and ran with it."

"Sorry about that. I use a string of hundreds of email addresses when I'm dealing with people I don't know well. They rotate through them at random intervals of never more than an hour."

"Wow, that's a lot of accounts to keep track of."

"It's not really a problem. I've created a program that allows me to use a central entry point to create my emails and then it copies the message and pastes it into an email from a random address. It works pretty well for outgoing mail."

"I might have to try that with my students. Outbound only email sounds fantastic for minimizing complaints and excuses." Eric smiled as Kate asked, "So is there actually a way to consistently send you email? I mean, I was able to send you the code via email, but that was it."

"Yes, but few people have that information. I specifically assigned the email address you used for the code to you and once the code was sent, the system deleted the address." Kate made an 'ah' type noise and nodded her understanding. "You will be happy to know we did not abscond with your code. In fact, we found it quite impressive and are interested in working with you, if you have an open mind."

"I don't know. I suppose it depends on what you mean by 'an open mind'."

"It means we work in nonconventional ways. I've done a little research on you and you appear to be somewhat libertarian in your thinking, so I suspect your mind is open in the way I mean."

"Okay, what did you have in mind?" Kate leaned forward a little as she sipped from her cup, her curiosity piqued.

"It means packing your bags and taking a road trip with me to the countryside. I'll be able to show you what I mean there."

"This isn't one of those ploys to lure me into the woods to slaughter me, is it. I've seen that movie."

"Oh no," Eric laughed, "it's nothing like that. I just want to show you where and how we work."

"Well, you're in luck. My bag is partially packed for tomorrow's flight so I can be ready quickly."

"Great, but be prepared, you might decide to cancel your flight for tomorrow. But that will be your decision. Is thirty minutes enough time to be ready to leave?"

"I'm intrigued enough to be down in twenty."

"I'll have the car brought around."

18
THE ROAD

The hotel had painfully slow elevators so Kate leapt up the stairs two at a time to her third-floor room. She rolled up the remaining loose clothes on the bed and tossed her make-up into a dopp kit before stuffing it all into her leather carryon bag. Never a minimalist by nature, the job had taught Kate to travel light. Eric was waiting next to his car in the hotel's porte cochère when Kate arrived.

"My goodness, is this a Saab 9-5?" Kate asked as she slid into it.

"Yes, the last model year made. They may be out of business, but they still have the best cup holders in the industry." Eric demonstrated by pushing against a slot in the dash to initiate the launch sequence for the drink holder. They watched as it slid out of the slot and turned itself ninety degrees to ready itself for a drink.

"Like a fine Swiss watch," Kate observed.

"Almost," Eric chuckled.

"So where exactly are we going?"

"I'm going to show you rather than tell you so you can back out at any time before we get there. If I tell you before we get to our destination and you decide not to go, things get a little more difficult."

"Now you're scaring me," Kate said shifting uncomfortably in her seat as she mentally grasped for some control over the situation.

"I'm not trying to frighten you. I just thought we could talk about the project a little on our drive and you could decide if it's something you'd like to pursue, otherwise you can say no and I haven't told you where we do business."

"Fair enough. So tell me how you think you can help me with the tumbler I've been so far unsuccessful creating," Kate asked trying to regain some control over herself and the conversation.

"We have several people who could help build that tumbler. I think the level of technical expertise we have available will surprise you. Some of the best and brightest programmers in the world work with us. I think you might be among them."

Kate gave a shy smile, "I don't know why you'd think that. What I've done is not particularly complicated and so far I've failed to independently produce a tumbler. That's the hard part."

"Ah, but it is not what you've done that intrigues me. You are a superior strategic thinker. It's not the wallet as much as the application. You've come up with a unique and innovative way to deal with moving money overseas for those of us who might have a need to do so quietly."

"I suppose I have."

"It's not only that. The way you programmed the protection and security back doors in your program was brilliant. We value people who put security and privacy first. It reminds me of someone who used to be with us…" Eric's voice trailed off.

"Who would that be?"

"Oh, it's not important." Eric gazed out the windshield and repositioned his hands on the steering wheel in a way that partially hid his face from Kate behind his right shoulder. He fell silent, lost in thought.

It was unseasonably cold and the drizzle of London had turned into a steady rain as they moved through the countryside. The cloud ceiling had gradually been falling in on them. The clouds now hung so low Kate unconsciously slid lower in her seat to duck under them. It would be foggy soon and the uncertainty of the weather and destination made her fidget and pick aimlessly at her fingernails. Eric's silence and the reliable squeak of the windshield wipers a fitting soundtrack to her rising fears. Kate closed her eyes and reminded herself she was not being kidnapped. *I'm not alone, I have a support team nearby, and I'm going to be okay.*

Memories Kate had suppressed for years began to well up as her central nervous system ran old scenarios through her mind as if to prepare her to respond to whatever danger might lie ahead. She tried to push them back down, but it only made the memories more vivid. She began to recall how the attack on the World Trade

Center, which happened the fall after Kate had completed graduate school, had prompted her to join the military. Like many of the things Kate had done in her life, her upper-middleclass mother did not support this decision. Kate rarely allowed thoughts of those years to reach her consciousness; there were more recent traumas to occupy her mind. Yet right now, without warning, she was back in Fallujah and the only female attached to a Delta Force unit.

She had been working in Fallujah to gain the trust of a forty-year-old Iraqi woman who had given herself the American name Lisa. Raised by a progressive father who perceived his daughter's intelligence at an early age, Lisa had been well educated both by her father and in the West. By the time she was four-years old, her father, with the help of a tutor, began to teach her English. When she was eight, her father's position in the Diplomatic Services took them to the United Kingdom where Lisa was enrolled in a British boarding school. While her father's UK assignment lasted only two years, he quietly left Lisa at the school, an act that angered Lisa's maternal grandfather.

During her time at the school, Lisa traveled throughout Europe and dreamed of one day improving the situation for all women in Iraq. She later studied Public Policy at Cambridge. "You will be the first female Prime Minister of Iraq. I just know it!" her father would say. And then, shortly after Lisa's university graduation, her father died.

Lisa arrived at her childhood home to grieve and help her mother as much as she could in the days following his death. "Go back to England," her mother implored, "never look back at Iraq."

Four weeks after she had arrived in Iraq, Lisa was at the airport to return to England and a summer job with a human rights organization before moving on to law school in the fall. Standing in line to board the plane, she heard someone yelling and turned to find her maternal grandfather shouting and running in her direction with the police.

The men grabbed Lisa and dragged her away to a waiting car where she was shoved into the back seat with her grandfather, "Your place is here. Now that your father is dead, it is your responsibility to marry and care for your mother. There are no other options for you."

The following morning Lisa was taken in chains and forced to marry the man her grandfather declared was "The only man in Iraq strong enough to manage Lisa and teach her to be a respectful wife and mother."

Lisa's husband was now a senior military leader of the Islamic State of Iraq and the Levant. Fuad al-Abadi was a cruel, vicious man who broke Lisa's spirit with whips, chains, stones, fire, starvation, and public humiliation. Living in fear, Lisa accepted her fate. She bore him three children, a son named Sivan and two daughters Marwa and Hadeel.

The U.S. government had become very interested in detaining Fuad al-Abadi for questioning, but they couldn't find him. Kate's job while embedded with Delta Force was to get Lisa to tell them where Fuad was or when he would be home. After staging several chance meetings with Lisa in public, Kate knocked on the door of Lisa's home. At first Lisa tried to slam the door in her face, but Kate pushed her way in. Surprised that Lisa wouldn't jump at the chance to rid herself of her husband, Kate spent several months visiting Lisa to help unravel the psychological damage her husband had done to her.

Once Lisa's self-esteem began to return, she expressed fears for her safety and that of her children if she cooperated with the U. S. At the time Sivan was ten-years old and the girls six and seven. With her husband away and Sivan at school, Lisa educated her daughters and also taught them English.

"My future is in my children's hands," Lisa would say, "I must keep them safe so they can make change in Iraq, it's too late for me. My husband's position provides us safety and he's gone so often now he rarely beats me anymore."

As the months wore on, Kate became frustrated with her progress until one day Lisa contacted Kate and asked her to come to her home immediately.

"What's wrong?" Kate asked when she arrived to find Lisa in a state of agitation.

"Fuad has contacted me, he wants me to prepare Sivan to be taken to the camp."

"What camp?"

"He wants him to go to the military training camp for children. Sivan is so young, but Fuad says he wants Sivan to be near him and begin his training to become a soldier. I will not let him take my boy."

"So you'll help us?"

"Yes, yes I will if, as you promised, you will take me and my children to America. I fear there may be less hope here for my children than there is for me."

"Of course, we will exfiltrate you at the same

time we remove your husband."

"I have one more request."

"Yes, what is it?"

"I want you yourself to take him away. I want to see the humiliation on his face by being captured by an American woman."

"I think that can be arranged."

Kate had never participated in a raid before. She practiced with the Delta team for weeks in a mockup of the Fuad al-Abadi home before Lisa contacted her with the information about his arrival.

The drone crew alerted the Delta team to Fuad's arrival and they barely let him get settled before swooping in on the home. Fuad was able to grab a rifle as they blew in through the front and rear doors and pointed it at the team. Since the order was to take him alive everyone in front of him momentarily froze, guns trained on Fuad. Those to his rear were still slowly and silently closing in on him. Lisa had gathered the children and was standing with them in the entryway to the dining area. Fuad shouted and waved his gun at his wife and children before yelling what Kate later learned was, "If you kill me, you kill women and children too," before abruptly shooting Sivan.

Before Fuad could get off another shot, he was knocked down from behind and bound. The entire scene had happened so fast, the events seemed to have occured simultaneously. Now, as time began to slow down, Kate ran to Lisa and dropped to her knees beside the wailing woman begging her son to wake up as his blood pooled onto the floor. So much blood. Kate took Lisa in her arms and held her while rocking and whispering how sorry she was. They needed to move quickly, but Lisa wouldn't leave Sivan's side. Kate picked up Sivan's body and threw it over her shoulders as she led Lisa out of the house and into the waiting helicopter. Kate could feel Sivan's blood running down the back of her neck and saturating her clothes.

After placing the body on the floor of the chopper, Kate moved close to Fuad. She had never wanted to kill someone out of anger as much as she did at that moment. Kate spit in Fuad's face before kneeing him in the groin and hitting him across the face with her left elbow. He rolled in a ball and begged for mercy. Stevens grabbed her arm, "That's enough Kate," as she removed her helmet to ensure Fuad knew he was being assaulted by a woman.

"Are you alright?" Eric asked jolting Kate from the memory.

Kate realized she was sweating profusely and her skin was bright red. It took her a moment to regain her bearings and unclench her jaw. "Yes, I'm fine, just one heck of a hot flash I'm afraid. I guess I'm getting to that age. May I?" she asked pointing to the air conditioning control.

"Of course, make yourself comfortable."

Quiet descended in the car's cabin once again and Kate willed herself to remain in the present. They were heading north/northwest and as they approached the coast near Liverpool a gusty wind began howling across the road, forcing the rain to take a ninety-degree detour and begin blindingly pelting the driver's side window. Eric removed his left hand from his knee and added it to the steering wheel.

They passed through the resort community of Blackpool, it's landmark tower obscured within the clouds. Eric offered no tour as they slowly drove past the town's promenade and pier, delayed by the late-day traffic.

"Not much farther," Eric offered abruptly, his bass voice creating a clearing inside the car as the thick, murky silence pushed out against the windows.

Throughout most of the journey the towns and villages melted one into the other, but as they moved north of Blackpool there was a country clearing. Eric stopped at a 4-way stop that seemed out of place in the rural setting.

He pointed right, "There's a large, modern industrial park up that road about four miles, but we're going left where the old industrial park used to sit. It was largely abandoned in the 1980s during the recession when manufacturing began moving to China. It's great oceanfront property, but not suitable for development due to ground contamination from heavy metals the foundries allowed to seep into the soil. There were concerns that attempts to clean up the land would lead to the destruction of the shorefront, so the government elected to just let nature clean it up over time."

He made a left-hand turn and continued, "At the time the government made the decision, we were squatting in the old shoe factory. They came in to tear down the buildings and clean the surface soil as best they could. We petitioned to take ownership of the building we were in and through a series of obscure squatters rights laws in Europe, we were able to buy the building rather than let it be destroyed. However, we had to make some improvements to the property, which we wanted to do anyway."

"But what about the ground contamination?"

"It's not a problem as long as we don't dig a well and use the ground water. We collect and process rain water and have large tanks filled with imported freshwater to supplement our needs."

The trees gave way to sweeping open spaces covered in field grass where the industrial park once stood. They rounded a corner to the left and a brick-walled factory rose up from behind the hill. "The building was built in the late 1800s," Eric added.

The old factory was a stately two-story building with tall stone-arched windows covering the façade on the lower level and smaller rectangular windows on the second floor. The stone arches on the first floor each contained three tall, narrow windows that were fixed at the top and tipped inward on the bottom quarter for ventilation. The individual panes included a mix of clear glass and opaque panes of blue, green, yellow, and red. The exterior walls of the building were reinforced by an iron exoskeleton with supports that jutted out like the third leg of an easel.

Rising up from the left side of the building were two dormant smoke stacks. An extensive green house had been added onto the structure's right side. Eric pulled the car into a parking space near the entrance, "Welcome to The Commune."

19
FALLS CHURCH, VIRGINIA

Faulkner kept blinking his fatigued, watering eyes, the strong aroma of garlic arousing his consciousness as he drove. 'Rugerio's' had let him pick up his food at the back-kitchen door thirty minutes after they'd closed.

"This is the last time!" Mr. Rugerio warned, shaking his fist and slamming the door.

"Hey, I improved my late time by twenty minutes!" Faulkner shouted at the door as the locks clicked inside. Apparently Mr. Rugerio didn't give credit for improvement.

What day is it anyway? Faulkner tried to reconnect with the world outside the Salt Mine. He steered his car around a Honda Civic with a broken taillight that protruded well beyond its parking space. *Thursday, I think.* The phone's calendar lit the car's cabin when he tapped it, *Yes, Thursday. Let's see, I haven't been home since Monday night, yes I left for the office Tuesday morning.*

The streets of his Falls Church neighborhood had been bustling with joggers, parents pushing strollers, school buses, and briefcase wielding commuters when he had left for work on Tuesday morning. Now, except for the shimmer of wet pavement in the pools of LED lamplight, it was desolate. The walls of his stomach begin to relax the closer he drew to home and hunger began to gurgle its accession for the first time in days. Every fiber of his body relaxed as he shifted the car into park in his driveway. He sat there, motionless, listening to the news on public radio as he succumbed to his weariness.

At first, the sound of jazz trumpeter Miles Davis' horn coming from the open front window of his house startled Faulkner as he stepped out of the car. Fear soon gave way to sentimentality for officer's clubs, the salt air of Guam, and a woman name Margaux. Faulkner inhaled deeply to prolong the fleeting memory before walking up the steps to the front door. The door was not closed tightly and he pushed it open slowly and silently. Faulkner peered in to find his close friend of so many years ago sprawled out on his sofa. His head was thrown back over the sofa's arm and his eyes were closed. One foot moved in time with the music as the ice melted in a glass of brown liquor swaying in his outstretched arm.

"Are you comfortable Admiral Reynolds?" Faulkner asked as he moved through the room and into the kitchen.

"Quite," Reynolds yelled after him not opening his eyes, "but let's cut the Admiral crap tonight, got it?"

"Roger that, but what brings you here tonight Reynolds? I haven't seen you in person since we were both Navy Commanders."

"Yeah, and if you would have stayed in the Navy you'd be leading the NSA instead of me."

"Not true. You were always better positioned with your combat and field intelligence experience, I was just a tech guy."

"Baloney, you were one of the best intelligence tech people we ever had. It's people like you we need to lead modern national security and warfare. I feel like a dinosaur from the prehistoric War College era when all you had to do was count the enemy's missiles, tanks, fighter planes, and bombers and you'd know who was going to win and whether you'd be home in time for dinner before the first bullet ever flew. Now, everyone has access to computers and social media and can organize an attack on a perceived enemy. You don't even need a country to go to war, just an ideology. No," Reynolds shook his head, "you'd be much better in the modern era of warfare than I am."

Reynolds sat up and sipped loudly from his glass as Faulkner arrived in the living room with his plated food.

"Still won't eat out of carry-out containers I see," Reynolds gave a snorting chuckle, "don't let me stop you from eating."

"I don't intend to." Faulkner set his plate of spaghetti and garlic bread on the coffee table. "So, to what do I owe the pleasure of your company with my dinner?" Faulkner began cutting his meatballs into bite-sized pieces. "I assume this isn't a social call and has something to do with the fact that you're now ultimately my boss." He stabbed a piece of meatball before scooping up some spaghetti and twirling it skillfully on a tablespoon until all loose ends were gone.

"My problem is, I don't know who I can trust. What if you're right and there is a mole? How will I know whom I can talk to about that theory? Hell Jason, you could be the mole!"

There was an awkward pause between the two men. Faulkner continued to stab meatballs, spin spaghetti, and chew. Reynolds let the silence hang until Faulkner couldn't take it any longer, "So, what's your point? We all have the same trust issues."

"I know, I know," Reynolds gestured dismissively at Faulkner. "But what's your impression of this person you imagine to be a mole? Where does he or she reside? What's their cause? Are they internal or external to the organization? I'm out of facts to deal with here. I'm ready to listen to gut instinct and I've always trusted yours."

"I can't really say I've formed an impression of the person yet, but there is one thing that's bothering me."

Reynolds leaned forward, "What is it?"

"Why hasn't the person releasing the information onto the dark web identified themselves?"

"What do you mean? Wouldn't they want to stay unknown?"

"Not usually." Faulkner dropped his fork onto his plate with a clatter so he could gesture with his hands as he talked. "Think about it. In every whistleblower case we've ever seen, the person releasing the information either identifies their real selves as in Julian Assange and Wikileaks or a pseudonym like Anonymous. The person supplying the information is usually the one who tries to remain unidentified. But whoever releases it is the vigilante who claims to be fighting for the public good. They're the one who craves attention and superhero status from the public."

"So what does that tell you about our whistleblower, The Executive?"

"We've all assumed The Executive is a single person who's stealing and releasing information, but what if it's more than one person? There might be multiple suppliers of information and another person releasing it. If that's the case, looking for the one person who's had access to all the released information isn't helpful because it's coming from multiple sources. Or, what if The Executive isn't a person or group of people at all, but a foreign government?"

"The foreign government angle might explain some of the misleading information designed to make the U.S. look bad in the eyes of the world. Today's whopper was that we're going to move troops and missiles to the Ukrainian border in a plan to push Russia out of Crimea."

"We've been so busy worrying about the release of secrets, when we should be figuring out who benefits from the lies." Faulkner picked up his garlic bread and took a generous bite.

Reynolds stood and began pacing the room. "It's difficult to immediately see a pattern of who benefits, but more detailed analysis might be in order. Jason, will you work on it?"

"Me? Are you kidding? I have enough to do."

"I'm going to pull you out of IT and make you a Temporary Special Assistant. I need you to look at two things: who's benefiting from the lies and where the actual data release is coming from."

"I thought you had a team in the field working on locating the source of the release."

"They were on a wild goose chase. I've told Lanser to have them stand down. Maybe I'm getting paranoid in my old age, but I need to keep the circle on this one small. You're one of the few people I believe I can actually trust. I also think you're one of the few people who can actually solve this thing."

Faulkner's weary eyes searched Reynold's face for something that would make him feel comfortable about taking on such a task, but he didn't even know what he was looking for. "I don't think so Doug."

"You don't have to give me an answer now Jason, you're obviously exhausted. Take the next three days off and rest up; we'll talk about it on Monday."

As the door closed behind Admiral Reynolds, Faulkner lay down on the sofa with the waves of Miles Davis still softly moving through the room. As he dozed he accepted that he'd be working directly for Reynolds come Monday morning.

20
NORTH OF BLACKPOOL, ENGLAND

The rain had ebbed, but the wind continued to rock their parked car. Something squeaked near the right rear tire as the car bobbed. Eric had turned off the car and absent the heater, the piercing wind squeezed through the car's crevices blowing thin streams of compressed icy air around them, raising goose bumps on Kate's flesh. In front of them the factory loomed, silhouetted around angular patches of yellow-lit windows, its steel exoskeleton creating the menacing appearance of a villain's lair in a Batman comic book. Thunder rolled across the sky and Kate struggled to suppress the reel of horror film highlights running through her head.

"Why do you call it 'The Commune'?" Kate asked to distract herself from the scene.

"We practice what we call neo-anarcho

communism. While we believe in the ownership of personal property, we don't recognize the legitimacy of the government to control our lives. Our group shares, collectively self-governs, and will never be allowed to grow to more than 150 members. Once the commune reaches that size, at least 10 members must break off and form a new group. Collective governance becomes far too difficult at numbers larger than that. We do retain relationships with other groups, trade and barter primarily in products, knowledge, and information."

"How does the sharing part work?"

"Quite easily really. While I technically own the building according to the government, I share it with everyone who lives here. We share knowledge and ideas, work collectively on projects, and use the individual gifts we've been given to support the economy of the collective. Individuals are allowed to keep any revenues they earn after a ten percent contribution to the collective. We use that money to expand our economy and security, pay for support people like cooks and accountants, as well as utilities and things like that."

"Interesting, but it's still somewhat difficult for me to wrap my brain around."

"Let's go inside and I'll show you."

The rusted hinges of the building's industrial metal door made a high-pitched squeal as it opened. They stepped into what had been the echoing lobby and administrative offices of the factory. The white linoleum floor tiles had weathered to a dingy shade of beige and were covered in black scuffmarks from the shoes of early 20th century salesmen. The institutional blue-gray paint flaking off the walls appeared original. The doorframes were made of steel.

Kate imagined secretaries, clerks, and managers with their desks lined up one behind the other down the long, narrow office space located to their right behind a wall-sized pane of glass. She wondered what the protocol was for whose desk was positioned at the front versus the back of the office space. To their left, instead of a turn of the last century smartly-dressed receptionist with her hair in a bun and a pair of pencils artfully threaded through it, a gangly young man with a red face and dirty blonde hair that stuck up unevenly was sitting behind the tall reception desk.

"Hey Eric," the young man said as he momentarily looked up from his computer.

"Kate, this is Benny." Benny poked his chin in Kate's direction and uttered a sound that wasn't quite 'Hey', but was in that general linguistic range. "We lock the door at 10pm, but have a community member assigned to sit at the reception desk 24-hours a day in case someone who lives here needs to get in or out and to keep curious interlopers away. We get all sorts of people who wander in here wondering what we do. The official answer is research and development in the fertilizer and pesticide industry, which is why we need the greenhouse."

Kate didn't exactly know what to say so she remained silent.

"We keep the lobby area in its original shabby condition to discourage anyone from thinking this place is worth robbing." Eric nodded toward the inner door, "We'll go in now Benny."

Benny pushed a button under the desk and there

was a buzzing sound. Kate expected the door to open, but Eric held his thumb against a small bio scanner before the door's bolt clunked open. "It always takes two people to open the door. It's a security feature."

"I see"

The secured door opened into a large, two-story brick room that had been painstakingly refurbished. The room's 19th century walls were made of handmade brick, ranging in color from dark brown, to terra cotta, to beige, joined by gritty mortar the color of sand. The space was capped with a four-sided dormer skylight that at this hour revealed the stars. Refurbished wide-planked oak floors gleamed below them in rustic elegance while dark green ductwork ran overhead where the first-floor ceiling would have been and similarly painted water pipes and conduit framed one of the walls. Small windows lined each side of the room where they met the second-story of the rest of the building.

Three 80-inch flat screen televisions were positioned around the dimly lit room. Two young women and a scraggly-bearded man were engaged in a video game on one screen. Movies were playing on the other two sets where a smattering of people had gathered in beanbag-style furniture. In the remaining corner of the room was a cluster of people tapping away on their computers. There were probably 20 community members occupying the space, yet it was nearly silent. Most of the occupants were wearing noise-cancelling headsets and while there was occasional laughter in the room, it was limited to facial expressions and never voiced. Occasionally the video game players whispered to one another.

"Why is it so quiet in here?" Kate whispered.

"This is part of our common recreation area, and sound carries up to the second floor from here. Since we have people sleeping at all hours, we try to be respectful. It also makes it nice for those who wish to work or meditate in a more relaxed environment."

They pushed through a door on the left into a smaller game room with a pool table, foosball, classic video game machines, a ping-pong table, and air hockey. Two women were playing ping-pong and three men stood around the pool table analyzing the geometry required to get the three-ball into the corner pocket.

"Everyone, I'd like you to meet Kate."

Realizing this wasn't a room she needed to be quiet in, Kate said, "Hello, everyone."

They came over to shake Kate's hand and introduce themselves as Maria, Anna, Abir, Xavier, and Joel. "Are you going to be joining us, Kate?" Abir asked with genuine excitement over a potential new community member.

"Slow down, Abir," Eric said, "I'm just giving her the lay of the land at the moment."

"We look forward to seeing you again Kate," Anna added.

"Everyone seems very nice," Kate remarked to Eric as they made their way back into the main brick room.

"It's much easier to be nice when we are all equal in power. It allows us to celebrate one another's accomplishments rather than engage in petty jealousy," Eric smiled.

On the far side of the brick room on the backside

of the wall was a set of grated metal stairs with metal pipe railings painted the same dark shade of green as the ductwork and water pipes. Eric led the way up the stairs.

"These are our living quarters. Every room is the same and there is a bathroom for every three rooms to share. This first room is mine," he opened the door and invited Kate in.

The room had one of the small rectangular windows Kate had seen from outside and she guessed in the daylight the room had an ocean view. There was a double-bed sized box spring and mattress on the floor, a low dresser with a mirror that looked like it came from a motel surplus store, a bookshelf, and a small closet. Some books and a few toiletries were present on the bookshelf, but the room was otherwise bare.

Sensing her observation, Eric added, "I'm a minimalist at heart, but community members may decorate their rooms any way they want. Some make very clever and elaborate use of the space."

They made their way back down the stairs and turned to their left, away from the brick-walled room. In this section, the front part of the building contained a commercial grade kitchen and dining hall.

"We believe it is the most economic use of our time to work rather than cook. Our operations allow us the luxury of a cafeteria and full-time staff. It's a bit like a university cafeteria, just on a smaller scale. We eat meals together at scheduled times and snacks are always available." Eric gestured in the direction of a long counter that was set up much like a hotel breakfast station with cereal, juice, and soda dispensers, pastries, a bowl of fruit, a toaster, and an assortment of breads and bagels. Next to the counter was a narrow glass-fronted refrigerator with bottles of water, small cartons of milk, yogurt, and hard-boiled eggs.

"Does the staff live on-site?"

"Most don't, but we give them the option of community membership and a room for a reduced salary. Only one of our current staff members has joined us."

Eric pushed through the double door that led toward the rear of the building. They entered a large open space with immense windows that in the daylight must have offered a spectacular view of the ocean. Outside the window was a vast patio lit by old-fashioned street lamps scattered throughout. In the center was a grouping of patio sofas and chairs around a large raised fire pit designed to shoot a gas fire out of a bed of glass. The rest of the patio was covered with groupings of tables and chairs with umbrellas neatly tucked away for the storm.

Three of the walls of the room itself were lined with a counter-like desk with chairs placed every five feet or so. The interior space of the room consisted of round pods of five desks separated by two-foot walls that rose up from the top edges of the desk's surfaces. Three men and a woman occupied one pod and seemed to be collaborating on a project. A second pod was occupied by three men each working independently.

"This is one of our work spaces. Many of our members write software, create apps or games, some even have regular jobs and are able to work from the community doing programming or research and analysis. Others have online retail or wholesale companies."

"What does he do?" Kate pointed to a solitary

angry looking man who had set up a hard drive, keyboard, and three monitors in a corner of the room. He was moving his head between monitors like he was watching a tennis match and clicking furiously between an array of charts.

"That's Condor. He's a professional whistleblower."

"What do you mean?"

"Condor used to be a floor trader on the London Stock Exchange. Around the time computers started taking over the floor trader's jobs, Condor allegedly had a nervous breakdown and was hospitalized. Eventually, he made his way here, but no one is really sure how he became a member of the community. We actually think of him as kind of a community squatter, but he contributes and doesn't cause any trouble."

"But how is he a 'professional whistleblower'?"

"Oh yes, well he does a little day trading to earn a steady income, but you see all those graphs and data he's moving through over there?"

"Yes."

"He's convinced that computerized traders are cheating and gaming the system somehow. Condor spends most of his day looking for indications of individuals and firms defrauding the stock market system. When he thinks he's found some evidence he reports it to regulatory agencies under their whistleblower programs. Every once in a great while he's right and gets payouts of millions of dollars from regulatory agencies for the money he saves markets. His contribution to the community for his last payout is how we paid for that kitchen."

"I understand why you let him hang around then."

"He's a good guy, but we suspect he's on the autism spectrum. You'll get to know him a bit if you decide to hang around for a while." Eric made it sound more like a question than a statement. "I've shown you the aspects of our community that are generally considered socially acceptable by the majority of the population, how are you feeling about it? Are you ready to open your mind and go deeper?"

21
UNKNOWN LOCATION

"What do you mean, denied?" The Executive jumped to his feet and tore the paper out of the man's hand.

"I mean, all your requests for asylum have so far all been denied."

"But I need protection from extradition and a place to start a new community. They'll kill me if they find me."

"Relax, you can stay here with us. We won't turn you over to the Americans."

"It's not that I'm not grateful, but I don't want to stay here. If the man who hired me knows I'm here that will only enflame the situation. Besides, you don't want to be implicated, do you?"

"There is absolutely no reason for us to appear involved unless you tell someone and you really don't want to do that." The man stepped uncomfortably close to The Executive.

The Executive retreated to the table and sat down. "One email from me is all it would take to bring you down. You have to make one of those countries take me."

"I don't think you fully appreciate your situation," the man said grabbing the Executive's shirt and pulling him out of his seat and into the man's face. "We are allowing you to live so you can continue to do some work for us. If you even attempt to communicate with the outside world, you will disappear, but not painlessly."

The man threw The Executive onto the floor. "We will provide you and your female companion with a comfortable home and you with a nice nine-to-five job. You'll eventually have free movement within the country and can use the money we've paid you to live a happy and satisfying life. Or, you can watch your woman be tortured and killed before we do the same to you. Those are your options. Choose wisely and quickly."

The Executive laid on the floor, stunned, the color having drained from his face.

22
THE COMMUNE

Kate had generally considered herself to be so open-minded that she often refused to take her own side in an argument, but now a range of frightening possibilities circled her mind. Was the commune counterfeiting passports, credit cards, and currency? Involved in the illegal arms trade? Trafficking children or illegal aliens? Kate suddenly felt naïve about the world and the things that go on covertly in its darkest corners. Granted, the Agency often engaged in activity that would not be acceptable to the general public, but it was for the greater good. At least that's what she told herself now. What things could possibly be going on in a place like The Commune?

"I'm somewhat concerned about how open you believe my mind needs to be," Kate was struggling to keep her face neutral.

"Well, let's begin the rest of the tour and if you want to stop at any time, just let me know."

With that Eric opened a door that led into a small room adjacent to the computer work room with two floor-standing industrial wash sinks and yellow jumpsuit-style coveralls hanging from pegs. He walked the short distance across the room silently before pushing through the door on the other side. Warm, humid air consumed them as the pair stepped inside an immense greenhouse filled with cannabis plants in various stages of growth. To their left, six people were de-seeding, sorting, and weighing marijuana before packing it into plastic bags of a variety of sizes. Each workstation had a computer and a label maker that were snaking out labels and rolling them loosely into a coil on the workbench. The labels were added to padded envelopes each containing one or more of the weed-filled plastic pouches.

"In addition to the people I've told you about who freelance, the commune runs two very large cooperative businesses. You may have heard of Silk Road, a company that sold drugs on the dark web?"

"Yes," Kate drew the word out into a question.

"We have a similar business."

Kate managed to suppress her shock and outrage, "Wow. I really thought much of the stuff you hear about on the dark web was just urban legend."

"No, there's a whole counter culture out there that really lives in a world of its own creation free from the harsh morals and oppressive laws of the rest of the world."

"But the people I've seen here don't strike me as

hardcore drug users, they seem quite self-motivated."

"You'll find that members of our community rarely indulge in anything beyond alcohol and pot. We require our members to be productive and peaceful and drugs usually diminish both qualities in a person pretty quickly. Every hard drug user that we've had in residence has been asked to leave at some point."

"But isn't that a bit hypocritical for a group that sells drugs?"

"We don't control what individuals can do when they're supporting themselves, but rules must be followed when part of a voluntary collective."

"Do   you   only   sell   marijuana?"

"No, our group specializes in cultivating several specialized and highly sought-after strains of marijuana, but we partner with other communities and drop ship other drugs directly from their locations. We run the retail side, but anyone can be a third-party vendor, we're just the storefront. Customers review the sellers and their products and consumers are free to select the product they believe is best for them. If products have strong negative reviews, we remove them from the website."

"Interesting." Kate refrained from adding 'and terrifying'.

Eric walked her through the greenhouse as he described the plants and introduced Kate to the people working there. When the tour of the greenhouse was finished they walked back through the dining hall, the brick room, and returned to the game room. Eric stood near a door that led out of the game room and into the far side of the building.

"I should warn you that you may not agree with

how many of the people in the community make their living, I just ask that you respect their right to do as they please."

Kate nodded.

Eric opened the door and they stepped into a long hallway with a row of doors on the right-hand side. The entire space was painted white, each door dotted with a gold doorknob. At the end of the hall was another door that looked just like the others. The duo walked through it and into an area full of electronic equipment that brought to mind a television studio. Except rather than screens full of various angles on a news anchor, about half the monitors featured predominantly women and a few men in various stages of undress playing to the camera in a variety of sexual manners. The other half of the monitors displayed the screen names of who was watching, how much they were depositing into the "model's" account, and occasionally a live feed from the viewer's webcam, which usually featured their genitals.

Realizing her mouth was agape Kate turned to Eric, "I admit, I'm a bit shocked."

"This is big business Kate, especially on the dark web. The men and women on this side of the building are making three to five hundred thousand US dollar equivalents a year."

Hearing those figures did not help Kate close her mouth, "You're kidding me?"

"He's right." The woman in a large swivel chair watching the monitors answered.

The shock had been so great, Kate hadn't even noticed the woman, "I'm sorry, I'm Kate."

"Georgia. Nice to meet you."

"So what is your responsibility here?" Kate waved a hand toward the monitors.

"I'm kind of a producer and bouncer. I monitor for abusive behavior by our viewers and when I see it, I cut them off. I also watch for what viewers seem to be into at the moment and let those who don't have a lot of traffic know so they can make some modifications, that sort of thing."

"Fascinating."

"I think you could pull it off, if you want to give it a try."

Kate blushed, "I'm not sure it's really my thing, but based on the traffic and money I'm seeing on those monitors, there certainly is a market. So, how does this all work from a business perspective?"

The woman pointed to a screen, "You see next to each viewer is an account that shows how much they've deposited. There's usually a small entry fee to the individual's room and they build up clients over time. As time goes on they build a relationship with the clients thereby making them more likely to tip. Additionally, the model might offer to perform a certain act if all the viewers offer the equivalent of say twenty to fifty dollars depending on what they're being asked to do. Sometimes they have 'special' parties with two or more women or a man and a couple of women. Those are big nights with high entry fees that bring in the clients from all the participating models into the room. They can triple their pay on those days."

"So why am I also looking at client's webcams on some of these?"

"That's a privilege extended to high rollers if it's

something they want to do."

"Please forgive me for saying so, but ick."

The woman laughed, "I know, but for what they've paid over time, I'd let them sit in the corner of my room if it makes them keep opening their wallets."

This did not ease the queasy feeling in Kate's stomach. "You talked about dollar equivalents, what does that mean? I ask because only the right column on those accounts is in dollars, I don't recognize the symbology in the left column."

Eric chimed in, "All of our dark web businesses take payment in the crypto-currency Luminiferon, more commonly known as Lumi."

"What's that?"

"Thanks Georgia," Eric nodded to the woman. "Let's go elsewhere to talk about it."

They walked back to the brick common room and found two cushioned chairs away from the others. "You've probably heard of Bitcoin, right?" Eric asked in a hushed voice.

"Yes."

"Well Lumi is another form of blockchain, digital currency. While Bitcoin has moved to the lit market and is more widely accepted, those of us in the deep end of the dark web use Lumi as our currency of trade."

"So how do you turn it into cash?"

"That's the other nice part about it. At first, we have to hold it as Lumi for a particular amount of time that varies based on how much is in circulation. After that time has passed, it can be converted to Bitcoin, which we have to hold for ninety days. Once the ninety days have passed we are able to sell the Bitcoin for cash."

"That sounds like a great way to create distance between you and your customers."

"It's the difference between staying dark and getting noticed. Your algorithm would help us not only distance ourselves from our clients, but distance our money from ourselves. That's why we're so interested in a partnership."

"I see." Kate's mind lit with clarity.

"So what do you think? Are you willing to join our community and let us help you finish the project?"

"It certainly seems as though we have a mutual interest. May I sleep on it?"

"Of course. Let's find you a room for the night or as long as you'll have it."

23
WASHINGTON, DC

It was Monday morning at NSA headquarters and much had changed over the weekend. Change was not something PDD Lanser adjusted to with ease. There were facts and reasons for change that must be explored, people to consult, bureaucratic processes that must be followed and tested. Major organizational changes didn't just happen in the dark over a weekend. It was for these reasons that PDD Lanser baulked when Harrison read him the memo from Admiral Reynolds.

"What the devil are you trying to tell me?" PDD Lanser looked over his coffee mug and across his desk at Harrison.

"I'm not trying to 'tell' you anything. The fact is that Faulkner is now working for Admiral Reynolds as a Special Assistant and Missy Ackerman as taken over the Cyber Security Division."

"But what the holy heck specks for?"

"I don't know exactly. The memo just says that Faulkner is going to report directly to Admiral Reynolds on The Executive case."

"Son of a pup. I wonder what that sneaky little splinter Faulkner knows that they're keeping from us?"

"I don't know that he knows anything, but I'm told the Admiral is closing ranks on this case. It's possible he's starting to buy into the mole theory and doesn't want too much gossip to get out. You remember the Aldridge Aimes case. No one even knew a mole was being investigated. I suspect the same is happening here."

"I'm not buying it. What if that snake Faulkner is trying to pin something on us? We should have never called off the field team."

"First, the Admiral has no reason to try and pin something on us and second, I didn't exactly pull in the field team, I just made them autonomous. However, I think we need plausible deniability on this. Let the field team see what they can dig up before we let on that we still know they're out there."

"Good man, Harrison. I still wonder what the Admiral's new team knows that we don't. The Admiral has cut off everyone except the President and the other Intelligence Community heads. It's time for us to do some good old-fashioned snooping and see what that son of a booger butt Faulkner is up to."

"The Admiral will be traveling with the President next week. That may be our opportunity to poke around. I have some thoughts…"

24
THE COMMUNE

The room Eric offered Kate for the night was one facing the ocean.

"The ocean side of the building is remarkably not very popular because of the wind," Eric explained. "But there are only three rooms still available. The other two are on either side of the shared bathroom and are subject to plumbing noise. Of all your choices, I believe this is the best room."

The room was identical to Eric's in size and had a similar brick exterior wall and rectangular window. The closet and motel dresser were also there, only this room had a single bed on a frame with a headboard, as well as a folded stack of sheets and a wool blanket. Kate spent the night tossing in the scratchy sheets as the ocean wind whistled, and the resurgent rain pounded against her window.

The next morning Kate arose early and sent Joe a message suggesting a meeting time and place along with two alternates. She received a confirmation of receipt. Breakfast was at seven and she met Eric in the dining room before moving through the food line. Kate selected eggs, bacon, smoked salmon and half a bagel, which she toasted while dispensing some cranberry juice.

They found a place to sit and Eric introduced Kate to the people around them. The room was nearly full and the people were jovial and in an upbeat mood.. The commune's members were a diverse group and she'd already met people from nearly every country in Europe as well as South Africa, Canada, Japan, China, and the United States. This was a happy place and it was contagious. Kate felt the tension in her shoulders disappear as she relaxed and enjoyed the company of those around her as they ate.

People began to peel away from the table at an unhurried pace, some to work, others to sleep.

When the group had thinned out Eric turned to Kate, "Well, have you given my invitation some thought?"

"I have and while I'm not sure if I'm willing to give up my job and move in permanently, I'd like to stay for the summer and finish the project within the community."

"Excellent!" Eric clapped his hands together and stood, "Everyone!" The remaining murmur in the room subsided before he continued, "I'd like you to meet Kate." Eric waved his hand in her direction. "She'll be with us for at least the next three months and perhaps beyond."

The room exploded into applause and people clamored to meet Kate and shake her hand. Many were already encouraging her to stay for the longer term. All Kate could do was wonder, *Who are all these people who are so happy living like this?*

After breakfast Kate asked, "Is there a way for me to get into town? I'd like to pick up some things, not the least of which are new sheets."

"Yes, of course. We have communal cars you can utilize, just check one out with whoever is working at the front desk. By the way, we'll have to get you on the front desk rotation schedule."

"Happy to do my part." Kate ran to her room to grab her purse before checking out a car.

25
BLACKPOOL, ENGLAND

Joe and Elliot ate their full English breakfasts at a seaside window in the Blackpool Hilton Hotel. The hour was early and aside from staff they had the dining room to themselves. Joe pondered why the English served beans with breakfast and concluded that, like eggs, beans are an inexpensive source of protein much needed before a hard day of physical labor. Since there were no plans for physical labor in Joe's day, he decided a trip to the gym would be in order at a later time.

The windows of the dining room were still rain-streaked, but the wind had subsided. Sea birds were diving in and out of the surf and picking through garbage bins in search of food. An oystercatcher was wading on the sandy beach hunting cockles in the receding tide as a gull launched off the deck below the window with half a soggy hot dog bun in its beak.

An outside door to the dining room had been propped open to facilitate the delivery of bakery goods, allowing the scent of the ocean to mingle with the aromas of coffee and pork sausage. It was a pleasant smell that aroused a sense of longing in Joe, but he wasn't sure what he was longing for. *Probably just a vacation*, he determined before pulling himself back to the task at hand.

"Kate has suggested a very public, outdoor meeting spot here on the promenade," Joe pointed to a map of Blackpool on his phone. "Since the mission is officially called off and we're down to just the two of us, I'm inclined to skip the meeting and use that time to check for any surveillance on her."

Elliot gave a sharp nod, "I agree."

"I'd rather take her up on the first alternate, which is in this building beneath the Blackpool tower."

"I like that better too, if for no other reason than to get out of the unpredictable weather."

"Good point. It'll also give Kate some time to get the lay of the land in case she needs to bug out for some reason."

The Blackpool promenade was lined with shops and tourist traps allowing Kate a day of browsing. At the appointed time, she exited the linen store with a huge plastic bag stuffed with sheets and a goose down comforter and took a seat on a bench at the far end of the promenade. Assuming the pose of an exhausted shopper, Kate leaned back on the bench and rolled her neck around on her shoulders.

She opened her large tote bag and pulled out her cell phone. There were no messages so she spent some time scrolling through her Twitter feed as a light mist began falling. After a time Kate returned the phone to her bag, threw her arms over the back of the bench, and watched. There were few people moving around in the area and Kate saw no sign of Joe or Elliot. After twenty minutes, she returned to the car to shove the comforter into the trunk before popping open her umbrella and walking briskly to a chocolate shop.

Joe and Elliot emerged from the two separate shadows they had been observing Kate from within. They each independently made their way into the building surrounding the Blackpool tower. One of the doors to the ballroom inside the building was standing open and the men went inside, closing the door softly behind them. After searching the room, including the overlooking baloneys, they gathered three red velvet chairs from the corner edge of the room and sat down to wait the hour and a half before Kate's arrival.

"The coast looked clear to me," Elliot remarked.

"I didn't see anyone who might be keeping an eye on her, in fact, this is a relatively quiet place on a rainy weekday morning in the off-season."

By mid-day the rain had died down and the sun was peeking out. Kate decided to eat her lunch at an outside table. She used the plastic bag her Chinese food had come in to shield herself from the wet seat. The venue allowed her additional time to watch the shoppers and pore over anyone who might be suspicious. Finding no suspects, she tossed her trash into the bin and walked toward the Blackpool Tower building.

The musty odor of cellulose decay reminiscent of an old library brushed across Kate's nose as she entered the aged building and made her way to the ballroom. Kate was momentarily awed by the gilded ballroom lined in three levels of balconies under a ceiling of ornate frescos featuring ladies of nobility in flowing robes resting on clouds and accepting flowers from admirers while others look on or play musical instruments. Elliot and Joe gave the appearance of clutter in the otherwise elegant and neatly ordered room.

"Gentlemen," Kate offered as greeting while she moved toward the open chair in their closely arranged triangle.

Joe responded, "Hello, are you well?"

"Quite."

"Then talk to us."

Kate described the commune and their activities, what little she knew about the residents, and why they wanted her computer programs. The men sat silently offering occasional signs of listening.

"So, I've decided to stay through the summer, let them help me build the tumbler for my program, and see what comes up."

"There's not much evidence yet to indicate this group is involved in the data leaks in any way, do you think it's worth our time?" Elliot had a strained look on his face.

"Look, I'm just starting to form relationships so I don't know much about anyone or anything yet, so it's much too early to tell."

"I agree with Kate on this," Joe added, "These people are deeply involved in dark web culture, even if the leak isn't coming from them, the leaked documents are being posted in the dark web community. This group is as good a place to start as any."

"Very well, we'll carry on," Elliot's reluctance was palpable. "How easy will it be for you to meet with us regularly, Kate?"

"Not particularly. I played dumb today and pretended I didn't know that I'm supposed to attach a posting to the communications board that I was taking a car into town in case anyone else was interested in going. I may not be able to come alone."

The three of them determined the next meeting time. For the next meeting, Kate would bring a written report. If Kate were alone they would meet, if she were not they would conduct two brush passes. The first pass to drop her report and the second to pick up Joe and Elliot's communication to her.

Kate handed Joe a typed page of paper with information she had about customer screen names and model handles she had observed when she was in the control room as well as the name of the commune's web-based drug business.

"This will give you something to dig around in for the next ten days. You guys have fun roaming around the depths of the dark web looking for all the tentacles that lead to the commune, but do it with only one eye open, it's a little scary out there."

Elliot scoffed, "I've seen Osama bin Laden's bookshelf, there's nothing on the dark web that can shock me now."

26
THE COMMUNE

The ten days passed and Kate worked with Eric and a woman named Vegas on the algorithm's tumbler. Vegas was a beautiful woman of African and Japanese decent whose grandparents met at the end of World War II after her Japanese grandmother fled Okinawa in a boat before being picked up by the Navy. A tattoo of a turtle graced her wrist, a symbol of intelligence in Africa and longevity and happiness in Japan. She remained noncommittal regarding her beliefs about what the turtle symbolized, but figured she couldn't go wrong either way.

Kate and Vegas worked a traditional eight-hour day, while Eric helped them in the mornings before moving on to other projects in the afternoons. Community meetings convened every Wednesday evening and the members took turns leading them. The sessions included revenue and budget reports, a count of current commune members, and updates by the membership on their projects.

Decisions were made by a consensus of all members, a process that seemed to work surprisingly well. Although the majority of decisions that needed to be made were somewhere in the vicinity of what to serve in the cafeteria and whether or not to turn on the air conditioning.

When a member would express a concern, the day's leader would ask, "What can we do to make this better for John!" or whomever the member was. Suggestions would be thrown out, discussed, consensus reached, and John was made happy again. The end of the meeting was reserved for expressions of happiness and gratitude.

The gatherings reminded Kate of a Rotary meeting and she grew increasingly concerned that she would begin to believe the commune *was* a utopia. Utilizing sex and drugs as a basis for an economy was bothering her less as she bonded with and began to better understand the members of the community. Dropping out of society seemed an increasingly viable option. The urge to drop out was particularly strong when sitting on the sprawling deck with a beer listening to music and watching the waves crash against the beach below the bluff while enjoying the company of the other members, all of whom were kind and generous.

For a group who professed to have left the world behind, everyone was surprisingly up to date on current events. Even political discussions were polite in the commune. Each person would take turns expressing their opinions on issues as the others listened politely. There were never any attempts to convert one person toward another's viewpoint, just an airing of ideas and a search for nuances in the position everyone could agree on. After all, none of what was going on in the "lit" world, as they called it, ultimately mattered in the world they lived in.

While Kate was quickly getting to know people, one person remained a complete mystery. She watched Condor toiling away at his computer screens daily, his head twitching and bobbing between them. She never saw him interact with the other members of the group.

Late in her second week, when she and Vegas had taken a break from their work, she approached him, "Hi, I'm Kate."

"Hi," Condor replied flatly, never slowing the movement of his head.

"I hear you're looking for anomalies in market data, that's something I enjoy too."

Condor stopped typing and turned his head in Kate's direction, but kept his face directed toward the ground with only momentary flicks of his eyes in Kate's direction, "Really? That's cool. Most people don't." He returned to his keyboard.

"Tell me about what you're working on."

What followed was a greatly detailed description of his work, told at a dizzying pace in a halting voice that bordered on a stammer, but never committed to it. He concluded by showing her the types of anomalies he was looking for by pointing at a small chart and saying, "Like this one."

Kate squinted and moved in closer to the screen, but couldn't see what he was trying to show her. "I don't see the anomaly."

"Oh…I'm sorry…let me…make the chart bigger." Condor blew the chart up to the microsecond level on the timestamp and the two-microsecond price plunge in the stock he was looking at emerged. "This is…what I'm talking about. When I find these kinds of anomalies…I try to figure out if someone did something to…momentarily manipulate the price."

"Interesting, but how on earth did you find that? Before you blew it up it just looked like a straight line to me."

"I know…it's strange…but I can see small patterns in things that no one else seems to be able to."

"Fascinating. That's a bit like a superpower."

Condor smiled shyly, "Yeah, kinda."

"Well, Condor, be sure to let me know if you find anything particularly interesting."

"Okay," his flat tone had returned and his head was darting across the screens again.

"I didn't see you at the group meeting. Do you spend time with the others?"

"No," he continued working, "People in a group are…too loud for me. Besides, I can hear the meeting from here."

"I see," Kate said softly.

"As long as they…let me work, I'm happy. People here are nice though…so are you."

"Thank you, Condor. I'll stop by and see you again sometime, if that's okay."

"Yes."

27
WASHINGTON, DC

Faulkner had been working directly for Admiral Reynolds for about three weeks, but the work was like slogging through thigh-high mud, his progress slow and arduous. What he had been able to pull together so far at least made him feel like he was asking better questions. It had been another long day, but fortunately his current position allowed him to sleep at home every night.

Banned from after-hours pickup at Rugerio's, Faulkner was forced to go to a 24-hour deli located in a convenience store near his office. He hated the place, but pastrami on rye and heartburn sounded fantastic after nine hours of work without food. Fortunately, the late hour meant there was a convenient parking space at the far end of the lower level of the small garage, just beyond the section reserved for guests at a nearby hotel.

Since there was no direct access to the exit from

that part of the garage, he was forced to walk back around the u-shaped level to get out. As he turned the corner near the ramp to the upper level, a woman in a business suit with long black hair rapidly approached him.

"Will you help me, please?" she asked urgently, "I think a man is following me."

"Of course, are you going out, or to your car?"

"I'm going out."

Faulkner asked a string of questions about the man who was following her before allowing the woman to take his arm. The two of them moved cautiously toward the door, on the lookout for the tall, slender man with dark hair and a brown leather jacket as she had described. What Faulkner didn't notice, was the man who had crept up behind him.

The valet returned to his post with two cups of coffee, one for himself and one for the concierge who had stood in for him. "Thanks for relieving me. I brought you a cup. Any activity?"

"No, it's still slow. I think most of our guests are in for the night. Thanks for the coffee." The concierge went back inside to his desk.

The valet leaned against his station and sipped coffee as the dead of night parade of Ubers, limos, and taxis slid past him. No one drives his or her own car after midnight in the city. A cab drew up under the hotel's porte cochère and absent a doorman at this hour, the valet opened the cab door so two margarita-infused young women could ooze out of the back seat. As the women moved past him, their momentary drunken flirtatiousness amused the valet and provided welcome relief from his boredom. He entertained a fleeting thought of pinching the behind of the woman in the burgundy dress, but thought better of it.

The hours slipped past uneventfully until just before dawn when a black Mercedes sedan glided up to the valet stand.

"Checking in, sir?" the valet queried the driver, a wide-shoulder man with slicked back black hair that glistened under the lights.

The man turned down his radio, "Yes, I'm afraid I arrived much later than I anticipated, I hope you haven't given my room away."

"I'm sure your reservation is safe. May I have your keys to park the car?"

"Here you go." The man set the keys in the valet's hand like a precious jewel, "Take good care of her."

"I shall."

The valet slid into the car, turned the radio's volume back up, and began bopping his head and singing along with the Red Hot Chili Peppers. His merriment was interrupted by the smell of rotten garbage coming from the dumpster at the side of the building. Crinkling his nose in disgust, he rolled up the window and hit the car's air recirculation button.

The parking garage was quiet as the Mercedes nosed its way into a parking space. The valet stepped out, closed the door, and pushed the button on the

Mercedes' key fob causing the lights to flash and a *beep-beep* to emit. Several flies buzzed around his head and a bad odor persisted. As the valet thrashed about swatting flies, he noticed large numbers of them buzzing in and out of a nearby car. A bad feeling welled up in his stomach.

"Oh no, oh no, oh no," he whispered to himself as he crept toward the car. "Oh damn!" He ran back to the hotel.

Harrison stood with the coroner over Faulkner's body, which had been removed from the car and placed into a still open body bag.

"My guess would be that he's been here less than 48 hours," the coroner stated matter-of-factly.

"Thirty-six hours would put his death right after he left work. I suspect he was going to stop for a sandwich at Smittie's like all of us have done so many times." Harrison couldn't stop looking at Faulkner's gaunt face, "He's going to haunt me. I just know it."

"Literally, or psychologically?" the coroner asked with a serious look on her face.

"He's going to show up in my office as an apparition and hound me about why I can't make PDD Lanser use a fucking computer." Harrison saw the scowl on the coroner's face and laughed lightly, "I'm sorry, but gallows humor is the only thing that gets me through days like this."

"Hmm, well you'd better be careful about that around Admiral Reynolds. I hear he's pretty upset about this."

"The coroner says he was murdered," Admiral Reynolds set his coffee cup down on PDD Lanser's desk as Harrison looked on. "He took a blow to the back of his head, which knocked him unconscious before he was strangled to death with a wire. They know it was a wire, because it was still embedded in his neck." Harrison winced as Reynolds looked at the carpet to regain his composure. "You know Faulkner and I were close back in the day, but we went in different directions. I stayed active duty; he left for a brief stint in the private sector before coming to work here. It was great to work closely with him again. I regret not having stayed in touch with him over the years." He hung his head again.

"I'm real sorry for your loss, Doug. It's a shame," PDD Lanser mirrored Reynold's head hang.

"So who's working on the murder case?" Harrison asked.

"Everyone," Reynold's picked his head up and acted reinvigorated by the discussion of action. "Our people, FBI, Capital Police, Local Police, everyone's lending a hand on the footwork."

"Were there security cameras? Did they catch anything?"

Admiral Reynolds made a huffing sound, "There

were cameras all right, but they weren't working. I'm convinced there is only a half dozen or so of those cameras in the country that function properly. Most companies don't bother getting them fixed because they think their presence is enough of a deterrent. Idiots."

After huffs of agreement Harrison continued, "Did it have something to do with what he was working on?"

"I am not yet prepared to discuss his project," Reynolds said rising to his feet. "I'll be in touch as things develop. In the short-term while I'm away I'll continue to lead the work Faulkner started. When I return from my trip with the President I plan to reestablish a small team to continue the work internally here. It was a mistake to have much of the case knowledge residing with one person. But I need to think deeply about how I wish to proceed first. Harrison, I need you to stand by, I might need your help on this one." He shook the men's hands and PDD Lanser ushered him to the door.

Harrison remained bothered by something.

As Admiral Reynolds stepped into the outer office, Lanser's administrative assistant stopped him, "Sir, your office called. They would like to speak with you briefly before your next appointment."

PDD Lanser motioned for Reynolds to use his office.

28
THE COMMUNE

He was chasing her again. The unknown man wore a hood, his face reduced to a dark, blank space beneath it and was coming for her. He had a gun this time and they were in a pine-scented campground. A camper, tent, or van occupied every camping space and they weaved between them in the dark, moonless night. She knew she could run faster than she was, but her legs felt so heavy and her feet were sticking to the patchy, grass-covered ground as if it were hot tar. Outrunning him would be fruitless; she'd have to hide.

She began checking the doors on the campers, but they were locked. Quite unexpectedly she recognized one of the trailers as her own and her legs began to carry her at a more rapid pace. Reaching the door, she threw it open and ran for the back of the camping trailer. As she did, the man appeared to take flight, moving swiftly

*through the door. He overcame her and leapt on top of
her as Kate's world faded to black.*

Kate awakened with a start. This was the third
time tonight she had been chased by the nameless,
faceless man who consistently lurked around the edges
of her frequent nightmares. She was sweating profusely
and peeled off her nightshirt before standing on a chair
to turn the metal lever that opened the window. The cool
sea air whooshed in, blowing papers off the dresser. She
gulped in the fresh air as both her temperature and heart
rate returned to normal. Now chilled, Kate climbed back
into bed and under the comforter near the edge of the
mattress where the sheets were dry.

The tormenting dreams had been worse this
week than they'd been in almost a month. Why now?
She felt safe here and Joe and Elliot were just a few
button punches away. Kate worried that perhaps safety
and security would always elude her and her
subconscious would never let her have peace. Sleep
continued to evade her and by five in the morning
hunger drove her downstairs to the snack counter where
she prepared a bagel and peppermint tea, which she took
to her room. The food brought on the sleepiness Kate
had been waiting for. A quick text message to Vegas
suggested they take the morning off and convene at one
o'clock to work on the program. She could barely type
the message before sleep overcame her.

Later, the sun's reflection off the ocean formed a
perfect line from the surface of the water, through the
open window, and onto Kate's eyelids, waking her. The
morning's sleep had been deep and restorative,
unmolested by the hooded man. It was closing in on

noon when Kate went downstairs and walked through the computer workroom on her way to the cafeteria.

"Kate," Condor shouted too loudly in the hushed room causing everyone present to turn and glare at him. Condor appeared oblivious to the attention as Kate walked toward him.

"What is it Condor?"

"I found a really cool manipulation. I thought you might want to see it." He stood as he said it and began shuffling his feet nervously as he watched them.

"Of course, but I'd like to grab my lunch first."

"Can you bring me a tuna sandwich?" Condor's excitement about eating a tuna sandwich once again caused him to be too loud.

"I'd be happy to bring you a sandwich," Kate said in nearly a whisper.

"Thank you," Condor said, mirroring Kate's volume.

"My pleasure."

Returning with two tuna sandwiches, bags of chips, and bottles of water, Kate sat with Condor for the next hour as he walked her through what he had found.

"That's really interesting Condor. I'm so glad you showed me."

"So do you think I should file a whistleblower case?"

"I think it has merit, go for it!"

Condor smiled widely, "Thanks Kate."

Vegas had arrived and Kate expressed her apologies about not being able to make it in during the morning.

"No worries," Vegas said pushing up the sleeve

of her sweatshirt to reveal a new tattoo of a rose with a tiny bumblebee attempting to light upon it on the forearm opposite the turtle. "You're usually the morning person, but I'm far more productive in the afternoon."

They were productive for several hours before being joined by Eric who wanted to make sure Kate was feeling all right and check on their progress. Vegas and Kate were nearing the conclusion of their draft product. They were walking him through what they still needed to do when Jeffrey, one of the community members who handles the finances, burst into the room and ran to Eric.

"It's gone, all of it," Jeffrey said breathlessly.

"What's gone? I don't understand?" Eric's face twisted into a question mark.

"The Lumi, it's gone, someone hacked in and stole it."

"Excuse me," Eric squeezed between Kate and Vegas, opened a browser and began typing.

He stared at the page, his mouth agape, "You've got to be kidding me! Come on Jeffrey, we need to make some calls." The two men bolted out the door

"What just happened?" Kate asked noticing Condor was standing up, covering his ears and walking in circles. "And is Condor okay?"

"Yes, he's fine. He just doesn't like sudden loud noises and commotion. He'll go back to his monitors in a minute."

"That's good, but what about the Lumi?"

"It looks like someone hacked into The Commune's accounts and stole our Lumi, but I find that hard to believe.

"Why is it so hard to believe?"

"Well, first of all for someone to find the account and hack in would be incredibly difficult. And it's not like they can steal it and then just spend it."

"Why not?"

"Whoever took it would have to keep it in their Lumi account for twenty-seven days and then if they tried to withdraw it all at once in order to turn it into Bitcoin, they'd expose themselves."

"How would withdrawing it expose them?"

"Because selling that much Lumi at one time would cause the overall value of the crypto-currency to decline and the client would become known. Their only really good option would be to use it to buy things on the dark web without converting it, but the amount of Lumi we have would last five lifetimes on the dark web. The crypto-currency is nearly useless to a thief. Stealing it just doesn't make any sense."

The next morning an emergency meeting was called and Eric announced the community's Lumi had, in fact, been stolen. It was all hands on deck to try and figure out who took it. Kate requested a meeting with Joe and Elliot.

29
WASHINGTON, DC

Following Faulkner's death, PDD Lanser seemed satisfied that Harrison would be added to the internal investigative team upon Reynolds return and ordered him to stand down on his independent investigation. But Harrison was restless. Even though Faulkner's files had supposedly been turned over to the Interagency Task Force, why hadn't Faulkner's work moved the task force along in their investigation? What did Faulkner know that possibly got him killed?

Failing to talk himself down, Harrison decided to covertly continue his investigation. He had to know what Faulkner knew. But he would need some help.

"But Harrison, we can't spy on the Director of the NSA." Missy Ackerman's voice was quivering, "I have a lot to lose. I really need this job."

"We're not spying on the Director, we're just trying

152

to discover what got Faulkner killed. Besides, I have a team in the field and they might be in danger."

'Oh come on! There's no difference. We're still spying on the Director's office."

"You're the interim Director of NSA Cyber Security Division and you have a right to be in the loop on this investigation, just like Faulkner was."

"But the Director is trying to keep the circle of informed small in case there's a mole."

"Look," Harrison leaned in close to Ackerman, "whoever killed Faulkner might assume you already know what he knew. Your life could be in as much danger as his."

Ackerman sat back in her chair twirling a stress ball in her hand forward, then backwards over and over. She stopped and studied a paperclip on her desktop as if it were a crystal ball ready to reveal the answers to the agonizing questions she felt in the pit of her stomach.

"How do you intend to pull this off?"

"I have a memo from the President's office instructing us to take up the cause."

"But it's not real, you've forged it! How will you explain it to Admiral Reynolds when he returns and finds out the President's office never sent it?"

"We'll just say it arrived via messenger, we called to confirm, and everything checked out. We had no idea it was a forgery."

Ackerman shuddered before standing abruptly and leading Harrison toward the elevator and the seventh floor.

"Good morning, Betty," Harrison smiled broadly at one of Admiral Reynold's administrative assistants as

Ackerman struggled not to look uncomfortable. "I have a memo here from the President's Office asking us to take over where Faulkner left off. We're here to extract whatever data was on his hard drive." Harrison held up a flash drive.

"Yes," Betty replied cheerfully, "I received a call from the President's Chief of Staff office letting me know you were coming. Let me unlock the door and open the safe. Log in here please," she tapped her finger on the Visitors sign-in sheet attached to a clipboard. Protocol dictated that Betty call the Chief of Staff's office for one final clearance before carrying out the request for materials, but she didn't. The lack of call undoubtedly left on edge Harrison's people stranding by ready to intercept the call and once again pretend to be the Chief of Staff's office.

Admiral Reynolds had converted a small conference room within his inner office into a space for Faulkner to work. Betty unlocked the door and used a master code to open the office safe where Faulkner's files and computer hard drive were stored when he wasn't in the office. The two infiltrators glanced around the room.

Their training at the Farm took over and they inventoried the sparse room. Swingline Optima stapler, standard Agency yellow notepad and telephone, three Pilot Gel Roller pens, two mechanical pencils of unknown brand, artificial fichus tree in the far corner, 36-inch round table, executive desk chair, and two guest chairs, one in front of the desk and one at the table. There was a light coating of dust on the top edge of the desk where the computer monitor, phone, and printer resided. It appeared undisturbed. There were no signs to indicate anyone had been into the office or moved anything since Faulkner's demise.

They watched as Betty swung open the safe door, "Two hard drives and three thin files. Would you agree that is the contents of the safe?"

"Yes," Harrison and Ackerman said in unison.

A series of formal protocols and paper signing commenced and once complete, Betty said, "I'll leave you to it then," as she pulled the door closed behind her.

"I'll copy hard drives, you handle files," Ackerman was now in full combat mode as she pulled the external hard drives from the safe and moved rapidly to the desk.

Harrison grabbed the unlabeled files and took them to the table. He began photographing the contents without reading them with a small digital camera a member of his covert internal team had borrowed from inventory. It was a larger camera than they gave to assets in the field, but it took clear pictures even in low light conditions.

Ackerman had nearly finished copying the files from the first hard drive when there was a sharp knock on the door. They both started and then froze, eyes locked on each other. The knock repeated and Betty's voice cut through the tension, "I forgot to ask if either of you would like some coffee?"

"No, thank you," Harrison replied as Ackerman remained wide-eyed. "We should be finished relatively quickly."

"Very well." Betty's heals clicked a retreat.

Ackerman had to force herself to breathe again

before returning to her work.

When they'd finished they returned the items to the safe, contacted Betty to confirm everything was in place. Agreeing it was, Betty locked the safe and Missy and Harrison returned to their individual work areas. Harrison would review and report on the documents, Ackerman on the computer data.

"I'll see you tomorrow, Missy."

Ackerman returned to her office and sat behind her desk, adrenaline still coursing through her. She tried some deep breathing excises to slow her heart rate. Looking for a distraction, she turned on the TV hanging from a ceiling bracket in the corner of her room. The news correspondent looked professionally calm as she announced,

The Executive has released more information and documents on his dark web site today. This time he disclosed specific CIA tactics in the war on terror and outed this man, Adria Galanos, as a CIA officer operating in Serbia. A woman, Duscha Moravec, has also been disclosed as a CIA operative running assets in Moscow.

Two official looking photo IDs of the alleged agents flashed onto the television screen. Ackerman could see they were genuine. She also knew the FSB in Moscow watched every embassy employee when they left the compound. They knew where they went, what they did, and with whom they met. Certainly some of their local friends and maybe even some assets had been compromised with this new revelation. More people would die due to The Executive's actions. With renewed determination, Ackerman shoved the first flash drive into her computer.

30
THE COMMUNE

Eric was working with the Luminiferon founder and the distributed autonomous organization that organizes the currency to try to find a way to get their crypto-currency back. Meanwhile, most computer geeks in the community were working on figuring out who stole it. Kate and Vegas continued working on their cyber-currency wallet and tumbler project. After all, the community now needed a more secure means of storing their Lumi and Bitcoin. To stay informed, Kate walked around and talked to people working on finding the thief.

It was during one of these walkabouts when Condor yelled to her, "Kate, Kate, come here!" He was standing and waving with both arms for her to come to his station.

"What is it?"

"Look here, do you see this code?"

"Yes. What about it?"

"Well, I was just reading through the code the hacker used to capture the currency and I started to hear a rhyming pattern."

"What do you mean, 'a rhyming pattern'?"

"I can't really explain it, but when I've seen code written by someone before and then see something else they've written, I pick up the rhythm of it. Everyone codes a little differently. The way we organize code into coding paragraphs, how we write shortcuts and how we use them, that kind of stuff."

"So what does this code tell you?"

"I've seen this code before, it rhymes with other code I've seen. To be sure I ran both codes through a program that is a bit like voice recognition for code. It analyzes the code for the same types of patterns I perceive naturally and it's almost a perfect match."

"Whose code is it Condor?" Kate leaned in to the computer screen running her eyes over the report generated by the program. A 98% match. "Who wrote both of these programs?"

"Anchor," Condor was nervously rubbing his hands together.

"Who's Anchor?"

"He used to live here, but he left several months ago. That's all I know."

"Thanks Condor, you did great!" Kate hugged Condor's shoulders and gave him a peck on the cheek. Condor smiled, and blushed.

Kate found Eric at a desk in the business office off the lobby. She could see through the glass that he was on a video call and leaned against the wall to wait for him to finish.

As he was wrapping up he waved her in, "Yeah, guys, I know. Let's talk again tomorrow, okay? See ya." He closed his computer. "Have a seat Kate, tell me you have some good news."

"Well, the wallet program should be ready for live test in a day or two, so that's good news."

"Yes it is, but I'm guessing by the look on your face that's not why you're here. What can I do for you?"

"Tell me about Anchor."

"Anchor? What makes you ask about Anchor?"

"You first. I want to make sure two plus two equals four before I say too much."

"Anchor's a great guy. He was here since the beginning. Programming geek. Did a lot of software development, helped set up our Global Defense System."

"What's that?"

Eric shifted in his chair a few times before looking up at Kate from under furrowed brows, "Since you're close to your first community contribution, I suppose it's time for you to know."

The two of them got up and walked to the lobby reception desk, "Hey Ingibjörg, why don't you take a fifteen-minute break."

"Sure," she grabbed her purse and went inside.

"Sit here," he tapped the reception desk chair.

When Kate sat, she discovered that built into the wall of the desk was a row of five monitors. They listed statuses she didn't understand. "What's all this?"

"We are tapped into every nuclear launch facility on the planet as well as major power grids, and water supplies. We can also access traffic controls and disrupt electronic communications."

"Holy shit! What for?"

"We are pacifists. This is our defense system. If someone gets ready to launch a live nuke, we know it and can shut it down. We can disrupt power and communications to make things even more difficult. Rarely do we use it for retaliation, it's just a defense system, but once we shut down power for fifteen minutes in Moscow after they invaded the Crimea."

"I can't believe this. What else do you monitor?"

"We have access to most intelligence and military satellites, but we only tap in when something else triggers our attention like communication traffic that indicates something is getting ready to happen."

"But this is impossible. There's no way you can get into all these classified systems."

"It's easier than you might think. Since several countries have each figured out how to get into certain systems, you just have to tap into a handful of master systems and you have access to most of the world."

"I don't know what to say. So the person riding the desk is also responsible for defense?"

"Yes, but not everyone does desk time. We rotate the duty between members who have been selected or approved by the community. Not everyone is comfortable with the responsibility. Do you think you'll be up for it when you're asked?"

"Perhaps, but I'll reserve my answer until the time comes."

"Fair enough."

"So Anchor put all this together for you?" Kate

pointed at the monitors as Eric nodded an affirmative. "Where is Anchor now?"

"I don't know, exactly. He said he had a big project that required him to work offsite for a while, but when he was finished, he'd have enough money to start a new group. We're filling up, it's time for some to break off."

"He didn't say anything about where he was going or for whom he was working?"

"Nope, but it did sound like he might be out of the country. He said he had to 'leave the boundaries of his government' and I assumed that meant he was going outside the country to work. But Anchor had an unusual way of speaking, so it's difficult to tell."

"So Anchor just, shall we say, pulled up and sailed away one day? Did he have strong attachments here? Would you expect him to come back?"

"Yes, of course, he wanted to start his own commune. And he had a girlfriend…dammit, what was her name? Lana! Yes, Lana. She worked in the back." He pointed toward the sexier end of the building. "But she up and left about a month after he did. Haven't heard from either of them since."

Ingibjörg returned from her break.

"Let's go back in the office and sit down," Kate suggested as she led the way.

Once the door was closed Kate asked, "Do you have any reason to believe that Anchor would want to steal from you?"

"You expect me to believe that Anchor took the Luminiferon? There's no way!"

"Condor did some analysis and found that the pattern of the code matched other code Anchor has written."

"Impossible!"

"Not impossible. In fact, 98% possible."

"But why? It doesn't make any sense. He always made good money and had saved up nearly enough of his own to build a new community. Why would he steal ours?"

"Could someone have hired him to steal it?"

"Never. Very few people know about our accounts and Anchor is the only one with knowledge who is not in the commune now."

"Could it be an inside job?"

"I don't believe it. And I'm not going on a witch hunt within our own home."

"Well, for now Anchor is our best lead. We should probably try to find him. There may be a way to trace the code. Would you like me to look into it? Vegas can finish the other project testing on her own."

"Who knows about this?"

"Just Condor and me. I can work on it with him and see what we can find. He's excellent at this kind of stuff."

"Go ahead. Discretely. I'll ask around and see if anyone has heard from him."

31
WASHINGTON, DC

It was nearly seven in the evening when Harrison shut down his computer and slid the folded papers into the front of his pants. He grabbed his briefcase and coat and said goodnight to the few people he passed in the hallway. Stepping off the elevator, he turned left and walked toward security.

"Good evening, sir," the officer greeted as Harrison handed him his briefcase. The officer flipped it open and inspected it. The contents were not very interesting, gym clothes and shoes, and a now empty insulated lunch box. "Thank you, sir. Step inside please."

Harrison hesitated slightly before stepping inside the body scanner, "I'm sorry, this has just been a little more embarrassing lately."

"Quite all right, sir," the security officer assured

him warmly.

The machine scanned and Harrison stepped out and waited. The officer watching the monitor called over the supervisor who had previously inspected Harrison's briefcase. They were pointing at the screen and whispering, "This will only take a moment, sir."

Harrison knew they were pulling up this morning's image to see if they matched. They would…he hoped. It felt like he had been standing there for an eternity as he watched the men fumble with the computer. Beads of sweat were trickling down his spine, but were interrupted and absorbed when they reached the edge of the incontinence underwear Harrison was wearing for the second time today. Only this time he was hoping the thick pad in front was concealing the documents. "Thank you sir. Have a nice evening. Be well."

"I will, thank you."

Walking briskly to his car, Harrison caught himself unconsciously holding his briefcase with both hands in front of himself. "C'mon, you know better than that. That's just the sort of tell that would tip someone off," he muttered to himself dropping the briefcase to his right side and swinging it lightly.

Once inside the car, Harrison drove out of the complex and toward downtown DC. He parked in a garage on Massachusetts Ave. near Dupont Circle and got out, leaving his briefcase in the car. He walked the circle, before getting off at New Hampshire Ave. NW. He cut across to L St., then over to 19th St. NW, before walking up to M St., and across to Connecticut Ave. Harrison was now certain no one was following him so he walked down Connecticut Ave. and into the lobby of the Mayflower Hotel.

He approached the desk clerk, "Good evening, my wife should have left a key here for me. The name is Ackerman."

"Yes sir, I have it right here. Room 616. Please enjoy your stay. The elevators are to your right."

Harrison rode the elevator up and let himself in to find Missy Ackerman standing nervously wide-eyed at the door, her hair in disarray from passing her fingers through it too many times.

Neither of them spoke until they were locked inside the room, "That was kind of risky, Harrison. Why not just come downstairs to the Salt Mine?"

"There's no way for me to justify still being at the office. It's just better if I can claim off duty status. Your work never ends, I'm supposed to work a respectable ten-hour executive's day and go home." He reached into his pants and pulled out the documents.

"Ick. Don't expect me to touch those"

"Very funny. I didn't bring all of the documents, just a few. They look like printouts of docs you probably found on the computer, he's just added some notes to them."

"Let's compare notes than, shall we?" Harrison nodded and pulled a chair up to the room's desk. Missy continued, "The week Faulkner was killed, he had discovered two important pieces of information in the case."

"Do they have to do with a cell phone and a hacker?"

"They do in fact."

"Then we are talking about the same information. What is your take?"

"It looks like Faulkner was the central point person on the investigation, but he involved other people as needed. Based on the work order memos, it seems like they didn't really know what case they were working on, they were just given tasks." Missy slid a couple of papers across the desk for Harrison to look at.

"I would agree with your analysis."

"It turns out he was using some of my people in the Salt Mine to look into the code used to hack into the UK's system. They did find a possible connection with a thirteen-year-old hacker who was working out of the basement in his mother's row house near Heathrow nearly a decade ago. Alfie Brand was his name." Missy slid a picture across the desk, "He was suspected in those days of running an electronic records modification service. For a small price he would modify grades for high school and college students and their scores on college entrance exams. His services expanded to modifying medical records for those who either wanted to qualify for disability or maintain job licensure they were no longer medically qualified for.

He came to the attention of the authorities when he attempted to modify the criminal record of a pedophile who was trying to get his teacher's license. Alfie denied any involvement in the hackings and MI5 was never able to definitively prove it, but they allegedly scared the hell out of him and his mother. His petty hacking discontinued after that."

Harrison was nodding his head, "Yes and Faulkner's notes on the document show that the analysis of the program used to hack into the UK's database found a coding signature profile similar to that of Alfie's. Is it possible he's in the big leagues now?"

"Seems odd," Missy observed, "that he would disappear for ten years and then resurface as a hacker. I've always thought of hacking as a trade that has to be practiced so you get better at not getting caught."

"True, but the code used to break into the UK's database was quite sophisticated by most hacking standards. It was a brilliant adaptation of an existing method that has made it so far impossible to trace its origin."

"We should probably visit Alfie's mother's basement. In other news, it looks like analysis of The Executive's released documents reveal that they appear to all be photographs, not scans or other formats."

"Yes," Harrison added. "That means either The Executive isn't in possession of physical documents, only photographs of them or that he or she is photographing them."

"It doesn't make a lot of sense that The Executive would be photographing documents rather than scanning them or using the digital copy. However, being in possession of photos, rather than paper or digital documents does support the theory that there is a mole and not a hacker."

"True. And Faulkner's handwritten notes indicate the tech who did the work believed all the photos were taken by the same digital camera. Also, based on pixel density, a somewhat older camera."

"Who's the tech who worked on it?"

"It doesn't say who worked on the photo angle.

Could be inside or outside the organization."

"That's curious. Faulkner is usually not that sloppy in his documentation, but perhaps it was intentional."

"Which might be significant."

"It seems unlikely that someone would be able to get a cell phone or digital camera into the building and through security to take pictures though."

"I suppose they could have brought it in through the loading bay somehow."

"Yes, I suppose they could have, but they'd have to have inside help or they couldn't get in, right? You can't just show up at the door and walk in. But right now I think we need to figure out who the tech was who worked on this and look closely at anyone else Faulkner had working on this project. I also think we should take a look at the loading dock employees," Missy was already pulling up the list on her computer.

"Yes. And we need to visit with Alfie."

"I agree, but how are we going to pull that off without Lanser knowing?"

32
THE COMMUNE

The long days of staring at computer code following restless nights of sleep were taking a toll on Kate. She rolled her head around her shoulders while massaging her neck. The speed at which Condor was moving through the lines and pages of code was spectacular. Kate could do everything Condor was doing, but at only one-fifth of the speed. Condor's keystrokes had a rhythm to them suggesting the keyboard was just an extension of his beating heart and the flow of electricity through his neurons.

Then all at once he was still.

"The IP address of the hack came from an Internet café in Latvia." Condor's voice lost its halting cadence with the revelation.

"Yes, but public servers are usually used as bounce points to make it more difficult to locate the originating server in the attack," Kate rubbed her eyes and pointed her chin toward the ceiling to ease her stiff neck. She looked at her phone and saw it was just after two o'clock in the afternoon. "We've been at this for six hours already and may still have to pick through hundreds of bounced public servers in the chain to find the origin. It's a long shot no matter what we do. I need to rest my eyes for a while and I would suggest that you do the same, Condor."

"Just…a minute," the hesitation had returned to Condor's voice. "Let me finish accessing the café's server log so we can start looking for the next hop in the chain."

"I need to go lie down for a while." Kate pushed away from the screens, "Take a break, let's resume in an hour and a half."

"Okay," Condor moved swiftly toward the cafeteria following his clipped response.

The grated metal stairs clanked beneath Kate's feet as she walked heavily up the stairs to her room. Opening the door released the blinding afternoon sun that was blaring in through her window. Kate brought her hand up to shield her eyes as she stepped into her room. As she turned her head to avoid the glare, the corner of her eye caught a glimpse of something moving along the wall. Kate jumped back and yelped before realizing it was just the shadow of the door passing across the wall as she closed it behind her.

The fright had punctuated her edginess and welled up in her a new awareness of how tense she was. Breathing deeply, Kate purposely tried to relax her muscles, but the more she tried, the more they resisted softening. A shudder ran through her body as she tried to shake off the tension. It just made her exhausted and achy.

She napped fitfully as a string of dreams tortured her subconscious. A pleasant dream of her life with her late husband Max ended with his having an affair and telling Kate he didn't love her anymore. A walk with her dog Zoe resulted in the dog being attacked and killed by a bear. There was a tornado that swept Kate away as her last breath was sucked out by the twisting wind.

But what woke her were the figures in hooded robes that surrounded her bed, floating, moving closer. The air of her dream became filled with the stench of evil as she was consumed by their vile wickedness and hissing shriek, unable to escape.

Bolting awake, Kate struggled to get air into her lungs as her muscles crushed her chest and ribs. She felt sick and brought a wastebasket to her face and gagged unproductively. Her stomach's heaving and the compression in her lungs slowly began to recede, and she gasped in air like a person revived after nearly drowning. Perspiration pumped out of her pores in throbbing rhythm as her mouth turned dry and her head felt like it was splitting.

Kate grabbed a bottle of water off her nightstand and gulped half of it down. "What is wrong with me?" she yelled to the dust motes dancing carelessly in the sunlight, "am I going mad?"

She tried to wash her delirium away in the shower before returning to Condor's side. He was sitting back in his chair balancing it on two legs, smiling at the computer and shaking his head.

"Didn't you take a break?"

"Yes, but just long enough to eat something. Look at this." He dropped the chair forward onto all four legs and pointed at the screen, "I can't believe it. Our hacker only made one hop on a public server. The log I'm looking at now is the originating server. What hacker does that?"

"You're kidding me? Where's the server?"

"Skolkovo, Russia, just outside of Moscow. Right in the midst of Russia's failed attempt at a Silicon Valley style science and technology district. Unbelievable."

"What happened to it? What's there now?"

"Typical Russian corruption combined with brain drain and a lack of funding killed the project. There are still a few die-hard companies functioning there though. Rumors have surfaced of government-funded troll shops and hackers also operating there. The troll shops write false or misleading news articles and leave propaganda-laced comments on anti-Russian articles published in the West. There's also an operational business school still in Skolkovo, so there's likely a community of college students."

"Only a rudimentary hack would go through a single bounce point. Maybe it's a college student."

"I suppose it's possible. Although the server the hack came from originated in a residential complex, not the student dorms. It's also unlikely that a troll shop would be operating out of a residence."

"You seem to know a lot about it."

"I…tried to…work there for a while when they were recruiting a bunch of people, but it didn't work out.

So I came here."

"Ah, that would explain it. I'll do a little poking around in the outside world and see what I can find out. Let's not tell anyone about this until I can check it out."

"Okay." Condor closed the coding screens they'd been working on and returned to his graphs and trading algorithm.

33
LONDON

Harrison decided the best way to deal with a visit to Alfie's home was to ask for forgiveness rather than permission. He phoned some close contacts at MI6 and found them to be surprisingly supportive of his plan and willing to help. They would send someone to meet him at the airport. All that was left was to get out of the office without raising Lanser's alert level, which was running high on most things these days.

"The trip will be short, I promise," Harrison was pulling together the files in his office and dropping them into his safe as he talked to PDD Lanser, "it's just a few days of protocol meetings with our colleagues at MI6."

"Good glob, can't it wait? You're going to have to work on The Executive case when Admiral Reynolds returns from his trip with the President."

"I'll be back before Reynolds, so this is a good

time to fit these meetings in. Relax. It'll be fine. Call me if you need anything." He headed for the door.

"Harrison!" Lanser called after him. Harrison stopped and turned around. "Be careful out there. Something about this whole thing doesn't smell right to me. It's got me on edge. I've got assets and deep cover agents being blown, or worse yet, assassinated on a daily basis and we haven't been able to dig up a doggone thing in the field. I just worry about you being out in the wild."

"MI6 will be with me the whole time, I'll be fine. Besides, I'm not clandestine, so I'm not a target of exposure."

"I'm more worried about assassination."

Now Harrison was too.

The plane landed smoothly at Heathrow. Harrison's slumber was interrupted by his seatmate's awkward attempt to dive for her cell phone, which was buried in her purse stuffed under the seat in front of her.

Two men, whom Harrison could have picked out of a lineup as MI6, met him at the gate. "Harrison Steyn?" the taller one asked.

"Yes," Harrison stuck out his hand. The tall one introduced himself as Henry Williams and the other as Phillip Allan. Harrison didn't bother to commit the names to memory; they likely weren't their actual names anyway. "Nice of you gentlemen to help me out on this."

"Well, we always love a rogue American." There was more than a hint of sarcasm in Mr. Tall's voice, but somehow sarcasm with a British accent always seemed more highbrow than it really was.

The trio walked out to the rental car lot and

Shorter pointed to a dark blue car, "That one's yours, Cowboy." Nice to see they hadn't bothered to commit Harrison's name to memory either. Tall threw a set of keys at Harrison.

"What is that?" Harrison stood next to his rental car and grimaced, "A Nissan Granule? It's so small I'm going to be eating my knees."

"You can walk if you'd be more comfortable, Cowboy," Tall suggested.

"No thanks, I'll just curl up into the fetal position and drive." It was obvious that all attempts at diplomacy between global cousins had been abandoned.

Harrison followed the men the short distance to the home of Alfie Brand's mother. The neighborhood was working class, but the homes were well maintained with miniscule fenced yards trimmed to a uniform height. Occasionally a garden gnome or whirl-a-gig ornamented a flowerbed. The Brand home flew a decorative flag depicting a spring flower with a bumblebee feasting on its nectar. The brick row house that belonged to Alfie's mother had a fresh coat of white paint on the frames surrounding the windows and door.

Tall rang the bell, but hearing no tone, opened the screen door and knocked loudly on the burgundy interior door. A square woman in orthopedic shoes and a floral apron answered the door.

"Mrs. Brand?" Tall inquired.

"Used to be a long time ago. Now I'm Mrs. Trotter. Not many Trotters left you know. It's a dying surname."

"Interesting," Tall said blandly, "are you the mother of Alfie Brand?"

"Who wants to know?" Mrs. Trotter began looking the men up and down. Introductions were made. "Oh, dear. You'd best come in. I'll put the kettle on." She led them in and scooted toward the kitchen.

The front room of the home was neat and pleasant with a few more floral patterns than Harrison enjoyed. Porcelain figurines were perched neatly in a corner curio cabinet and a few more were scattered about the two small end tables. Against the far wall a Kawai K-series professional upright piano stood looking uncomfortably out of place in the working-class home. A bowl of cellophane-wrapped hard candies rested on the coffee table.

Tall and Shorter sat on the rose-patterned sofa together and Harrison selected a rather uncomfortable narrow upholstered chair with slender wooden arms. The room's dusty rose color scheme beckoned the 1980s and Harrison half expected an official portrait of Prime Minister Margaret Thatcher to be hanging above the mantel. He wondered if Tall and Shorter were sitting together reminiscing about Margaret Thatcher or if they were the type who yearned for the rampant chaos of garbage and coal strikes that plagued Britain in the 80s. Shorter just appeared to be pining for the candies as he stared at them while tapping a small leather-covered notebook on his knee.

Mrs. Trotter soon arrived with a pot of tea, four cups with saucers, some butter cookies, and scones.

"I could fix some finger sandwiches, if you'd like."

"Thank you, Mrs. Trotter," Tall responded, "but what you've already served is more generous than we deserve."

"Very well." She had poured the tea and seemed confused about whom ranked highest and should be served first.

Smaller noticed, "Left to right will be fine, ma'am"

Mrs. Trotter was visibly relieved and Smaller secured a scone and balanced it on his saucer. Harrison made a mental note, *Smaller's the observant one, Tall's the jackass bad cop, got it.*

Once tea was served, Mrs. Trotter sat in a winged-back chair and waited until everyone had taken a sip before speaking, "So tell me, what is your interest in my Alfie?" She looked at Tall with her head cocked to one side.

"At this point he's not in any kind of trouble, we just think he may be able to answer some questions for us and/or point us in the right direction on a problem we're trying to solve."

"Does it involve computer stuff?" Mrs. Trotter set her cup and saucer on the coffee table and procured a butter cookie.

"Yes ma'am it does."

"You're not going to tell me what exactly this is about, are you?"

"No, ma'am I'm afraid it's classified, but your son may be a great help to us."

"Why the American?"

Harrison mustered a warmish smile.

"We are working jointly with the Americans on the project."

Mrs. Trotter pointed her nose toward the ceiling

as she considered what to do.

"I haven't laid eyes on Alfie in about a year," she frowned and blinked heavily. "He finished university and went on to graduate school. Graduated with a degree in Computer and Information Sciences. He's very smart my Alfie." The men nodded attentively and leaned in. "He worked here and there for a while, but never stayed anywhere very long. Made good money though and saved a lot. Decided he wanted to start his own…oh what did he call it," she squeezed her eyes shut and rolled her hand in the air, "an information analytics company." Her eyes popped open, "Yes, that's what it was."

The men deployed body language that indicated they were listening, but remained silent.

Mrs. Trotter continued, "He went west to the coast. Said he had met some people who lived in a community that functioned a bit like a business incubator. You know, a place where you can go to a common workspace and work with others while you get your business off the ground. He'd been there about two years and seemed to be doing well, but I haven't heard from him at all for about six months. I've tried to call his mobile, but he doesn't answer or return my messages. Frankly, I've been a little worried about him, but your visit has raised my level of concern." She began wringing her hands.

Harrison spoke up, "We don't have any reason to believe he's been harmed in any way. He might just be very busy on a big project. We just want to talk with him about his work and see if he can help us out at all."

"You can try the incubator, it's just north of

Blackpool. I don't know where exactly."

"Thank you, Mrs. Trotter. Did he leave anything here at all when he moved out?"

"No," she shook her head as if she were trying dislodge a memory from her brain, "he took or sold everything he had. I'm pretty sure."

The men rose and Tall offered his hand, "Thank you for the tea, Mrs. Trotter, we won't take any more of your time."

As they turned to leave Smaller poked his head questioningly at the candy dish.

"Of course, dear, help yourself."

He did, dropping two pieces into his shirt pocket and unwrapping a third as they walked.

Harrison stopped at the door and turned toward Mrs. Trotter, "That's a very nice piano. Do you play?"

Mrs. Trotter seemed momentarily flustered, "Yes, I can plunk a bit, but I'm not very good. Alfie won the piano in a contest."

"Very lucky, it's lovely."

They departed.

Tall huffed as he closed his car door and spoke to Harrison through the opened window. "All right, Steyn, you got what you came for. Now you're well outside my jurisdiction. I'm going to contact MI5 and let them know what you're up to. I assume you're going to want to go to Blackpool, am I right?" Harrison motioned an affirmative. "Well, you're not going out there without someone from MI5. Are we clear?"

"I hear you quite loudly," Harrison yelled over his shoulder as he defiantly marched toward his own car. He drove away as he plotted a course on his GPS for the nearest Poppies.

A gloomy blanket of grey covered London deepening the shadowy corners of the city. Shadows make lonely company, but Harrison's mood drove him to eat outside to commune with the consuming bleakness of the street. He drenched his fish in malt vinegar and tested a chip for salt level. They were crispy, just the way he liked them. The fish and chips provided a momentary jolt of satisfaction to his weary soul. He was regretting his decision to come to London. He feared things might get too far out of his control. Had he gone too far? Was he in too deep?

His meal finished, Harrison sat in his car for a few moments, engine running, considering whether to point it in the direction of Blackpool. In another six years he'd be fifty-five and could take early retirement. It would be the first time in his long career in intelligence that he would be in total control of his choices.

The career field didn't allow many autonomous decisions. A seemingly endless chain of higher-level management allocated assignments, and procedures were often firmly fixed. It wasn't like in the movies where an agent could do whatever it took to complete his or her mission. There were rules that must be followed and a well-practiced rhythm and flow to everything they did. Every move was run up channels before it was executed.

Yes, retirement would offer choices. Harrison could return to intelligence as a contractor, assuming he didn't screw things up too badly, or he could sell hot dogs at a National Park or on a beach in the Caribbean. He alone would get to decide. But there was also a decision to be made now. Should he return to Washington, wait for Admiral Reynolds to return, and form a team to pick up where Faulkner had left off?

At this point his deceptions were still recoverable, yet his gut told him the situation was more urgent than Admiral Reynolds seemed to believe. What might be coming next from The Executive? More lies or the U.S. nuclear launch codes? *This is why we have processes and structure*, he thought, *to deal with the endless uncertainty.* He put the car in drive and headed toward the airport. Process needed to be followed and he had wandered off the trail.

After driving about three miles, Harrison looked in his rearview mirror at the dark sedan three cars behind him. He made three quick left turns around the block and the car was still following him. *They're coming for me. This is it.* The muscle memory of repetitive training in evasive maneuvers cut through the fear and Harrison made a last-minute lane change in heavy traffic, sped up, and turned right eliciting a chorus of honking.

Realizing they had been made, the sedan dropped all pretenses and actively engaged in pursuit. Harrison didn't know the city well, so he tried to move toward a high point thinking he could see his best evasive move from there. Unfortunately, he could find little more than a low rise. He frantically poked at buttons attempting to turn on the car's navigation system as he weaved through traffic. During a brief moment of unconscious competence, Harrison hit the right combination of buttons and the screen lit up and he zoomed the screen out for a broader perspective.

At the next block Harrison again crossed traffic,

but turned left this time. Four blocks later he looped left and drove until the Ringway's on-ramp came into view. He exited right onto the London Motorway Box and merged into traffic. The two cars settled into a pursuit at the speed of traffic. Now on the loop, he could call for backup as they rounded the city as long as his pursuer didn't try to run him off the road. Harrison dialed Tall's number off the card he had handed him. There was no answer. He left an urgent message.

As Harrison was trying to decide whom to call next, he noticed in his rearview mirror that traffic was parting, followed shortly by the repetitive *bee-boo, bee-boo* of a police siren. As the lights grew closer, the sedan chasing him pulled over and stopped. When Harrison pulled over, the police car pulled up behind him. The black sedan pulled out and whooshed past them.

PDD Lanser answered his ringing emergency line, "Lanser here."

"Principal Deputy Director Lanser, this is Air Force One, please hold for Admiral Reynolds."

The line clicked to dead air for thirty seconds before opening to the muffled sound of jet engines and Admiral Reynolds talking to someone in the room, "That's right. Close the door on the way out, will ya? Thanks. Lanser, is that you?"

"Yes, Admiral, how may I be of service?"

"It has come to my attention via the Brits that you may have disobeyed my order and still have someone working The Executive case in the field."

Lanser immediately wondered what the devil Harrison was up to in London. He tried to muster some sincerity, "Who would that be, sir?"

"You know exactly who I'm talking about. Kate Adams! You've reactivated her and put her on The Executive case."

Lanser was briefly stunned when he heard the name, he was unaware of Dr. Adams involvement. "Who told you that?"

"I'm the Director of the NSA, it's my job to know these things! Now, I'm not saying that I wouldn't have done the same thing you did, but be glad some time will pass before I see you again." Lanser didn't know what to say, so he remained quiet, which had never gotten him in any deeper trouble before. "But hear me Marc, you have a major problem with Adams, she may have been blown. You need to bring her in immediately; my source on this is highly reliable. She may be in danger."

Lanser hung up and leapt up from behind his desk, but the dizziness and stabbing pain in the center of his chest forced him back into the chair. The thought that he might be having a heart attack crossed his mind as he broke into a cold sweat.

"Dear God, please no," he said as he slid off the chair and onto his knees. A few moments later a thundering belch emerged from his chest followed by stomach acid, which burned his nose and throat. Grabbing the wastebasket from under his desk, he spit out the bile that had gathered in his mouth. He swallowed hard to try to keep the rest of it down and removed a bottle of liquid antacid from his bottom, right desk drawer. Chugging the chalky liquid straight from the bottle he eased back into the chair and hit the intercom button on his phone.

"Yes, sir?"

"I need you to get ahold of Harrison for me right away."

"Yes, PDD Lanser, I'll try his cell phone."

34
BLACKPOOL, ENGLAND

The kitchen was cramped in the rented caretaker's cottage on Annesley Avenue adjacent to Layton Cemetery. The two men had learned to dance around each other, their arms held in the air, surrendering to the room's diminutiveness. There was a chicken stuffed with onion, lemon, garlic, rosemary, and thyme roasting in the oven. It was basted in a bourbon sauce of their own creation, inspired by the drinks they had poured when the antique grandfather clock in the hall had struck five.

A plate of sliced cheeses and smoky sausage was extracted from the refrigerator and placed on the coffee table next to the crackers as well as a dish of olives, tiny sweet pickles, and marinated mushrooms and artichokes. The bottle of bourbon and an extra glass were added to the array.

The dining table was set and candles were gently

inserted into their holders. A pot of potatoes boiled on the stove. Carrots and green beans rested in a steamer basket waiting for the flame to be lit beneath their pan. One of the men looked at his watch and went to the front window. He lifted the edge of the curtain ever so slightly with his middle finger and looked out, motionlessly, appearing not to breathe, "She's here." The men went to the door and opened it before Kate could knock.

"Something smells good." She pointed at Joe, "I see who wears the apron in this partnership."

"Very funny."

"Seriously though, it looks like the two of you have settled into domestic life in your little hideout quite nicely. Anything I need to know about you two that you haven't told me?" Kate smiled mischievously.

"You've made it very clear you don't want to know anything about my personal life, so you'll just have to make stuff up to satisfy your imagination."

Elliot had retreated to the kitchen in embarrassment during the exchange. Kate wondered about the two of them, it had never occurred to her before.

"In the meantime, let me fix you a drink. Is bourbon okay?"

"Bourbon is great. On the rocks please."

"There are some appetizers on the coffee table, help yourself."

"This is so much better than trying to meet in a public place, I'm so grateful you and Elliot found this cottage."

"It would have looked suspicious after a while for a couple of guys with nothing to do hanging out in a hotel. It wasn't practical. But two guys looking for a summer rental is a much better cover." He handed Kate her drink. "Any trouble getting dark?"

"No, I don't have any reason to believe I'm being followed either in the car or on foot. I followed protocol, but I'm mostly just tired from walking around for three miles to go to a destination two blocks from where I parked my car. The coast has been clear the whole time I've been here. My cover seems to be holding." Kate sipped her drink.

Elliot poked his head out of the kitchen, "Dinner's almost ready. May I get some help please, Joe?"

Joe hopped up, "Of course. Kate, enjoy your drink & appetizers, we'll save business until after dinner." Before leaving, Joe loaded a plate with cheese, crackers, and pickled items and took them with him to the kitchen. Elliot popped out of the kitchen to fill his own plate from the coffee table.

The atmosphere and bourbon were filing away Kate's sharp edges and her tension was at last relieved. The tension would return, it always did, but she relished the feeling of relative weightlessness overcoming her. It was nice to enjoy dinner and a glass of wine with no mention of work. They were just three friends talking about art, politics, and life as if they were the only things that mattered. After dinner, Elliot offered to clean up and Joe and Kate retired to the tiny living room and sunk into the pine green sofa.

"Before we talk business, how are you feeling, Kate."

"Under stress, but this evening has helped a

great deal."

Joe nodded slowly, "How are the panic attacks?"

"Nearly nonexistent, until I have a nightmare."

"Would you describe the nightmares as being worse or more frequent than usual?"

"Both. They're coming multiple times a night and some have taken on characteristics of night terrors that result in panic attacks and momentary confusion when I wake up."

"Are they impacting your ability to do your job during the day?"

"I'm somewhat tired during the day, but as long as I can take a nap I'm usually okay."

"Do you have the dreams when you nap?"

"I've started to."

Joe engaged in more thoughtful nodding, "The good news is, since things weigh on your subconscious, I can conclusively state that in my professional opinion you are neither a sociopath nor a psychopath."

Kate laughed, "What a relief. At least that's one issue I can tell my subconscious not to worry about."

"Is there something within your control that you think would help ease your tension?"

"Maybe. There's something I find interesting that I would like us to work on."

Joe sat forward in his chair, placing his forearms on his thighs, "That's not really what I was looking for, but tell me."

Kate told Joe about the theft of the Luminiferon and the man named Anchor. "The crypto-currency wallet project is pretty much complete. We just need to launch it. I think we should go to Skolkovo and try to find out who took the Luminiferon."

"Isn't that a bit outside our mission?"

"Maybe, maybe not. This is the first hint of suspicious activity I've found in the group. Assuming you overlook the black-market activity, that is. Plus, this guy has gone off the grid along with his girlfriend. My gut tells me to follow up on this."

"Who else knows about the location of the hack?"

"No one, just Condor and me. I trust Condor to keep it a secret. It was a long shot anyway that we'd be able to trace the hack back to its originating point. Everyone else will just assume he's still working on it anyway."

"What's Eric doing about the theft?"

"He's working with the developers of Luminiferon to get them to develop a hard fork so they can get their currency back."

"What's a 'hard fork'?"

"It's complicated, but think of it as creating a fork in the road of programming code that takes the program back to a previous state, when the Luminiferon was still in the commune's account."

"I see. I think. If there really is a connection with The Executive case, I'm not sure it makes sense to pull you out of the commune at the moment. It might look suspicious."

"I'm not a prisoner. I'm free to come and go as I please. With my project wrapping up it makes sense that I might want to take a break for a couple of weeks and travel a bit. It's not like I'm pulling myself out of the commune, I'm just taking a vacation with some friends."

"How will we keep track of what's going on at the commune? What if there are developments?"

"Condor can keep me up to speed. Besides, I need to do this and I have to stick with my team. If either the two of you or I go off and do this alone, I'll be stuck without any backup, surely you don't want that. We're autonomous, it's not like they're going to send replacements. I'm going with you to Skolkovo. Or, perhaps more accurately, you're coming with me because I'm going with or without you."

35

LONDON

Harrison sat stone still with his hands resting in plain sight on the top of the steering wheel, the squad car idling behind him, the lights still flashing. Passersby slowed their cars to look at the scene while competitively constructing stories about the man behind the wheel of the car. Harrison was suddenly self-conscious. Did he look nervous? Guilty? Confused? He felt all of these emotions simultaneously, but was trained to look earnest, controlled, and confident. There was doubt in his mind that he was pulling it off.

Why aren't the officers getting out of the car? A dozen reasons ran through his head, but the one that frightened him most was that they were holding him for an assassin. A short time later, a second police car arrived and parked in front of Harrison's car. A male and female officer stepped out of the car at the front of his, each holding an expandable baton. They stopped when they reached the rear corners of the squad car. Two male officers stepped out of the rear patrol car and slowly began approaching Harrison's vehicle, one on each side.

As the officers approached, the cell phone lying in the passenger's seat began to vibrate and buzz. Harrison's hand twitched in an automatic answer response before settling back onto the steering wheel. The last thing he needed to do was to be seen reaching for something in the car. *Do British police carry guns yet?* He couldn't remember, but glanced over at the phone to see PDD Lanser's number lit on the screen. *Shit!* He hit the steering wheel sharply with his palms.

The officer on the driver's side tapped the window with the rubber handle of his baton. Harrison rolled down the window.

"Good afternoon, sir. I'm Officer Cox and this is Officer Elwyn," Cox poked his baton toward the officer on the passenger's side of the car. Elwyn touched his hat in greeting as he continued to look around the inside of Harrison's vehicle. "We're very sorry to disturb you, but we have reason to believe you are Mr. Harrison Steyn, is that correct?"

"Yes, I'm Harrison Steyn."

"Would you step out of the car please, sir." Harrison complied. "Again, I'm sorry to inconvenience you, but you're going to have to come with us."

"What is this about?" Harrison demanded.

"I don't really know, sir. We've just been asked to bring you in for a brief meeting. Will we need the cuffs, sir? Or, will you be coming along?"

"The cuffs won't be necessary."

"Excellent. Officer Elwyn, will you please gather Mr. Steyn's cell phone and other personal items and bring them along?"

"I'd be happy to, sir."

"Thank you Officer Elwyn. Mr. Steyn, one of the other officers will follow us in your car. Come along, please."

When they arrived at the police station, Harrison was placed into a small waiting room usually designated for waiting families and witnesses rather than an interrogation room. He took this as a good sign and poured himself a cup of coffee, his confidence returning. About an hour after he arrived, three men in dark suits entered the waiting room, locked the door, and closed the blinds. The men were nearly indistinguishable from one another and made Harrison think they could have been the male version of the Robert Palmer girls. Harrison fanaticized about the men standing behind a vocalist with bored looks on their faces, pretending to strum guitars and swaying stiffly to the music. The men said nothing until they had poured themselves cups of coffee.

"Have a seat Steyn." The man who spoke, squinted as he sipped the scalding coffee, "Oh, that's awful," he added as a review.

"Relax Steyn, we're not here to kick your ass, we just want to talk. Who we are exactly is not important, but I can tell you we are part of a special unit of MI5."

"Good, I would like to report that someone is following me."

The speaker laughed and looked at the others, "Don't worry, that was us. These guys in fact," he point at the other two men. "We really hoped things wouldn't come to this, but we did want to keep an eye on you."

Harrison remained silent, but decided Speaker's long arms would look better with a bass in them. He made Speaker dance sullenly in his mind while plucking a bass. Harrison could feel the smirk creep into the corners of his mouth.

"So, here's our problem Steyn. We understand you have some interest in the commune north of Blackpool and that you're looking for one Alfie Brand, correct?"

"I'm looking for Brand, but I don't know anything about a commune."

Speaker forced a laugh, "The business incubator you've heard about is actually a commune."

Interesting, Harrison thought to himself before asking, "So what about it?"

"We need you to stay away from there, you may jeopardize our operation if you go running in there all Yankee Doodle Dandy." The other two Robert Palmer guys laughed and shifted their feet as if standing their ground.

"Since you guys are obviously still busy fighting the Revolutionary War, I can't imagine how my going out there to ask for Alfie will harm your operation. Unless," Harrison stepped in a little closer, "he's working for you."

"Listen here Yank." Speaker stabbed a finger in Harrison's chest, "We don't give a flying fig about Alfie Brand, we are only interested in the commune. But if you go running in there looking for someone, they might be tipped that something is up and you could ruin years of our work."

"So what's your interest out there?"

"That is none of your business."

"I think it is. Since we both have an interest in the place, perhaps we could share intel and work together."

"Okay, you first. What do you want Alfie Brand for?"

Harrison smirked, "What's going on at the commune?"

"I see we've come to an impasse. We've booked you on a flight that leaves in two hours. These gentlemen will see that you're on it."

36
BLACKPOOL, ENGLAND

The night was cool and Kate walked quickly down the sidewalk away from the cottage, the heels of her running shoes beating heavily on the pavement. *Slow down, look around, and watch*, she told herself as she executed breathing exercises to calm herself. Kate turned right and then took another immediate right into the cemetery. *Schools and cemeteries make good neighbors*, she remembered being told once by a real estate agent. There was a single light post at the entrance to the cemetery and the remainder was bathed in the sooty darkness of the tombstone's elongated shadows.

It was in one such shadow that she sensed it. Kate didn't know what it was her subconscious had detected. The scuff of a shoe? The brush of a sleeve against a hip? A wisp of cologne? A glint of light hitting a watch? She reached into her purse and fished around for her flashlight, which while small, lit up like a collapsing sun. A broad-trunked maple tree loomed ahead and she ducked behind it and listened. A single footfall, a whisper, at least two people were moving in her direction. *Just wait, a little closer.* As they stepped near the tree Kate jumped out and lit the flashlight in their direction. Two twelve-year-old boys, each looking out from under a lifted white sheet, stood wide-eyed in the beam before beating a retreat.

Kate clutched at her chest and tried to catch her breath.

"Assholes," she yelled to the dead, her voice echoing endlessly across the night, "Fucking little assholes!"

Exhausted and irritated, Kate exited the cemetery and went straight to her car. If anyone else had been following her surely the commotion had chased them off.

The drive back to the commune had failed to quiet the edginess Kate was feeling. As she stepped inside, the clang of the commune's weighty metal door closing behind her caused Kate to flash back to her cell in China. The brick room disappeared from her sight and she heard the cell's metal door close as she crawled across the concrete floor and picked maggots off a rotting rodent before stuffing them into her mouth to prevent starvation. She caught her breath and stepped backwards to prevent a fall and reached out to brace herself on the cool metal of the commune's door. The physical jolt brought her back to real time. *Pull yourself together, Kate. They were just kids in a cemetery trying to scare people. There was never any real danger.*

It was late and the common rooms of the commune were quiet, even Condor had abandoned his screens full of charts. Kate made her way to the cafeteria for a cup of peppermint tea to calm her nerves before bed. The fright in the cemetery had left her unsettled and the flashback didn't help. *Why am I so afraid? Why do I feel so out of control? What would make me feel better about going to Skolkovo?*

Kate took out her cell phone and rolled it aimlessly forward and then backwards in her hand until she dropped it onto the floor. It landed face-up, the phone's contact list on its screen. Reaching down to pick it up Kate noticed one of the contacts and bit her lower lip in thought. She pressed one of the numbers and waited until a cheery woman answered, "Sainsbury Market, how may I help you?"

"Good evening," Kate responded, "this is Peggy Albright for Mary Fenn please."

The following morning, Kate awoke well rested having slept uninterrupted the entire night. She showered and went downstairs to find Condor. Passing him in the computer workroom Kate asked, "I'm going to grab a bagel and some tea, may I bring you something?"

"Juice. Apple Juice." Condor's focus on his computer screens endured.

Returning with Condor's apple juice and her breakfast, Kate inquired, "What's new?"

"Nothing."

"Did Eric ask how we were doing last night?"

"No."

"I've been thinking," Kate took a bite of her bagel and sipped some tea, "we need to make it look like we're still trying to find the originating location of the hack. I want to try to find these people, but I don't want anyone to know we've figured out where they are in case they're working with someone in the commune."

"I've already taken care of it." Condor woke his far-right monitor from sleep mode, "I wrote a simple algorithm that can be used to search server logs to trace bounce locations. Once it finds one, it pings me so I can pull up the next log in the chain and run it again."

"I don't understand how that works since we've already found the endpoint."

"I started in our server and I have the algo searching for basic protocol that links computers together on the Internet. We'll have to ping every computer in the world before this program quits. I think we've got some time, but if for some reason we reach the end, I'll just start it over again."

"Condor, that's brilliant! What a great idea."

"Thank you." He gulped down some juice and went back to clicking away at his keyboard.

"Good morning, Kate!" Kate turned to find Vegas walking toward her.

"Hey, Vegas! Condor has done a brilliant thing and automated our bounce trace process so what do you say we work on getting that crypto-currency wallet launched?"

"Sounds great! Get things fired up and I'll be with you in a minute. I've only had enough caffeine to power two-thirds of my brain. Can I get you anything?"

"No thank you." Kate went to work powering up their computers.

Over the next three days, Vegas and Kate completed the beta testing on the program. Near the end of the third day they decided it was ready to go live and be shared with the open source community. With a few keystrokes they released the new standard in crypto-currency money laundering within the dark web economy. What Vegas and the rest of the dark web didn't know was that it also contained a backdoor that allowed the NSA to track everything that moved through it.

That evening after dinner, as many community members lounged on the patio, Kate walked across the lawn to the edge of the shallow bluff to watch the waves crash against the sandy shore. Kate finished her beer and inhaled the sea air. The scent of an ocean breeze evoked pleasant childhood memories in Kate. The anticipation of summer camp on the shore of Lake Superior and the joy being there with her friends had brought her. She also recalled being a teenager surfing in Hawaii on the family's annual winter vacation and a native Hawaiian boy named Jake whose brown skin and red aloha shorts made her heart skip a beat. Kate smiled to herself, she should have been coming out here to relieve her stress all along.

"Am I interrupting anything?" Eric was walking up behind her, but had stopped to ask the question.

"Of course not. Good to see you Eric. Come on over."

"I noticed your drink was gone, would you like

another?" Eric handed Kate one of the two beers he was carrying.

"Thank you, that's very kind."

"I see you and Vegas launched the crypto-currency wallet today. That's excellent news, you should be celebrating, but you look a bit glum. Is anything wrong?"

"No, not at all. With the project finished, I'm just feeling a bit of a loss."

"Well, that's understandable. Don't worry, you'll soon find your next project."

"I'm sure I will. Where are you on the missing Luminiferon?"

"We think we might have a solution, but it has never been tried before so it's risky."

"I hope for the commune's sake it works out.'

"Speaking of the commune, have you given anymore thought to staying here with us? We all think you'd be a great addition to our community."

"Actually, that's what I was talking to the sea about."

"Has the man in the sea provided any answers?"

"He has actually. What he advises is taking a brief vacation from the commune to explore The Continent before making a final decision. I think I've been lulled into a comfortable inertia here and I need to step away to make sure staying is what I absolutely want to do."

"Quite understandable. I'll save your room for you. When do you think you'll leave?"

"Having made the decision, I think I'll get underway tomorrow. Condor has written an algorithm to continue the bounce trace, so he doesn't need my help combing through code."

"Have a relaxing vacation and we look forward to your return."

37
WASHINGTON, DC

The corridor reminded him of a submarine. A narrow hall of gray walls with darker gray metal doors, their bio scanners and knobs a winkingly brilliant silver under the steady glow of LED bulbs. The only deviation from the gray was a strip of Old Glory Blue carpeting running down the center hallway, absorbing his every footfall.

Occasionally an administrative assistant perched in an outer office would glance up at him through a narrow bulletproof window and nod in greeting. There was never any bustle here. No people moving in and out of offices hurriedly executing official duties. Just people locked behind doors doing whatever it was that bureaucratically caged people with security clearances do.

But the most unnerving part of the journey was the absolute soundlessness. The passageway was a vacuum sucking all sound into the acoustic paneled walls and dense carpeting. The people behind the thick glass were mute and the space lacked even a whisper of ventilation. By the time PDD Lanser had reached the CIA Director's office and picked up the telephone receiver resting beside the door, he feared the corridor would capture the sound of his voice before it reached the microphone. Fortunately, one of Director Wolf's assistants noticed Lanser in the hall and buzzed him in before he had time to find out.

A whoosh of noise greeted PDD Lanser as he opened the door to the busy outer office of CIA Director Nancy Wolf. Five busily buzzing people had joined Wolf's three assistants in the undersized space. The flurry of activity was like oxygen to Lanser and he could feel his lungs heaving in relief. By the time Lanser had gotten his bearings, his presence was already being announced to Director Wolf.

"You may go in now, sir," the woman at the desk to his right said as he was buzzed into Wolf's inner office.

"Marc, how are you?" Director Wolf had come out from behind her desk to shake Lanser's hand. The light coming in from the specially coated exterior windows designed to prevent anyone from seeing in or sound from getting out, cast a sickly greenish glow across the Director's office.

"I've been better, but it's good to see you, Nancy." The sounds of the outer office slowly disappeared behind the closing door.

"Have a seat," the Director motioned toward one of the guest chairs as she sat in the other. "Tell me a bit more about your problem?"

"Not much more to tell then what we discussed on the phone. Harrison had been running a field team working The Executive case on our side. Admiral Reynolds called the team in to move the investigation in a different direction. Harrison, however, decided just to pull back all the team's support personnel and leave the core team of three out on an autonomous op. I had no firsthand knowledge of who was on the team, but I was quite surprised when I found out Kate Adams was out there and might be blown."

"I think Adam's involvement was a decision made on our side. Your Elliot Poe has been working with one of our psychological profilers and I believe he found a possible role for Adams and asked me to activate her. I agreed. But I'm sorry to interrupt. Please, continue."

"Once Admiral Reynolds told me Adams was in danger, I tried to contact Harrison who had flown to London for a brief meeting with MI6. Now I can't find him. I thought we should compare notes and see if we can figure out what's going on and where the team and Harrison might be. Unfortunately, Harrison is the only one who has any details on my side about the team. This is really your project."

The Director of CIA reached across her desk and slid a file folder toward him. "Here's all I know about the team. When support was pulled, they were operating around Blackpool on the west coast of England. After that they went totally dark. They dumped their cell phones and probably switched to burner phones and started using cash. The last Agency charge we have for them was for rent of a house in Blackpool."

"Are they still there?"

"We had some of our folks go out and knock on the door, but there was no answer. They kept eyes on the place for three days, but didn't see anyone."

"Did they go inside?" Lanser's gut was churning about the possibilities.

"Yes. No sign of clothes, toiletries, or suitcases, so it looks like they're either gone or away, but no clues as to where. They're good at this, you know."

"They certainly are. Do the Brits know anything?"

"Not that they're sharing with us."

"What about Harrison?"

"We were able to track his cell phone and it looks like he didn't get too far away from the airport at first."

"Then what?"

"Then his movement patterns, most likely in a car, look like he was trying to shake a pursuer." Wolf opened the folder and showed Lanser the map.

Lanser closed his eyes and quickly prayed after he saw it. "So the signal stops there on the Ringway then.   No   additional   signs?"

"I'm sorry, Marc, but that's all we have."

"Again, I assume the Brits are no help?"

"Actually a police officer recalls pulling the car over and taking Harrison to the station, but your man seems to have disappeared after that."

"Nancy, it strikes me that there is too much compartmentalization of information going on in this Executive case. Everyone is so terrified to share information, even internally, at the risk of tipping off a mole. Heck, even I don't know everything that's going on in my own agency. And now the one person with the most knowledge about an autonomous op is missing and we have people in the field in danger. I think, at least between the two of us and within our own agencies that needs to stop now. My plan is to gather all the information I can get my hands on and share it with you so we can figure this whole thing out and put it to an end. I think right now no one has the big picture, just fragments of information. Let's form an Executive Task Force and find The Executive."

The airport's dampness was releasing the smell of long banned cigarettes from the pores of the building's structure. Or perhaps one of the Robert Palmer men sitting on either side of him at the gate was on fire. Harrison smirked as the image of smoke rising from their collars crossed his mind.

He'd previously been occupying his mind with methods of escape, but there was only one option that was even plausible. Yet, as he visualized himself bolting out of the ground crew's jetway door and sprinting across the tarmac, the men to his sides always overtook him. When he imagined successfully fleeing from the men, Harrison found himself penniless and wandering the streets of London aimlessly. Yes, it was better to return home to the safety of his pension. He did not have the stuff of a field operator and had resolved himself to the fact that he wasn't hero material, but a bureaucrat who appreciated the value of structure and process. Now all his mind's eye could see was the grief he was going to get from Lanser.

The plane landed at Dulles International Airport at sunset. Harrison solemnly shuffled down the aisle with the other passengers to deplane.

"Oh, wait a minute Mr. Steyn," the flight attendant near the door grabbed his arm. "I have some things for you." She went to the first-class closet, removed a suitcase, and rolled it toward Harrison. After passing him the handle of the case, she slipped his cell phone and the battery that had been removed from it into his pocket.

38
SKOLKOVO, RUSSIA

The stars crackled around the fingernail moon making Kate feel like God was pointing an accusatory finger in her direction. *I know this might be a bad idea,* Kate repented as the cab careened down a steep hill on its way to Heathrow Airport, *but it's the only action I can take at this point. You didn't make me capable of passivity.*

"I have assigned you seat 12B and your flight will be departing from Terminal 5, Gate B-53. Will you just be checking one bag today?" The British Airways agent smiled hopefully as if Kate's response were the answer to the universe's most important question.

"Yes, just the one please."

The agent efficiently tagged and dispatched the suitcase and Kate proceeded toward the gate stopping to pick up some soup with a side of French bread along the way. She was the first of her party to arrive at the gate and was sipping tomato soup off a plastic spoon when Elliot appeared and sat near the window. Shortly before boarding, Joe materialized looking frazzled. This was Joe's usual airport arrival time and state even under the best of conditions. His frayed appearance upon entry always made Kate smile, an expression she was unable to suppress even today. Kate stifled a giggle as she tried not to look at Joe as he awkwardly maneuvered his carry-on bag, knocking over another man's drink before flopping into his seat and panting heavily. Kate always wondered if this was the real airport Joe or a character he played when on assignment.

The flight was uneventful, yet Kate was feeling keyed up. She found herself taking an unusual number of trips to the lavatory, alternating between the forward and rear facilities, to look at the faces of the people on the plane. If something was awry, she didn't find it.

When they touched down in Moscow, Kate positioned herself away from the rest of the team at the baggage carousel. Standing near the opening, she watched the bags drop monotonously onto the circular belt. Two identical bags with pink yarn tied to their handles dropped in next to one another. Kate lifted the cases off the carousel, extended their handles, and dragged them toward the exit where she hailed a cab.

The team reconvened in a room at the Marriot Grand Hotel after sweeping it for cameras and listening devices. They didn't find any.

"Elliot, will you give Kate and I a minute alone, please?" Elliot nodded and returned to the adjoining room.

Joe's voice was stern and his arms were crossed

in front of him. "What's going on?"

"What do you mean?"

"What I mean is, you were wearing out the carpet in the aisle of the airplane on the way over."

Kate turned and went to sit on the bed, "I don't know exactly, but something doesn't feel right and it's making me anxious. Looking around the plane for anyone who looked suspicious made me feel better."

"As it turned out, the only thing suspicious on that airplane was you. If there was anyone from any foreign intelligence service on that airplane you are now on his or her radar. You acted like someone getting ready to set off a bomb in a crowded market. I'd have profiled you from a mile away."

"I'm sorry Joe. I don't know what's gotten into me."

"Kate, your instincts are good and I trust them. If you feel like something is amiss, there very well might be. But let's talk about it. Don't bottle it up and carry it around with you. Remember and practice your training and we'll all be all right."

"Okay. I'm a bit disappointed with myself frankly. I'm usually more together than this."

"It's all right, we all have challenging moments in this business. So tell me, what are you concerned about?"

"I'm not sure exactly, but I feel like we're missing something right under our noses. As soon as I'm able to refine that feeling I'll be sure to let you know."

"That's a deal. But tell me, do you feel strongly like we should call this off and go home?"

"No, I'm not ready for that."

"Okay, our rental van should be here, so let's all take a drive out to Skolkovo and get the lay of the land."

The 24-kilometer drive from Moscow to Skolkovo took the trio from the urban heat of city pavement and into the flat, tree-lined coolness of the Soviet era suburbs. In the absence of trees, it would have been difficult to know where the city ended and the suburb began. The Innovation Center was ringed by the community of Skolkovo and guarded by military-style gates and personnel. Casually driving onto the property wasn't going to be possible.

"I guess we'll just have to be technology entrepreneurs looking for a location to incubate our ideas," Kate stated matter-of-factly. "What would you gentlemen like to produce?"

They threw around some ideas before continuing the conversation over hamburgers at an American-style lunch counter. Joe's face lit up, "I've got it! What if we just want to develop a technology think tank designed to aggregate ideas from the expertise inside the Innovation Center?"

"That's a great idea," Elliot added, "it would also explain our small staff and minimal office needs."

"Well gentleman, now we just need to find some office space adjacent to our suspect. Perhaps we can find a local person who deals in such properties."

Kate used her limited Russian to ask the man flipping burgers behind the counter where they could find a real estate agent who dealt in rentals at the Innovation Center. Apparently, Kate's Russian was so poor that the man both misunderstood her question and felt compelled to answer in English.

"The bus tours for the Innovation Center leave every two hours. You can get tickets at the cash register. The nearest tour bus stop is one block that way," he pointed behind them.

They decided the bus tour was a good place to start. Moving through the Innovation Center gate, the tour guide began her presentation, "Innovation City measures approximately 400 hectares and is able to house a permanent population of 21,000 people. It is also within a 40-minute drive from Moscow and will attract many commuters from the city. It is a modern planned city with two primary elements: a University and a Technology Park."

They had passed through the surrounding grassy field and were entering the "city." The guide directed their attention to a 7-story square building sitting on a large parcel of land, "This was the first building built in Innovation City. We call it the Hypercube. It is the center of our philosophical eco-system. The gross floor area of the building is 6,000 square meters and is environmentally friendly and energy efficient with many autonomous utility systems. The exterior of the building is 3,200 square meters of architectural wire mesh, which includes a 415- square meter transparent media façade."

The building's media façade was playing a series of video clips of people skiing, skydiving, and swimming. At the end of the presentation a giant human eye filled the screen, an image Kate associated with the omnipresent government surveillance of Big Brother in George Orwell's 1984. Was the eye designed to stimulate or intimidate the residents of Innovation City?

"Behind Hypercube is the main public building

in Skolkovo called MATREX," the guide continued dryly, "both buildings were designed by prominent Russian architects."

The area beyond Hypercube and MATREX was occupied by a housing area surrounded by buildings arranged into five clusters by technology specialty areas: information, energy-efficiency, nuclear, biomedical technologies, and space technologies and communications. The tour group was let out of the bus in a town square that resembled a Universal Studios back lot. Restaurants, a Starbucks, and several specialty stores ringed the square and many of the fifteen or so tourists went off in search of coffee. Kate grabbed Joe's arm and dragged him down the steps toward a three-sided kiosk at the center of the sunken plaza. Elliot trailed behind. The sides of the kiosk contained a map of Innovation City, a guide to dining and shopping, and on the third side, a map of buildings with space available and the contact person for each.

Kate pointed at the city map, "Right here, in one of the buildings on this side of the housing complex, is where the hack on the commune's Luminiferon originated. We need to set up shop in this building on the other side of this grassy area and the road."

"That building is in the space technologies and communications cluster and it does appear to have several vacancies," Elliot said from the real estate side of the Kiosk as he wrote down the contact phone number.

"Great, we'll give them a call in the morning."

Returning to the hotel for the evening, Kate switched on the room's television.

There's more fallout from documents released by

The Executive. Sky News received word late today from Brussels that thirty-two seasoned American diplomats are being expelled from around the European Union on suspicion of spying. This action comes two days after the U.S. expelled twelve European diplomats for the same reason...

39
WASHINGTON, DC

The sun had set on Dulles, but twilight's glow still lingered. Harrison was tired, but felt compelled to check in at the office. He needed to touch base with the safety and normality of his life. Fumbling to reload the battery into his phone, Harrison hailed a cab to take him home to retrieve his car. Harrison was grateful the phone's battery was dead so he didn't have to listen to the string of voicemails that were likely residing on it.

Once in his own car and on his way to his office, Harrison groped around in his center console for his charger and then clumsily plugged it into the cigarette lighter as he drove. The phone's battery charging indicator lit up, but it would need to charge a while before he could use it.

The security clearance area of the building was a brightly lit beacon in a dim building immersed in nighttime energy conservation mode. A ridiculous concept considering the building operated 24-hours a day. Harrison went through the security protocol before being approached by a security supervisor, "Sir, I need you to step in here please." He pointed toward a small holding room adjacent to the bag scanner.

A jolt of panic lead to beads of sweat on Harrison's hairline and spine, "What's this about?"

"I'm sure it's nothing, sir. We've just been asked to hold you until someone can talk to you." The guard closed the small room's door with Harrison inside. He immediately tried the handle. Locked.

They know about the documents I smuggled, ran on a loop inside his head. He sat on one of the plastic chairs in the room and tried to calm himself, but he was resolved: *This is it. My career is over. I should have lost my pension being a hero in London, not for wearing an adult diaper full of classified.*

What seemed like an eternity later, PDD Lanser burst into the room, "Where on earth have you been?"

Harrison, mouth agape, could do nothing but stare at Lanser in confusion.

"What the devil is the matter with you? Did you become mute while you were away?" Lanser's voice boomed in the small space now lit by the red glow emitting from his face.

Harrison contemplated his hands, "I have some things to confess, but I need you to be my confessor." He thought he heard Lanser growl under his breath. Harrison looked at him, "Can you offer me absolution and leave what I tell you in this room?"

Lanser spit out, "Spill it!"

Harrison stared at the table as he told Lanser everything that he had done. Breaking into Faulkner's office using a forged memo. Smuggling documents. His ill-fated trip to London and the man named Alfie Brand. When he had finished his body rested in an exhausted heap on the tabletop, his eyes pleadingly fixed on Lanser. Lanser didn't respond. Instead he turned on his heel and left the room. Harrison watched in anguish as Lanser walked out the front door of the building. Harrison rested his head on his arms and quietly cried himself to sleep.

Harrison thought he was still on the airplane when he awoke. As the fog of sleep lifted, the weight of dread descended. A portable partition screen had been moved in front of the window of the room he was imprisoned in. He went to the window and pressed the side of his head against the glass to try to see beyond the edge of the screen. The orange glow of morning sun was reflecting off the tiled entry floor. It was early and he could hear a steady stream of people arriving for work. He was grateful for the privacy screen.

Harrison kept checking the sun, and listening to foot traffic. He guessed it was near noon when Lanser returned rolling Harrison's suitcase behind him.

"You look like a turd, you know that, right?" he barked.

"I am a turd," Harrison stared down at the tiled floor.

"Before I try to pick you up by the clean end, let's get you showered and put back together. I'll meet you in my office. Try to look like nothing is wrong." Lanser skipped Harrison's ID across the table and left the door open as he left.

Everything Harrison did seemed to take too long. His feet were like lead weights reducing his movements to jerky, slow motions. Images of what was to come flashed through his mind. The thought of never being able to step foot in the building again filled him with remorse. This wasn't how he had wanted his career to end. He was in mourning.

Harrison entered the Principle Deputy Director's area and walked past his own office toward Lanser's Administrative Assistants.

"Are you all right, Mr. Steyn?" one of them asked, "You look like you've had a shock."

"I'm quite all right, thank you." Harrison managed a weak smile, "I'm just lost in thought."

"PDD Lanser told us to send you straight in," the other assistant chimed in as she slid a sideways glance toward the first assistant.

"Sit down," Lanser commanded before holding up the coffee pot he had just used to fill his own mug, "I'll pour you some."

"No, thank you."

"Well, you're going to drink some coffee and learn to take orders while you do it." There was a light rap on the door, "Come in!"

One of the assistants brought in a cafeteria tray and set it on the office table before silently leaving the office.

"You're going to eat too." Lanser pointed toward the food.

"But I'm not…"

Lanser interrupted, "Shut up and eat the food!

You're following orders now, remember?"

Harrison nodded and moved to the table. Using a fork, he broke off a small portion of omelet, put it in his mouth, and chewed mechanically.

"Let's get something straight. I am peeved to a point that I am actually incapable of describing."

Harrison was now grateful the food gave him something to do other than just look at Lanser.

"What you did is a terminable offense. But you're lucky. You actually helped us out in your own way and this case is too important to allow a good man to be put out on the street."

Harrison set his fork down and looked at Lanser, "Are you saying you're not going to fire me?"

"I didn't say that. Let's call it a probationary period before I make up my mind."

"Thank you, sir."

"Eat your food. We have an appointment in an hour with CIA Director Wolf."

This trip down the long, gray hall Harrison's nervous, shallow breathing broke the silence of the walk to Director Wolf's office. Harrison told Director Wolf everything he knew about Alfie Brand.

"Well, we need to find him," Director Wolf agreed. "It sounds like the Brits aren't going to be much help. I'll contact our London station and have them start poking around Blackpool and the area computer and hacking communities."

Lanser added, "I'll have our people run him through the database and see if we can build his network of connections. Someone knows where he is. If we're lucky, maybe we'll find an associate with something to hide who's willing to give him up in exchange for the silence of the U.S. Intelligence community."

"Harrison," Lanser added, "I also need you to tell me everything you know about Kate Adam's whereabouts. Admiral Reynolds says she might be in danger. We have to find her."

"Let's get this moving. It's all hands on deck." Director Wolf picked up her phone and stood as means of dismissing the men.

40
SKOLKOVO, RUSSIA

The Skolkovo real estate agent met Kate at the entrance to the building and walked her down a wide, window-lined hallway. The agent's office was at the end of the hall at the back of the building. The agent ushered Kate inside. The view from the office's floor to ceiling windows was of brown overgrown grass and a concrete pond with a water feature that was bone dry and infested with leaves, dirt, and food wrappers. Beyond it was a field of desiccated grass that led to the highway. Technology City looked unfinished, as if abandoned by it's contractors on a hot, sunny day in August after lunch.

As if sensing Kate's thoughts, the agent spoke to her in English, "You have selected a lovely office for your work. The view on that side of the building is quite nice. Shall we start the paperwork?"

Once the lease agreement was signed and Kate had the key, she walked to the MATREX building. After a few forms and a photograph, Kate was handed her Technology City employer ID badge. She texted the men and asked them to meet her at the main gate. Once inside she escorted them to the MATREX building for their own credentials.

The trio backed the van up to the freight door of their new building and began unloading their supplies: folding chairs, a card table, cots, sleeping bags, pillows, and their personal suitcases. The office space was on the second floor and was made up of three rooms. In front was a reception area that overlooked the housing complex. Through a door behind it was a large workspace designed for cubicles. Off the large space was a bathroom with a stall shower.

They would be the first occupants of the office space and it appeared that when the contractors abandoned the building, they forgot to clean up behind themselves. Every surface was covered in gritty drywall dust. There were finishing nails, scraps of brown paper, bits of insulation, rags, and paint cans scattered about the floor. Kate walked down to the agent's office to inquire where the building's dumpster was located and was told there were only central quadrant dumpsters located in each section of the city. Kate was aggravated to hear such a centralized Communist-style dumpster policy still existed in Russia's allegedly most modern and innovative city.

They set up the folding chairs and table in the reception area near the window as their lookout station. The building's reflective glass made it impossible for anyone to see in during daylight hours. Cots were set up in the larger room and the eight-hour lookout shift schedule was agreed upon. Elliot took the first shift. Kate began cleaning. Joe borrowed tools from the building agent in an attempt to fix the shower handle that fell off in his hands the minute he touched it. During the four-block return trip from the central dumpster, Kate stopped by the housing complex to see if there were names on any of the mailboxes or buzzers.

The complex was set in a circular pattern and had a common brick lower level with entry doors for each of the apartments. The upper levels were made of individual rectangular boxes painted in pastel colors set perpendicular to the lower level. The upper boxes cantilevered over each side of the lower level. There was a well-manicured courtyard in the middle of the circle with grills, fire pits, horseshoe pit, and volleyball net. Each upper level had two balconies, one facing the courtyard and one facing outward. There were no names on either the doorbells or mailboxes of the complex, only numbers. The lack of names would make identifying who Anchor really was more difficult. Eric had given Kate a picture of Anchor's girlfriend, but all she knew about Anchor came from a description derived from Condor's remarkably detailed memory.

Three days of cleaning, fixing, eating takeout, and watching the housing complex later Elliot alerted the team, "Guys, I think we've got something. Sorry Kate, I know you're not a guy. I meant that in the upper Midwestern gender inclusive sense. But look, that might be our target. That looks like the right woman with him."

A slender woman in a sundress made tall by four-inch wedge sandals was walking with a man wearing a hoodie and a baseball cap, hiding his face with his hand.

"That certainly looks like Lana," Kate agreed, "but it's hard to tell who's with her."

"This is your show, Kate. How do you want to proceed?" Joe asked urgently.

"Let's follow them, try to get a positive ID, and see what they're up to. Elliot, hang back in case there's more activity   from   that   complex."

It was nearing seven o'clock, overcast, and a light rain was beginning to fall. Kate and Joe shrugged on their raincoats and threw their hoods up as they walked out the door. Joe moved across the street and Kate hunched over and shoved her hands into her pockets while following directly behind the couple keeping at least a hundred yards between them. The couple didn't seem to be at all concerned about being followed and walked directly to a restaurant in the town square and were seated near the back.

Kate went inside, sat at the bar, and ordered a glass of white wine. A short time later, Joe entered and sat on the stool next to her and introduced himself as if he were coming on to her. The bartender asked what he'd like to drink and Joe smiled warmly at Kate.

"I'll have what she's having. Can we get some menus? I think I'd like to buy this lady dinner." So began their heads together hushed voice conversation.

The man with Lana had removed his hat, and Kate leaned into Joe. "I'm pretty certain that's our man."

"I think you're right. Soup and salad should get us out of here quickly if they move, don't you think?"

"Yes, I'll have the potato and sausage soup,

please."

Joe ordered for the two of them, "Nothing seems particularly unusual over there. They just seem like two lovers out for dinner."

"They do, but why tonight? Is it a special occasion? Are they meeting another couple? I guess we'll have to wait and see."

Kate and Joe had time for another glass of wine after their meal before Anchor signaled for the check. Joe did the same. They followed the lovebirds as they walked arm in arm back to the apartment in the rain. Nothing seemed out of the ordinary.

Elliot reported no activity at the apartments.

"I'd like to make contact when he's alone," Kate told the men, "When he's with the Lana we follow and observe, but if he's alone, I'm going to find a way to talk with him."

"Are you planning to approach him as a member of the commune or as American intelligence?"

"I don't know yet. I'll play it by ear."

The next day, Anchor left the apartment during a steady downpour. "Elliot, stay here and follow Lana if she goes out."

"Roger that, Kate."

Anchor walked much faster without Lana and made a beeline for one of the coffee shop. He ordered an espresso and sat alone with an English language newspaper.

"Let's go." Kate led Joe to Anchor's table and sat down. "Are you Anchor?"

Setting his cup back onto his saucer, "Yes, I'm Anchor? Do I know you?"

"I have reason to believe you may have stolen the Luminiferon of a commune of which both you and I are members."

Anchor looked relieved. "Thank goodness you found me," he said in whispered excitement. "I plan to give the Luminiferon back, I just took it in hopes that someone at the commune would find me and help me. I need to speak to American intelligence urgently."

"Why do you need to speak with American intelligence?"

"I'm into something way over my head. I've lost control of the situation and I'm certain I'll eventually be killed."

"Why don't you just contact the U.S. Embassy? And why U.S. intelligence, you're British? Just get ahold of MI6.

"I'm being held here against my will and my movements and communications are monitored. You don't understand, my situation is extremely urgent."

"Make me understand."

Anchor leaned in close and whispered, "My name is Liam Tremblay and I'm The Executive."

"How do we know you're really The Executive?"

"Get me to U.S. intelligence and I'll prove it."

Kate and Joe looked at each other briefly before Joe said, "We are U.S. intelligence. Prove it."

Anchor's voice was shocked and excited, "If you're really American intelligence I need you to leave now. I need help. I'll tell you anything and help in any way I can, but I'm meeting someone and I can't be seen with you."

"If you need help, why don't you come with us

now?"

"Because they'll harm Lana if I do. We'll figure something out. Come see me later. I'm at number 49 in the housing complex. Now go, please," Liam gritted his teeth, "I beg you. Please leave my table."

Joe leaned into Liam, "Frankly, we don't give a shit about Lana. You'll have to give me a better reason not to drag you out of here."

Liam's face turned serious and his swagger returned, "Because if I don't enter a randomly generated code into my computer twice a day, all the documents I have stored on my computer will automatically be released. You and much of Europe will no longer have any secrets left to protect."

Kate jerked her head toward Joe and they retreated to the bar. A few minutes later two men sat down with Liam, but they couldn't hear the conversation.

41
WASHINGTON, DC

The CIA's London station had discreetly descended upon Blackpool. Staff members remaining at the embassy were working assets and friendlies looking for anything that would connect Alfie Brand to Blackpool. After several false starts, a picture was slowing beginning to emerge of Alfie and his known associates. It was time for London to call it in to Langley.

"Yes, ma'am we think we know where Alfie might be." The London-based agent's face loomed large on the high-definition screen at the head of the conference table. "We've discovered a compound of sorts out in Blackpool. Alfie has likely been there, but we'll need to set up an operation to determine if that's where he still resides."

"And we have reason to believe Alfie has many associates there with much to hide," PDD Lanser added.

Director Wolf nodded in the affirmative, "We'll need to send a team out to ask for him. What I'd like you to do…"

Lanser interrupted, "We need to send Harrison in. He's met Alfie's mother and may have some intimate knowledge your team doesn't have."

The room fell silent and the giant head on the screen averted his eyes before speaking, "Look, I'm not sure bringing in a…," the head paused as he chose his words carefully. "I'm not convinced bringing in someone from the home office would be wise. Our sources tell us Steyn is already on the radar here anyway and we frankly need someone with more field experience."

Reenergized by his possible participation in the mission, Harrison spoke, "I know you think I'm just a pencil pusher, but I've been on the ground there and have a feel for Alfie's roots. I really think I can be of help here."

"I have to say I agree," Director Wolf guided. "Work on an approach plan and we'll send Harrison out."

Wolf disconnected the video call. Lanser glared at Harrison, "Don't screw this up. This is your best chance at redemption."

Harrison arrived in London on a cargo plane under the cover of darkness. The face from the video call picked him up at the cargo company's terminal.

"Sorry about what I said on that call. I'm Duke by the way." He offered his hand, which Harrison shook. "We've talked about it here amongst the team and see the value in having you go out to the commune to ask for

Alfie."

"No apology needed. What do you have in mind?"

"We want to send you out as a friend of the mother who's worried about her son."

"Great idea, I can pull that off."

The two men drove in silence to Blackpool. Duke tossed Harrison a room key once they arrived at the Blackpool Hilton, "Go get some sleep. We'll talk details after you've had a few hours of rest. I'll wake you when we're ready."

Exhaustion drove Harrison into a deep sleep that was interrupted three hours later by a firm rap on the door. Harrison let Duke in.

"Our people are in place. You're job today is simply to find out if Alfie is on the property. You're just an acquaintance of his mother's, a new neighbor from across the street who sells trinkets to the Blackpool gift shops. His mother just asked you to check in on him since she hasn't heard from him in a while."

"Got it."

"Don't be specific about anything. Not even the length of time she hasn't heard from him. Keep it casual. Remember, we don't know if he's actually done anything." Duke gave Harrison a list of known associates at the commune. "Are you ready?"

"Ready."

Harrison's electric car lacked the motoring sounds he found reassuring as a driver. To reduce the feeling of a golf cart, Harrison turned up the volume on the radio. The vibes of Drowning Pool failed to suppress the electric whir as he approached the compound.

Three agents disguised as lab-coated scientists

were taking soil samples in a nearby field beside a panel van. When Harrison saw the building, he relaxed a little. The place didn't look particularly menacing in the bright light of the day, but then again Auschwitz looks like a country boarding school from afar absent knowledge of what actually happened there.

Stepping into the shabby lobby, Harrison imagined no successful businesses would dare be incubated in such a locale. It looked like a place where dreams and ambitions went to die. A young woman with red hair arranged in layers of orderly corkscrews was sitting at the desk feverishly pecking at a keyboard.

She lifted her head and merrily asked, "Hello, how may I help you?"

"Hi, I'm looking for Alfie Brand. Is he here?" Too quickly Harrison added, "I'm a friend of his mother, Mrs. Trotter, and she asked me to stop by and check in on him."

"Aww, how nice, I love Alfie," she responded like a woman who drew little hearts over her "i's" and squeed at the sight of puppies. "Unfortunately he hasn't been around for a while. We don't really know where he went."

"Does anyone know what happened to him?"

She shrugged and whined, "Not that I'm aware of."

"May I speak with whomever is in charge?"

The woman bristled and her tone transformed from that of a teenager to a schoolmarm, "This is a co-op, no one is in charge."

"I'm sorry, I didn't mean to offend. He had a friend here named Eric, I think. Is he around?"

"I'll see if I can reach him." She picked up a phone

and dialed. Reaching Eric, she let him know an acquaintance of Alfie's was looking for him.

Eric gave Harrison a jovial greeting and offered him a seat in the adjoining office.

"I'm sorry, no one has heard from Alfie in five or six months."

Harrison pressed him, "Any idea where he went? His mother is concerned."

"No. He just said he had a job and wanted to set up his own location like ours, but he just sort of disappeared. I've actually been informally looking for him myself, it's a bit concerning. Will you let me know if you find him?"

"Yes. I assume you'll do the same?" Harrison handed Eric a business card from Harvey Bender, Novelties.

"Of course. Good luck."

Harrison briefed the team in the hotel room about what he had discovered.

"I think they're telling the truth, but they could be hiding him either inside or elsewhere."

"Let's do this analytically," Duke suggested as he began drawing a grid on a piece of paper.

Thump! Thump! Thump! All heads turned toward the hotel room's door where it sounded as if a fist was beating against it. Duke made some hand signals and all present stood and quietly moved around the door.

"Who is it?" Duke yelled.

"MI5. My badge is in front of the peephole."

Duke looked through it before opening the door. The speaking member of the Robert Palmer Men entered, alone.

"Well, well, well. It looks like Harrison Steyn brought some friends this time. Are you going to introduce me?"

He did so. Reluctantly.

"Gentlemen, MI5 has been working a major case against the commune based on a plethora of illegal activity taking place at that site. Unfortunately, your poking around out there is causing us to have to push up our raid date. This does not make me happy."

Duke moved forward, "What type of activity?"

"That is not for me to discuss until after the raid. However, while I think it's a terrible idea, my boss seems to think we should cooperate and bring you along on the raid to see if you can find your man Alfie Brand. If he's of interest to you, we expect he may be of interest to us. We'll share what we know after the raid."

"What's the timing on this?"

"Grab your popcorn, it's going down now."

By the time they had arrived at the commune the raid was well underway and the people on site had been rounded up and were being held in the cafeteria. Harrison and the team did a walk through, but did not find Alfie or anyone willing to admit they knew him and volunteer where he might be.

They met with MI5 Director O'Brien on site, "I'm sorry you didn't find your guy. We've had a couple of agents inside for about a year. They've put together a list of known community members during their time inside who are not currently in the building. Your man Brand is on the list."

"May we see the list?" Duke held out his hand.

"I'll let you take a look, but you can't take it

with you."

O'Brien handed the list to Duke as Harrison looked over his shoulder. The name "Kate Adams" was at the top.

Harrison looked at O'Brien, "May we talk to your agents on the inside?"

"Sorry. They're covert and this case is too big. We're not willing to risk blowing their cover. They're both too good at their jobs. Share your questions with MI6 and I'll let them interview our agents."

And find out what we're looking for at the same time, Harrison thought.

42
SKOLKOVO, RUSSIA

The two men paused to look around the coffee shop as the door closed behind them. Liam's eyes slid sideways toward the bar where Joe and Kate sat huddled together looking at a cell phone and laughing intimately.

"We have a problem," the more muscled of the two announced, though both men could have been professional wrestlers.

"Won't you sit down," Liam offered. "What seems to be the problem?"

"Our boss is telling us we have to move you. Something about too much communication traffic or something."

"Don't be silly. I'm perfectly safe here. Who on earth would look for me in this place? Heck, no one but you and your employer even know who I am."

"The boss doesn't want you compromised," the

spokesman said as the other man played the part of 'muscle' by staring down anyone brave enough to make eye contact. Muscle noticed a couple taking selfies at the bar and turned his back to them, positioning himself between the couple and Liam. "We still have a lot of work to do together before we can give you up."

Give me up? I think you mean kill me. There's no way Lana and I get out of this alive. Liam fidgeted.

"Let's go." The men each grabbed an arm and lifted Liam from the chair and led him out the door.

Joe and Kate followed behind. The men walked Liam back to his residence and Joe and Kate returned to their lookout post.

"Hi guys," Elliot chirped, "what's up?"

"We have a situation, but we don't know what it is." Kate pointed at Elliot, "They've already seen us at the coffee shop. I need you to go keep an eye on Number 49 from inside the housing complex and see what those men are up to with Liam. Follow them if they leave on foot, regroup with us at the van if they leave by car. We'll take over here."

"Who the hell is Liam?"

"Liam is Anchor's real name." Elliot dashed out the door without asking any more questions.

Kate looked at Joe, "I've managed to get some pictures of the men in our selfie. I'm going to crop us out of the photos and see if we can find out who they are."

"Who exactly are you going to send them to? We're an autonomous op, remember?"

"Don't worry about that." Kate cropped the photos and messaged them to the Mary Fenn contact on her phone with the note '*Identify*?'

About thirty minutes later, the men led Lana and Liam out of the apartment and into a waiting car. Liam's nose was bloodied. Locking the couple in the car, the men went back into the apartment and returned with a computer hard drive and monitor. They stuffed the electronics into the trunk and drove away.

Joe grabbed the three bug-out bags and Kate dragged a suitcase to the van. By the time they reached the van Elliot was already jogging in their direction. They met him halfway, opened the side door, and Elliot jumped in without making them slow down.

Elliot pointed at Kate's suitcase in the back of the van, "Really. You can't travel without your makeup? What exactly wouldn't fit in your bug-out bag that requires you to bring your suitcase?"

"Shut up. Joe and I need to brief you." They shared what they had learned in the coffee shop.

Following someone with a single vehicle is not easy, but the men who had taken Liam didn't seem to be testing to see if they had a tail. They were able to move easily between lanes alternating between two and five cars behind. The car was heading directly toward Moscow and slowed once it reached a *mikrorayon*, a suburban micro-district of Soviet-era gray, flat-paneled concrete buildings. The driver appeared to be looking for the street they were supposed to turn onto.

After a series of sharp turns, the car stopped in a narrow alley between two concrete paneled Khrushchyovka-style apartment buildings. The pursuing trio continued past the alleyway and turned into the next parallel alley.

"Park here, in front of this building that backs up to the alleyway they took Liam down," Kate instructed. "We can go inside and look out at the alley to see where they're taking him."

When they reached the building they found each of the entry doors locked with a coded keypad, but a woman was exiting at the far door.

"Hold the door!" Kate yelled in what she hoped was convincing Russian.

The woman held the door and the trio scampered up the stairwell to the third floor. They looked out the window from the landing in time to see the men lead Liam and Lana from the car and into the building across the alley.

"See where they're taking him," Kate whispered to Elliot.

Kate and Joe watched Elliot cross the alley and try the door of the Khrushchyovka Liam had been taken to. The door was unlocked and Elliot disappeared behind it. A few minutes later, Elliot was walking back across the alleyway and bounding up the stairs two at a time to Kate and Joe's landing.

"They're on the third floor in an apartment facing the alley. That one," he pointed, "with the red cloth covering the window."

A piece of thick, shabby red cloth crookedly covered the window leaving a slanted gap at the top. The slender window in the door leading to the shallow balcony was covered entirely in newspaper. Kate grabbed a pair of binoculars from her bag and held them to her eyes.

"The newspaper covering the window is local,

so no clues there." Two additional men pulled up in a beige sedan. "What kind of car is that?"

"Russian origin, I'm guessing, but the branding information has been removed. They must be going for the 'non-descript' beige car look. It's working." Joe was taking pictures with his phone as he said it. The two men from the car took up a security stance on either side of the entrance to the Khrushchyovka.

A couple exited an apartment adjacent to the trio's stairwell lookout point and squeezed past them on the narrow landing eyeing them suspiciously. *Why is everything produced during Soviet-era Russia narrow?* Kate wondered.

"We won't be able to stay here much longer without drawing attention to ourselves. Elliot, will you please do some recon to see if there are other locations we can rotate through to keep an eye on the place?"

"Roger, that." Elliot ran down the stairs.

About fifteen minutes later another car crept down the alleyway between Khrushchyovkas. The driver got out and opened the rear door and as Joe continued to take pictures, the man in the backseat stepped out and looked around. Startled, Joe and Kate pulled in from the window and against the wall on either side.

"Holy shit!" Joe whispered, "What the hell is he doing here?"

"I don't know, but I think it might be time for us to call home."

43
WASHINGTON, DC

At Langley, scraps of abandoned sandwiches and crumpled napkins littered the clear plastic plates scattered around the conference room table amidst stacks of paper and files. A steady stream of people had been moving in and out of the room on this Saturday morning dropping off files containing pieces of information and briefing the team on snippets of seemingly random data. Only those around the table understood how it all might fit together.

CIA Director Wolf returned to the conference room, "MI6 claims they have no relevant information to share other than confirming that Kate was at the commune and may have gone to Moscow in pursuit of a man who may have stolen money from the commune."

PDD Lanser looked at Harrison, "Tell her what we've been able to piece together."

Harrison took a deep breath and began, "Alfie suffers from polymorphous light eruption, more commonly called sun allergy. The form he has is quite severe and causes him to turn red and break into hives and blisters within minutes of exposure to direct sunlight. This disability qualified Alfie for disability compensation and vocational training from the British government. He dabbled in several indoor hobbies & vocational skills and eventually became an accomplished pianist and programmer."

"Sounds like a guy who likes to work with his fingers," Lanser chuckled, solely amused by his joke. "Sorry to interrupt. Continue Harrison."

"Likely acting on a tip from a cooperating professor, the British Intelligence service took an interest in Alfie during his time at University and began the slow process of recruiting him. He had demonstrated exemplary programming skills and was unusually skilled at building security systems. MI6 knew that would also make him good at finding weak spots in their own systems and penetrating the systems of others. They were keen on having him in their cyber division."

"So did he join?" Director Wolf squinted her eyes in curiosity.

"No. About 18 months into the recruitment, his recruiters developed a bad feeling about him and decided to back off."

"Do we know why?" Wolf was running the long list of reasons CIA would back off a recruitment they'd already spent 18 months working on. Several of those reasons caused her great concern.

"We don't know, but MI6 likely does and I think

we need to ask for that information specifically. If they know we know, they might be more willing to fill in the blanks. Anyway, after the failed recruitment Alfie started to drift. His friends during that time described him as discontent. They also say he started hacking for fun again, but this time he wasn't changing grades, he was hacking into military and other government targets just to see if he could get in. He didn't poke around in the systems or steal anything once he was in, he just wanted to see if he could get past the firewall and then slip out."

Lanser added, "It was his low-profile hacking that probably kept him off the radar. By the time most systems knew he was there, he was already gone."

"That's right. His friends thought it was a bizarre hobby, but didn't feel like he had any nefarious intentions. We don't know if or when he would have escalated his activity on his own, but one of his employers nudged him along a bit."

"What happened?"

"Alfie's global government hacking had become so routine, that he openly talked about it at work. Most people didn't believe him, except for his boss. You see, the company he was working for, a farm supply company, was in serious financial trouble. His boss threatened to report him to the authorities unless Alfie helped him out by hacking into their major competitor's computer system and sabotaging their order system during a busy time of the year. Alfie agreed to do it and keep quiet for a generous fee.

"Word of mouth spread and Alfie started getting industrial espionage jobs from other companies, but he had a rule that he would never sabotage or hack a company he had worked for. It was his personal brand of honor among thieves. Some companies just put him on the payroll and paid him not to hack them. Eventually, he took on the alias of Liam Tremblay and began working as a cyber mercenary for governments large and small. If you needed someone to hack a political candidate or a government office and make it look like a specific person or country had done it, Alfie was your man."

Director Wolf turned slightly pale, "Has the U.S. used him?"

"No, ma'am we have internal talent for that sort of thing. But we do have reason to believe that during his time at the commune he was the one who developed the defense system and gave the group access to many of the major power grids and nuclear launch facilities around the globe."

"So, we're back to the very real possibility that another country who benefits by revealing America's intelligence secrets has hired Alfie as a cyber mercenary." Wolf looked toward Lanser, "Would you agree, Marc?"

"It's possible, but let's not forget that by revealing actual secrets that can be proven, Alfie also gives credibility to the false information he's spreading. So, both the true and the falsified information must benefit whomever hired him."

Harrison added, "Yet there's no evidence of a hack on our side, so where are they getting the information from?" The team knitted their eyebrows and stared at the table in thought.

"Maybe we need to approach this from a

different angle," Harrison rose to write on the whiteboard. "We've been assuming that an outside actor is spreading true information to give value to their false information, but what if the actor actually came from within the United States? What if someone within our own government hired The Executive? Someone who wants to harm the President's power."

Wolf perked up, "Okay, then the information that would be important to them would be the real information, but they would allow the false information to make it look like it was coming from outside the U.S."

"That could happen, but who would benefit from harming the President? It's not likely the President himself, but someone unhappy with current National Security policy perhaps?"

"Maybe, but our investigations haven't found anyone, not even at the highest level, who have electronically accessed every piece of information that was released."

"Hold on." Harrison dashed back to the conference table and began frantically searching through the piles of folders. Finding his target file he began rifling through it. He pulled out a piece of paper and held it to the light before flopping back into a chair. Harrison's face had lost color and his mouth was set agape.

"What's the matter with you, Harrison?" Lanser barked.

"Sir, you still type all of your reports and correspondence, correct?"

"Yes, of course. You know I don't trust

computers, especially email."

"And after you type them, your staff scans them into the computer system."

"Yes, yes, get to your point."

"Well sir, the documents you authored that have been released are photographs of the originals, not scanned copies."

"So what are you saying? Do you think my staff is feeding information to The Executive?"

"No, sir. I'm afraid I'm considering someone else. When the President calls you for a meeting, where do you meet?"

"In the Oval Office or the Situation Room depending on what the meeting is about. What are you getting at Harrison?"

"When you have a meeting with the Director of the CIA, where do you meet?"

"In her office like we are now. You know that! Protocol dictates that you meet in the office of the superior who has summoned you, except..." Lanser's voice trailed off and he looked up at Harrison in horror, "Holy shit, it can't be. Can it?"

44

MOSCOW

Admiral Reynolds stepped out of the car and into the alleyway behind the driver. A second man from the front passenger's seat fell in behind him. The three men systematically scanned the alley and its surrounding concrete walls and curtained windows, each beginning their observations from a different direction. Satisfied, they moved toward the door of the building where one of the guards punched the entry code into the keypad. The stairwell of the Khrushchyovka was dim, lit only by the windows at the landings. The leather soles of the Admiral's shoes scrapped along the concrete stairs. *Shi...shi...shi...shi,* he paused and uneasily craned his neck to look up the stairwell and then down.

"You're certain we weren't followed?"

"Yes, sir. We had two chase vehicles looking for tails, but no one followed us here."

"Huh," the Admiral shuddered and resumed. *Shi...shi...shi...shi*, until he reached the third level.

The driver knocked at the door to the left of the staircase and a solidly built man with a crew cut let them inside. The short, narrow entrance hallway had a small bathroom to the right and opened into what a real estate agent might puff as a cozy sitting room. Off the sitting room and behind the bathroom sat a utilitarian kitchen with a large wash sink and a squat refrigerator. A single row of whitewashed plywood cabinets were set into the exterior wall under the window, the wide windowsill serving as the countertop. A small microwave, hotplate, and spice rack occupied most of the scarce counter space. On the wall hung an on-demand water heater slightly larger than a family-sized box of cereal. The entirety of the apartment needed some fresh air, a good cleaning, and a coat of paint.

Admiral Reynolds had always perceived Russia to be a country of shabby, small and narrow spaces laid side-by-side to form a country. His bias was confirmed as he looked around the Khrushchyovka with Alfie huddled over a laptop computer perched on a TV tray in the corner of the sitting room, rattling away on the keyboard. The sleeper sofa was open with two pillows and a tangled blanket resting on its bare mattress. A tiny 50s-style chrome dining table with a peeling white laminate top and a single red vinyl chair were pressed against the wall next to the kitchen door, enveloping the remaining of the space in the room. The Admiral asked the men guarding Alfie to step outside and turned the vinyl chair 90-degrees before sitting down and resting his arms on the back of the chair. Alfie ignored his visitor as he worked on his computer. Lana remained in the kitchen, her back against the cabinets.

"So we meet again, Mr. Tremblay. I'm sorry about the accommodation. It is grim, isn't it?" Alfie remained silent. "Perhaps you would prefer that I address you by your given name, Mr. Alfie Brand."

Alfie stopped what he was doing and turned sideways in his chair to face Admiral Reynolds. "What do you want? I'm certain you're not here to get me out of this stinking hell hole."

"Yes, it has come to my attention that you are increasingly discontent and continue to seek asylum outside of Russia. What you don't understand is that I had to make a deal with the Russians to keep you safe. You should be glad I didn't send you to North Korea. The truth is, there will be no asylum outside of Russia. You will stay here."

"That was not our agreement!" Alfie stood and slammed his fist against the concrete wall. There was a loud crunching sound as Alfie winced and then cradled his hand.

"You should consider yourself lucky. Continuing to work for Russian intelligence once our business is complete means you get to stay alive, at least for a while longer. The Executive has become an iconic symbol Mr. Brand, a brand name as recognizable as McDonalds. You should be proud that as long as you cooperate you will be the place where those who wish to expose government wrongdoing come to have their secrets revealed. If that means helping the Russians once in a while with some *kompromat,* so be it. But if you become uncooperative, I make no guarantees about your safety."

"If anyone harms me and I don't log onto this computer twice a day, enter a code, and properly answer the questions the computer generates, all the years of information I've stolen through hacks of governments around the world will be released. That information includes voice recordings of your involvement."

Reynolds forced a laugh, "Mr. Brand, eventually it will no longer matter. The wheels of change will already be in motion and no one will be able to stop it." Reynolds stood, "But for now, the heat has been turned up and we need to escalate the document releases. I have some specific memos and people I want you to focus on."

45
MOSCOW

The heavy evening traffic added a vacillating hum to the air as the clouds began to part and reveal the stars. Admiral Reynolds had left the Khrushchyovka and Kate decided the team should abandon the apartment building's stairwell before the working-class residents began to return home. They moved outside and Kate and Joe had positioned themselves against the side of one of the concrete buildings where they could still keep an eye on Liam's apartment down the alleyway. The evening air was cool and Kate was chilled and bored as they waited for Elliot's return from his recon mission.

"It's times like these when I wish smoking wasn't an unhealthy habit." Joe cocked his head at Kate quizzically. "It would give me something to do rather than think about how cold and hungry I am. Just imagine the time I could kill out here with a cigarette."

"I'd begin by reaching into my handbag and slowly pulling out a silver cigarette case. Maybe it would be monogrammed with a calligraphic 'A' for Adams. I'd hold it in my hand for a while, gesturing with it as we talked. Eventually, I'd open the case where inside the lid would be an engraving, 'Thanks for the memories' signed 'D'. You'd notice and wonder who 'D' was and what memories we shared. Was it David, a former lover? Perhaps the case was from Diana, my college roommate? Or, could it be from a man named Devlin whom I pursued vigorously for the Agency before he slipped from my grasp and taunted me with the gift? You'd likely never know, but it would immediately make me more mysterious and interesting in your eyes."

Joe smiled at Kate as she continued.

"Finally, I'd gracefully slide out a cigarette from beneath the elastic band and hold it between my fingers before clicking the case closed and returning it to my purse. I wouldn't light it at first, but would again gesture with it, at times pointing at you with the two fingers that held the cigarette between them. This pause before lighting would be important. A lady always waits to see if a gentleman is going to offer to light her cigarette for her. Because you're not a smoker, I assume you would not be offering me a light so again I would reach into my handbag. This time I would have to rummage around a bit looking for the lighter that would have inevitably made its way to the bottom depths of the bag.

"Once I found the lighter I would strike it, momentarily lighting up my face for anyone who was watching to see. If any observers had been wondering what we were doing out here, they would now say, 'Oh, they're just out there having a smoke' and would turn from their windows."

Joe reached into his front pants pocket, "You would be wrong about the light." He held up a book of matches for Kate to see. "One thing they teach us is to always carry a book of matches from a local establishment. There's no better excuse to approach a woman who smokes than with a light."

"I stand corrected, but still cold and hungry."

"Yeah, there's nothing like a good old-fashioned stakeout to make me wish I'd listened to my grandfather and become a plumber."

"I have a hard time picturing you crawling around under a house unclogging sewer lines. But actually, that sounds like a better alternative right about now."

"The stakeouts aren't even the most unpleasant part of this career field. The worst part is that those of us in the field never get to see the bigger picture. We usually just provide pieces of the puzzle and forward them to some faceless person at headquarters who puts all the pieces together to figure out what's going on."

"That's true, but I always thought I felt that way because I was a contractor and not an employee."

"No, that's not a phenomenon unique to contractors. Now if I were a plumber, I'd get to see my work from start to finish. Even if a project took multiple days, I'd see my progress each and every day. In this business, I never have any idea whether I'm helping a mission progress or just spinning my wheels."

"Being a roofer always seemed satisfying to me in that respect. A roof is like a grid and at the end of each day you would be able to see how much of the grid you completed, whether you were taking a roof off or replacing it."

"Yeah, the linear nature of the patterns would appeal to my obsessive-compulsive side. We all have one, you know."

"I feel better about myself already."

"Is that Elliot heading for the door?" Joe whistled and Elliot bounded over.

"I didn't expect to find you out here." Elliot huffed trying to catch his breath.

"Kate thought we should get out before too many people got home. We rigged the lock though, so we can get back in. What did you find as alternatives?"

"It was a bit slim with pretty much only these two buildings on this side of the alley until I made an interesting discovery about that building." Elliot had turned 90 degrees and was pointing to the building across the next alley.

"What about it," Kate asked.

"You'll notice they staggered the buildings in each row so there wouldn't have a straight line of open space running between the buildings."

"Yes."

"From the far side of that building, you can see between these two buildings and get a pretty good angled view of Alfie's apartment, but that's not the best part."

Joe was growing impatient, "So what's the best part?"

"The apartment with the view is for rent on Airbnb."

Kate clapped her hands together, "You're kidding me. I didn't even know they had Airbnb here."

"I don't know if they do, but the owner is in Germany and renting it out from there. I've taken the liberty of renting it for a week. I think it will be a good base of operations and we won't have to stay on the move so much."

"Excellent!" Kate was feeling warmer already. "Where do we get the key?"

"Already have it from the neighbor."

Once inside the apartment, Kate sent Joe out for food and briefed Elliot on Admiral Reynold's visit.

Elliot was as alarmed as Kate and Joe had been, "We need to call this in, but to whom?"

"That's the challenge. It's difficult to know whom to trust. However, it strikes me that we should probably not contact the NSA. That seems like the greatest risk since Admiral Reynolds leads the organization."

"I had no idea," Elliot implored. "You have to believe me, I had no idea Reynolds was involved in this."

"Of course not," Kate smirked, "if you did you would have already killed us for getting too close."

"Yes, I suppose I would have."

Joe returned with vegetable soup and pelmeni.

"I've been thinking," said Joe as he popped the Russian meat-filled dumpling in his mouth and chewed, "I think we need to contact CIA rather than NSA on this. We don't know how deep this goes over there."

"Elliot and I had just discussed that very thing."

"Good. When I finish eating I'm going to head

over to the American Embassy and talk with the Agency Station Chief. Perhaps between the two of us we can come up with a plan. It's time to come back into the light."

"Agreed."

"I feel terrible, though. I really screwed this up."

"What do you mean?"

"My profile was completely wrong on this one. I would never have guessed such a high level intel community member would be involved in this."

"Joe, I don't think at this point we can conclude that Reynolds is the bad guy. He may be here on a mission. We don't know. But if he is involved, your profile may still be correct and Reynolds is just an outlier."

"Well, it will be interesting to analyze his motives once this is over to build a better profile."

As Joe prepared to head for the embassy, Kate went to take a nap as Elliot stood watch. The dreams had returned. Kate fought the sheets, as a faceless figure in a hooded robe hovered in front of her in a field. Looking around for somewhere to hide, she saw nothing but open field surrounding her. She turned and began running through the dry, brown grass as it cut her legs to shreds. Out of nowhere, the silhouette of a dark forest appeared in front of her and she quickened her pace, her feet now barely touching the ground. The figure was still behind her, but not getting any closer.

By the time Kate reached the forest, she was gasping for breath and soaked in perspiration. The forest floor was like quicksand, sucking her feet in with each step. Her legs were heavy as she struggled to run. A voice called out to her, "Over here!" A small one room cabin materialized and Kate managed to run inside and bolt the door.

She frantically searched the cabin for a weapon as her chest heaved and burned from lack of oxygen. There was a hunting knife on the mantle of the fireplace and Kate clutched it in her hand ready to defend herself. The figure seeped through the crack between the door and its frame and glided in Kate's direction as it shrieked. She lifted her arm above her head to plunge the knife into her pursuer, but her arm remained frozen overhead, unable to strike the blow. The figure's head was down as it moved in closer. There was a foul stench in the air.

It was at that moment Kate felt herself giving up; the pursuit in her dreams had gone on for months and her psyche was fatigued.

"Get it over with!" she yelled at the fluttering robe. It was then that the figure raised its head and lowered the hood. Kate bolted awake and said aloud, "Brad."

46
MOSCOW

Joe emerged into the moonless night. Traffic had subsided, but nearby two drivers had stopped in the middle of the road and were blaring their horns and shouting obscenities out their windows. A woman in the adjoining Khrushchyovka threw open her sash and joined the chorus of insults as she pelted the cars with garbage. An ambulance with sirens blaring was making its way down the street, but no one pulled over to let it pass.

Joe made his way up the main road to a nearby shopping district where he hailed a cab. It was unlikely that anyone would be following him, so he handed the driver a note in Russian with an address five blocks from the embassy. During the drive, Joe pretended not to speak any of the four languages the driver tried addressing him in.

"Spasibo," Joe nodded to the driver as he exited the cab and walked up the stairs of a government building. With the driver out of sight, Joe returned to the sidewalk and made his way toward the embassy.

His American passport got him through the embassy gate. Once Joe was within the compound he was ushered into a low, drop-ceilinged lobby with a row of embassy service agents assisting the remaining visitors with visas and lost passports from behind bulletproof glass. Seeing no other options, Joe fell in line with the others. The lines, bulletproof glass windows, and bureaucratic superiority of the place made Joe feel like he had been dropped into a DMV inside a convenience store in downtown Detroit.

At his turn, Joe stepped up to the freckle-faced woman at the glass and as discreetly as possible said, "Good evening. Echo 8486 is here to see your Station Chief."

The woman was a bit flustered, but tried to hide it as she reached under her desk and hit a button. "It will be one moment, sir."

In less than a moment a young Marine stepped up next to Joe, "How may I help, ma'am?"

"Please take this gentleman to a holding room."

"Right away, ma'am. Will you come with me, sir?" The woman picked up the phone as they walked away.

The Marine led Joe through a secured door, down a hall, and deposited him in a room with a metal table and two chairs. The young Marine took up a guard post outside the door. Joe knew the Station Chief had been notified and that the agents on duty were moving in front of the detention room's monitor to see if anyone knew the identity of the visitor. Joe carefully scanned the room trying to find the camera. It took him a while, but he eventually found a slight lens reflection embedded in one of the holes in the drop ceiling. It was likely he'd be kept waiting a while, so Joe put his head down for a quick nap.

The door opened sooner than he expected. An agent he knew well from his time in Afghanistan walked in and greeted him warmly.

"Joe, you son of a gun, how can you be in Moscow without me knowing it?"

"Ethan, what a pleasant surprise! I was expecting to sit here for hours while the station ran me through a half-dozen databases trying to verify my identity as a good guy."

"Well, since I wasn't expecting you, I did run you through the system to make sure you weren't on a wanted database or something. It's good to see you, but you haven't answered my question. What are you doing here?"

"Chief's ears only I'm afraid. Is the Station Chief available?"

"On her way. I'll take you up."

Ethan excused the Marine and punched the elevator's button for the 6th and top floor. Instead of a quaint ding as they moved through each floor, the elevator emitted an irritating buzzing sound.

"Are you trying to discourage people from spending too much time in the elevator with that sound?"

"Fucking Russian elevator. Everything here is a

bit harsh."

At the 6th floor they exited the elevator and Ethan swiped a card to open the door to a stairway. The pair walked up another set of stairs.

"Welcome to floor six and three quarters."

Ethan banged on the door at the top of the stairs before a man of late middle age with a ruddy complexion and a gin blossom nose opened the door for them. The space was aglow with activity considering the hour. The communal office space was large and cluttered with government-issued metal desks awash in papers, coffee mugs, and other detritus. Around the perimeter were a few private offices, a secure conference room, and two other smaller workrooms.

Introductions were made and hands were shaken around the room before Station Chief Patty Arnold arrived. The Chief was blond with plain features and a full-figured, athletic body. She arrived at the station dressed in yoga pants and a long t-shirt.

She skipped formal introductions, "Pardon my appearance, I was just working out."

"Quite all right. I may fall asleep before I finish a sentence, so I hope you'll pardon that in advance. Is there somewhere we can talk privately?"

Chief Arnold led the way to the conference room, "We've been looking for you."

"Really, what for?"

"Langley had reason to believe your team was in town and wanted us to intercept you to share information. They also wanted us to bring you out of the dark."

Joe paused. "What kind of information?"

"Well, first of all there's some concern that Kate Adams has been blown. But the bigger issue is that the Director has some reasons to believe that Admiral Reynolds may be involved in The Executive case…as an actor."

"I can confirm that. We found The Executive and tracked him to an apartment in Moscow. I was here to report that I and others personally observed Admiral Reynolds make contact with The Executive in Moscow."

"Then it's true. Langley has been able to confirm up to the level of the President that Reynolds is not on any sort of mission. He is likely rogue. Our orders are to observe and try to turn The Executive, who uses the aliases Liam Tremblay and Anchor, but whose real name is Alfie Brand. We are to bring The Executive in alive and on our side. The Executive is smart, I'm sure he has a dump program on his computer that will have to be deactivated and he's the only one who can do it."

"We spoke with him briefly before his handlers moved him to Moscow and he is afraid for his life. The guy is in over his head. He wants our help so turning him is not outside the realm of possibilities. We didn't pick him up because he does, in fact, had a dump program and needs to sign into the computer twice a day or else all information gets immediately published to his website."

"We can offer surveillance support, but our orders are to stand down on contact until we hear from headquarters. Where is The Executive located?"

Joe shared the details of the location and his contact with Alfie.

"That's going to be a hell of a report you're

going to write for me tomorrow, right Joe?"

"Yes, I suppose it is. Ah, the joys of being back on the Agency's grid."

"Now you need to head back and get some sleep. We'll work on positioning."

Joe was headed to the stairwell door when Chief Arnold stopped him, "Wait a minute! I almost forgot. Orders are for you and Kate Adams to have these satellite phones."

He took the phones and began what would be a long journey back to their rental. Leaving the embassy without being followed by Russian agents would be impossible since they followed every exiting American. After darting in and out of cabs, trains, buses, and alleyways for two and a half hours, Joe felt he was free of tails and it was safe to return to the rented apartment.

The next morning Joe stumbled out of the bedroom to find the apartment inundated with Moscow station personnel. A laser listening device had been set up with the beam aimed at Alfie's window. A man and woman were wearing headphones and writing notes as they monitored and recorded any sounds or conversation bouncing off Alfie's apartment window. Kate and Elliot were talking with two men, one of whom was pointing at things on a map and yet another man was typing on a computer resting on the kitchen counter.

"Good morning, Joe!" Kate waved him toward her group.

The man who was talking continued, "So, this is the perimeter we're covering. I have three teams of two or three rotating in and out of street level. Our teams have identified two people likely doing the same for our target, but they don't seem to have many people on the street. The people they do have down there are moving in and out of the apartment and community like pros. They are most likely FSB. We need to be careful that we make our teams look like residents, not tourists. We also have a utility van down there, but we need to keep it moving within the perimeter and keep our 'utility worker' moving from unit to unit. The folks in the van have eyes on the street and are also monitoring the listening device."

"I'd be happy to sit in the van and help profile people on the street to see if we can pick out any more agents on their side and give my impressions on conversations," Joe offered.

"Happy to have your help. I'll call down and let them know you're coming."

"Everyone remember, our current orders are not to move unless Admiral Reynolds reappears. If he does, we'll move in, grab Alfie, and bring Reynolds in."

"Roger that," Kate said as Joe headed out to the van.

Joe settled in with the team in the van. Alfie's apartment was quiet so they watched the street, memorized faces, and looked for anyone not moving in the classic glum and rushed, heads-down Russian style.

Hearing another ambulance and remembering the previous evening, Joe wondered aloud, "I wonder why no one in Russia ever pulls over for ambulances?"

The man next to him grunted, "That, my friend, is because Muscovites believe ambulance drivers use their down time to give the wealthy rides to the airport in exchange for large sums of money so the privileged can avoid sitting in choking traffic. The residents of Moscow no longer assume a medical emergency is the reason for the sirens, so they refuse to yield. Whether this is true or an urban legend is unknown, but it has become engrained in the culture."

"Fascinating."

47
MOSCOW

Having again been moved to the periphery of the mission, Kate wandered up to the roof to escape the nervous energy in the apartment and get a breath of fresh air. The grids of streets laid out before her were topped with a sea of Khrushchyovkas running east to west up a hill. Her lack of role in the current state of the operation left her feeling useless and fidgety.

The Agency team was running surveillance and waiting for something to happen. The only useful information that had come from the listening device so far was that Alfie would be moved again in two days. That intelligence had been up-channeled to Langley and they were awaiting orders on whether or not to grab Alfie during the move even if Reynolds didn't show beforehand. The Executive's document releases had become heavily focused on political candidates and the tempo of the releases had increased.

An agent working out of Moscow station who spoke flawless Russian had joined the team and plans were being made to get him inside the building to talk with Alfie. Kate worried that such a move would be too risky, but remained silent. As she stood on the rooftop running all the things that could go wrong during such an operation, the chiming of the satellite phone in her pocket startled Kate and pulled her out of her head and back into the real world.

Assuming Joe was calling she answered casually, "Hey, what's up." She regretted that decision when the voice on the other end asked her to hold for the President.

"Hello, Mr. President....Yes....What did MI6 say?...Yes sir, that's true.....If not quietly, yes....Uh huh, I hear you and understand....Yes I can....Goodbye, sir."

Kate took a deep breath and exhaled loudly just as Joe opened the roof door and poked his head out.

"Hey, Kate. We're going to try to get our guy inside. You wanna watch?"

"Of course, I'll be there in a moment." Kate returned the phone to her pocket and with some effort willed her feet toward the door.

The team was gathered around a computer monitor to watch the live feed from the infiltrator's tiny camera discretely embedded in his pen. A microphone had been implanted into his watch and the sound was always a fraction of a second ahead of the video giving the scene a dubbed movie quality.

The same type of drab, beige sedan that had delivered Alfie's guards pulled up to the

Khrushchyovka, their infiltrator sunk low in the backseat. The two men guarding the door came to attention and reached inside their jackets.

"We can confirm they're armed," the woman taking notes observed as she wrote it down.

The driver remained in the car as the man in the backseat exited away from the building and walked around to the back of the car. He raised his hands to shoulder level and spoke to the men at the door in Russian.

The translator in the room began his interpretation, "Gentleman, no need to be so jumpy. The American sent me to talk to our man."

"Do you mean the General sent you?"

"Shit," Joe exclaimed before turning to Kate, "we don't know if the Russians know Reynolds by his real name and title or something else. We've only heard them refer to him as 'The American'."

The agent answered in a mocking tone that could or could not be taken seriously depending on its accuracy, "No, the Admiral, what do you think. Come on, you know who I'm talking about."

"Who's that?" the same guard nodded toward the driver.

"An American. He doesn't speak any Russian, he's here primarily to keep an eye on me." The agent shrugged. "He's an idiot, but loyal to the boss."

"Why didn't the boss come himself?"

"They've found a common descriptor, that's good, very good," Joe whispered to Kate.

"The boss needs to lay low. He can't be seen coming and going from this place all the time. I'll be his representative on the ground here temporarily."

"I'll take you up." The team listened to the scratching of the men's feet as they walked up the stairs without speaking.

At the top of the stairs, a similar conversation occurred, only this time the men were resistant to letting him in. "What proof do you have that you are who you say you are?"

The agent answered forcefully, "Look the boss isn't happy with some of the stuff our man has been releasing. I'm here to give him some guidance, do you really want to get in the way of the boss's orders?" The men looked at him sullenly. "You might want to wait outside in case I have to scratch him up a bit. If I go too far the boss won't be happy and you need to be able to say you weren't in the room. Got it?"

The guards relented and urgently stepped out into the hallway.

The agent entered the apartment and in Russian accented English yelled, "You two, get up and got sit on the bed, now!

Alfie and Lana scrambled to sit on the bed as the agent went around the room sticking listening devices into a lampshade, behind the toilet tank, and on the side of the kitchen cabinet. The duo on the bed watched him with wide eyes.

The agent pulled a chair up to the bed, sat down, and turned his attention toward Alfie. Allowing his American accent to return he said softly in English, "I understand you met a couple of our people at the coffee shop in Skolkovo, correct?"

Alfie's mouth moved, but he couldn't seem to make

any sound come out.

"Relax, man, I'm with them. I understand you stole the Luminiferon from the commune in hopes that someone would find you and help you out. Well, I'm that guy."

"They're going to kill me. I just know it," Alfie blurted. "I only have about two weeks worth of releases for the American and then he will be finished with me. The Russians have already been using me to hack into some facilities, but they're learning from me as I do it. Before long they'll have everything they need and they won't have any use for me either. I figure I've got a few more months, that's all. You have to help me."

"That's what I'm here about, we'd like to help you out if we can."

"I'm so sorry," Alfie sobbed, "I thought I was working for the American government, but at some point I started to realize I wasn't. This guy has a personal agenda and was willing to turn me over to the Russians to do their bidding as well as his. Apparently the false information the Russians are spreading actually benefits both of them somehow. The Russians keep trying to reassure me that they'll keep me alive, but I'm certain there's no way I get out of this alive."

"So Alfie, would you agree that you're no longer a free man?"

"No, I'm a prisoner on death row."

Would you rather continue to work for the Russians or would you prefer to work for the Americans?"

"I never wanted to be here, doing their bidding. I just needed money and asylum to create a new commune. Please, take me with you. I want to go to

America."

"We can help as long as you realize you've already lost your freedom. If you come to America, you'll work for us."

"Yes, yes, I understand. I'm in over my head here, I have no other options."

"I understand you have a dump program on your computer that will release everything to your website if you don't log in twice a day. Is that true?"

"Yes, it's true."

"Would you consider disabling it temporarily to help facilitate our getting you out of here?"

"Absolutely not, that program is the only thing assuring my short-term survival. If I turn it off, I might as well jump out the window to my death. There would be no difference."

"That makes it harder for us to get you out of here."

"I'll turn it off if you take us with you now."

"No, we'll both have to wait to get what we want."

The agent quickly stood without warning and grabbed Alfie by collar as Lana gasped. He threw Alfie against the apartment door and slapped him hard across the face before throwing him onto the bed.

"Sorry man, I've got a cover to protect. We'll be in touch. Get back to work."

48
MOSCOW

The crinkle and tear was followed by the chinking sound of sugarcoated particles cascading into a bowl. The milk gurgled in after it. A spoon could be heard pressing the cereal downward into the milk making sure every piece was saturated.

"Banana?" a woman's voice asked gloomily.

"Just half of one," a man's voice replied.

In the distance, the springing sound of hot toast being released from a toaster was heard as a second bowl of cereal was poured in the foreground. A knife scraping butter across toast was accompanied by the clinking of a small spoon in a jam jar.

The internal listening devices provided much greater detail about the routine aspects of Alfie and Lana's life, but little additional information of value by the time moving day arrived. It was early, just past 5 am, when the phone belonging to the Agency's team leader first rang.

"Gather around everyone," the terseness of his order caused a murmur to rise amongst those turning their attention to him. "I have some good news and some bad news. First, the good news. It appears that Admiral Reynolds may not be aware that we are on to him as he continues to be in contact with NSA, making routine decisions, and carrying on as usual. However, he has indicated to headquarters that he deviated from the President's overseas trip in order to personally check in on a major operation, implying it's a NSA project. That leads me to the bad news. About two days ago he contacted NSA to request a specialist in dump programs claiming he needed one for the operation he was personally overseeing. That specialist is believed to have arrived in Moscow last night. He is not briefed on the situation."

"So Alfie's days are numbered," Joe stated matter-of-factly.

"It would appear so. It is the opinion of headquarters and I concur, that this specialist has been summoned to try to shut down Alfie's dump program. If he's successful, they'll be able to separate Alfie from his computer at any time they desire. Since we don't know if the Russians intend to continue to use his talents or not, that means we have to assume Alfie's life is at risk. That leads us to operate under the premise that if they move him today, it may be to kill him. Therefore, we have the order to grab Alfie during the move even if Admiral Reynolds fails to show. If at any point it appears that they plan to kill him inside the flat, we will attempt to get inside and grab him there. So with that, I'll send everyone to their go and hold positions. You know the drill, let's execute it just like we rehearsed."

Joe approached Kate, "I'm heading out to the van, I guess you can just hang out here and watch on the monitor. It might be a long day though. I'll see you when it's done."

"All right, I'll just curl up with a good book until things get exciting. Let me know if you need anything."

"Will do."

The sounds in Alfie and Lana's apartment went on like they did every day. The clicking of a computer keyboard, dishes being washed, and the persistent *swoosh, swoosh* of a carpet sweeper being pushed and pulled around the room. It was during a light-hearted conversation about the habit of Lana's mother to pick lint and other debris off stranger's clothes in public that everything changed.

The beige sedan turned into the alleyway crunching gravel under its tires. The brakes emitted a staccato squeak as it rolled to a stopped.

"Two in the backseat," the team leader broadcast into the earpieces of the hovering team including Kate's.

The driver hopped out and ran to the back door, opening it with a snap before the first man stepped out.

"That's our specialist," the earpieces crackled. As the second man stepped out the team leader added, "Admiral Reynolds is on site. Repeat. Reynolds is with the specialist."

The waiting began. At noon a food delivery truck pulled into the alleyway and plastic bags full of Styrofoam containers were taken into Alfie's apartment.

The listening devices initially recorded protests by Alfie, but he'd not been heard from since. The team leader wondered if he might already be dead. As two o'clock approached, they heard what they were waiting for.

"The program is disabled, it's safe to move the computer now."

"Alert, alert. We should see movement soon."

A breathless urgency crept through the team as a white panel van arrived with blue Cyrillic lettering and a clip art plumber on the side. Kate imagined it to say *Vlad's Plumbing and Heating, 24-hour Service.* The perimeter of the team closed in. To the west a car with its hood up and steam pouring out of the engine compartment now blocked access to one end of the alleyway.

Boxes were being moved from the apartment to the van. A man who happened to be walking by on the street held the door for the men as they came out of the building with their loads. The same man taped open the door's latch bolts and fluidly stepped inside the building and up to the second-floor landing.

Seven men surrounded Alfie, Reynolds, and the specialist as they emerged from the building and moved toward the van. Alfie's hands were tied and he had a pillowcase over his head. Reynolds held him firmly by the arm as if he were making an arrest. The van's driver started the engine.

An attractive young woman approached the group and the men all turned to look at her as they let her pass through them. She coyly offered a hello and a wave as she walked past and moved toward Reynolds before whispering in his ear, "I'm CIA, I need you to come with me. It's urgent."

Reynold's eyes went wide as he pulled Alfie in front of him as a human shield before pushing Alfie toward the van. Several stun grenades exploded and in the blinding flash of light, the man inside the building took two steps out, holding the door with his foot, as he pulled the specialist inside by his arm. Reynolds and Alfie dropped to the sidewalk next to the van as the rest of the men drew their weapons and ran for cover. Out of Reynold's grip, Alfie shimmied into the gutter and halfway under the van.

A firefight ensued and two of Reynold's men who had not immediately found cover were taken down. The remaining four continued to lay down enough fire to make it impossible to get to Alfie or Reynolds.

The van driver began to try and pull away from the curb as Reynolds yelled out to him, "Stop!"

The driver stopped, but only because two large caliber bullets had silently pierced the van's grill causing engine fluids to spill out onto the ground. Another of Reynold's men fell to the ground dead and the ground team moved in closer. Becoming increasingly desperate, Reynold's removed a gun from his belt and stood in crouched position next to the van. He raised his arm and shot an approaching ground team member in the shoulder before pulling a still blinded Alfie out of the gutter and dragging him toward the rear of the van.

Shouts were heard from the ground team as another agent tried to move in, but Reynolds shot him in his bulletproof vest, knocking him backwards, the wind knocked out of him. There was a brief pause in the shooting while Reynolds shoved Alfie into the back of the van. Reynolds stepped up on the bumper to get into the van himself, but as he propelled himself upward, the back of his head abruptly erupted into a plume of blood and tissue as he waveringly fell to the ground. In the stunned confusion that followed, Reynolds remaining men bugged out as the team grabbed Alfie.

49
MOSCOW

Lying in the prone position for so many hours takes a toll on a sniper. This time was no exception. Even though the sniper's back was throbbing, the rifle's scope still provided the best view of the mise-en-scéne below. Alfie was in custody and on his way to the embassy and it appeared all immediate threats had been eliminated. The team was beginning to split up and bug out in different directions.

Kate lifted her head from the scope of the Russian-made ASVK sniper rifle and used her arms to push herself across the flat roof and away from the rifle. A silhouette of her torso remained in the rooftop dirt, her breasts delineated by clearly defined circles. She used her boot to rub away the impression before pulling the sniper rifle back from the edge of the roof. Sirens screamed in the distance, but Kate's movements were deliberate and unhurried. She knew Moscow's traffic wouldn't yield even for the police. With care, she removed the rifle's suppressor and slipped it into her vest pocket.

Standing, she pulled out her phone and snapped a picture of the rifle where it sat on the rooftop. She carefully inspected both the area and photo for incriminating evidence. Finding none, she turned and walked past her open suitcase and down the stairs to the ground level and exited opposite the alley and walked west. Kate weaved up and down numerous alleyways before removing her gloves and tossing them into a dumpster behind a restaurant near the edge of the vast sea of Khrushchyovkas. Removing the phone from her pocket, she texted the rooftop picture to a Caribbean phone number with a single word: *Done.*

At the next corner, Kate hailed a cab and in Russian directed the driver to an address near the city center. Exiting the cab, Kate checked her watch and briskly walked several blocks arriving in time to step directly onto the city bus. Abandoning the bus eight blocks later, Kate hailed yet another cab, requesting a ride to a department store in a shopping district about two miles away. She entered the main entrance of the department store and walked through the store to the rear door where she exited, turned left, and entered a coffee shop.

Once inside, Kate ordered coffee and walked up to a side counter selling handmade chocolates. She picked out a few pieces for a plate and selected a large giftwrapped box of dark chocolates and a coffee mug, which the clerk inserted into a bag, tying the handles together with ribbon. After placing her plate of chocolates and coffee on a rear corner table, Kate proceeded to the restroom. She entered a stall and removed the silencer from her vest pocket and slipped it into the bag, flushed the toilet, and returned to her table.

The room smelled of vanilla roast coffee, chai, and citrus, and clamored with conversation over coffee grinders, the slurp of milk foamers, and wooden-legged chairs being dragged across hardened linoleum tiles. The café's patrons were a mix of young upwardly mobile Russians and grizzled, stubble-faced Communist-era men who used the privilege of age to commandeer four tables for a raucous game of dominos. A flask was being passed between the men and a splash of vodka was added to each mug of coffee. It was the first time since Kate arrived in Moscow that she saw people happy and seemingly enjoying themselves. The surroundings made the tension in her shoulders slip away and the corners of her mouth turn ever so slightly upward as she sipped her coffee and pushed up her sleeve to check her watch.

The next tinkle of the entrance door's bell revealed a slight man with closely cropped sandy-brown hair and a square nose. He smiled at Kate and waved as he made his way toward her small round table.

Kate stood and the two of them embraced warmly, "You look wonderful my darling, Peggy." He winked at Kate in a sexy way that only a British man could pull off. Her face reddened at the thoughts that flashed through her mind.

The man pulled his chair around to Kate's side of the circular table to both appear intimate and to watch the room. He discretely scanned his surroundings. "Sounds like there was a little trouble across town today.

I hope all ended well."

"Yes, I heard about that. I'm certain it will be on the news tonight."

"Indeed. I just hope we get a briefing soon."

"I expect that at the U.S. Embassy, information is being extracted from an individual and electronic devices as we speak. There should be something to share by morning. I assume you had an observer on scene?"

"Yes, it appears the hardware as well as the experimental device we provided worked well in the field."

"I would agree. Your new device produced nothing but a faint whisper. Happy Birthday, by the way, I bought you a present. But, be sure to hold the bag from the bottom, it's heavier than it looks."

50
MOSCOW

It had been 48-hours since the event and Kate had been biding her time in and around a cheap Moscow city hotel with dark paneled walls, yellowed sheets, and rust-stained bathroom fixtures. She had rested well during her time there and her nightmares had disappeared and been replaced with dreams of flying and beaches filled with bright sunshine.

From behind his barred reception window, the hotel's manager assumed Kate was either a prostitute or a drug dealer. To pay for a room for two whole days in a hotel where they usually rent by the hour implied money, and there were only two ways to get cash in this particular Moscow neighborhood. On the last day of her stay, the manager mustered the courage to ask which profession was hers, a salacious grin spreading across his face like cracking glass. Without admitting to either profession, Kate checked out and spent the afternoon sightseeing. At five o'clock sharp she entered the HopHead Pub and perched on the barstool next to Joe.

"What are you drinking?"

"Some local brew recommended by the bartender. It's good, but a little hoppy for me."

Kate signaled the barkeep, "Whatever he's having." She pointed to Joe's beer.

The Happy Hour crowd had not yet arrived and the place was quiet except for a few locals who had likely been there since they switched the lights on that morning. Joe seemed distracted; his head hung low over his beer as he spun his glass right, then left, then back again, a cocktail napkin sodden with condensation stuck to the bottom.

"Did you know that if you shake a little salt on the napkin before you place the beer on top, the napkin won't stick to the bottom of the glass?"

Joe turned his head toward Kate without lifting it and smiled mischievously, "Not your first time in a bar, is it?"

"Is everything all right? You look troubled."

"Just this case. There are some things that just don't add up."

"Like what?"

"Well, for one thing, why did Reynolds try to save Alfie? When the shooting started he would have been better off putting a bullet in Alfie's head so he couldn't talk. Not shooting him was a terrible tactical move."

"Good question, I don't know. What are you learning from Alfie?"

"Only that he and Reynolds considered themselves

whistleblowers. They justify their actions by believing they were blowing the whistle on U.S. actions in the Middle East. Particularly that the U.S. government knows it can't possibly win the war on terror, but continues to justify ongoing military operations to shore up Department of Defense funding while continuing the illusion of making a difference. Reynolds' goal seemed to be to tear down the existing anti-terrorism structure and rebuild it using his personal vision. Basically, he envisioned less military involvement and more intelligence community engagement. The Admiral also falsely believed the Department of Defense had intentionally blown many of his agents in the field, so he was willing to publicly out them in order to rebuild his covert operations."

"And Alfie believes all this too?"

"Of course. Cyber mercenaries all believe they're serving the greater good of the little guy. I fear they often have no depth of understanding of the implications of their actions. Alfie is no exception. He thinks of himself as some sort of superhero."

"So what happens next with him?"

"We'll take him home and pick his brain. Alfie seems to understand and accept that he works for us now. We figure he can train the trainers on his methods and help us out on specific issues that arise." Joe yelled to the bartender, "Hey, turn that up, will ya?"

The bartender clicked the volume button on the television where an international news station was broadcasting in English with Russian subtitles.

"The Director of the U.S. National Security Agency, Admiral Douglas Reynolds, was killed Tuesday in

Moscow while visiting the home of a friend. The name of the friend is not being released pending investigation, but sources at the NSA tell us the friend was a retired Russian naval officer who was experiencing terminal health problems. A Russian made ASVK rifle with sniper munitions, as seen in this picture, was found on the rooftop adjacent to the alleyway where Admiral Reynolds was killed."

Kate's stomach clenched when the picture she had taken on the rooftop appeared on the screen.

It is widely believed within the intelligence community that Reynolds may have been the target of an assassination by the Russian government and that Reynolds dying Russian friend may have provided Reynolds with information implicating Russia's Federal Security Service as the source of the documents being released by The Executive. Since Admiral Reynolds death, the document releasing website has been taken down and no additional documents have been publicly exposed.

Russian officials are denying the reports and have protested assertions that the Russian government assassinated Admiral Reynolds.

The scene cut to a video of a Russian FSB official.

No, we were not at all involved. It is our belief that the Americans killed their own man to cover up a conspiracy and the Admiral's involvement in the document release. The real Executive, as they call him, was exfiltrated from somewhere in Europe and taken to the U.S. We have evidence of this. We know the truth.

They cut back to the anchor.

Two additional Russian-made handguns and other

munitions were also found on the rooftop, but there were no explosives present. It is unknown at this time whether Admiral Reynolds was the intended target, however, a terror attack is not suspected at this time.

"That brings up my other two questions, who took Admiral Reynold's head off? And where the fuck is Lana?"

"Lana wasn't in the apartment?"

"No, by the time we got inside she was gone. I can't figure out if she shot him, if it was the Russians, or if someone on our side took the shot. Any order like that on our side would have come directly from the President. It would have to be someone deep inside the operations section. Someone we didn't even know was at the scene."

"Hmmm…could Lana have been ours?"

"No, we've checked that angle, but she doesn't seem to belong to the Russians either. We have every reason to believe she was who she said she was. But again, if she were a deep cover agent on our side…" Joe's voice trailed off in thought.

"So an inside player then, not an outsider or someone simply peripheral to the operation shot Reynolds."

"That's right."

"Interesting. You certainly know more about those types of operatives than I do."

"Maybe, maybe not." Joe looked Kate straight in the eyes.

Unflinchingly, Kate changed the subject, "Have we figured out why MI6 told Reynolds I might be in danger?"

"MI6 claims they never told Reynolds any such thing. We think that through Faulkner's investigation, the fact that you were still in the field may have come to light. Or, Reynolds just eventually put two and two together. We believe his primary objective was to have you pulled in so he could complete what he was trying to accomplish."

"I guess that makes sense."

Joe remained silently thoughtful as the TV droned on.

In related news, information continues to be released regarding the British government's raid on a commune in Blackpool where a significant illegal drug operation was underway...

On the screen lines of people were being escorted from the building, their hands zip-tied behind their backs. Faces downcast and familiar to Kate.

"I feel bad about the commune." Kate sipped her beer.

"What on earth for, they were drug dealers."

"Not all of them. There were some really great people in that place. And they were blissfully happy in their ignorance of the bigger picture."

"Do you have Stockholm syndrome or something?"

"No! I wasn't kidnapped and held against my will for goodness sakes. I'm just saying that since I've had time to reflect on what was happening there, Eric was the real criminal. He used everyone else to support his drug trafficking operation, which I'm quite certain was bigger than just a website and a greenhouse full of pot."

"That's certainly what the news reports are indicating."

"I wonder if I could write a letter or testify on behalf of any of those people charged erroneously. Hell, one of the commune members was materially involved in solving this case. I'm not sure his autism made him capable of understanding the bigger picture. He kind of lived in his own world."

"That's one of the downsides of this business we're in I'm afraid. The covert nature of our work doesn't allow us to do such things." Joe noticed Kate's crestfallen look, "Look, it stinks, I know. But trust me, things often work out."

"Not to change the subject, but I've been thinking about my work at the university. It just doesn't seem as important anymore after being involved in trying to save the free world."

Joe smiled, "Yeah, if you do this long enough you'll discover everyone's trivial complaints about their lives will seem downright silly when put into perspective. Of course, we deal with this stuff so the rest of the free world can continue to engage in petty grumbling without worrying about the big stuff."

"That's true. I'm considering retiring to Emeritus Professor and taking a more active role in running my late husband's software and cyber security company, MAK Inc. It'll give me more flexibility in my Agency contract assignments and more time to work on prevention. I think I might be able to add more value to the country there."

"That's a big step, but I'm glad you're considering what will maximize your happiness and contribution. Just don't rush into anything. There's no great hurry, we never run out of work."

"That's true. Don't worry, I'll give it some time before I make a decision."

Joe raised his glass, "Here's to a job well done and more success in the future. Whatever it is we do." They clinked glasses and Kate took a sip while Joe drained the last of his beer. "I'm going to take off. I think there's someone here to see you."

"Hi, Kate."

Kate turned around, "Condor!" She leapt off her stool and gave him a hug.

"May I have a seat?"

"Of course."

Kate turned to ask Joe what Condor was doing here, but Joe was already gone. The stammering pauses of Condor's speech and jerkiness of his motions were gone. He was relaxed and making eye contact.

"What's going on?" Kate slid Condor a sideways glance.

"I just wanted you to know I'm okay and maybe have a beer." The upward inflection at the end of his reply made it sound more like a question than an answer.

"Let me guess, you work for MI6."

"MI5 actually."

"You're not autistic either, are you?"

"Well, I'm on the spectrum. My Asperger's is mild and I had a great occupational therapist as a child, so most people don't notice. The primary manifestations are that I have difficulty keeping a desk or apartment neat and I don't always appropriately respond to social queues. Plus, if I get something stuck in my head I can be a little obsessive. I have not, however, ever had a nervous breakdown or worked on Wall Street. I did, however, play a whistleblower at the commune for over three years and I do possess a great ability to detect patterns, it's the gift Asperger's gave me."

"So you were playing a character?"

"Yes, I needed to be someone who could be a loner within a close-knit community. My brother is actually a little farther along the autism spectrum than I am, so I played him."

"I'm not sure if what you did was brilliant or cruel."

"I never meant any harm or disrespect. In fact, I asked my brother before I did it. He thought it was a hoot. When you grow up in a family with two kids on the spectrum, you learn to see yourself for who you are and get on with life. My brother is actually quite a successful software designer."

"So *you* were one of MI5's people on the inside of the investigation. I'm still surprised. Who was the other?"

Condor just sipped his beer.

"Were you watching me?"

"I was watching everyone, but when you came along MI5 needed to truly understand what you were building for the commune. Turns out we were on the same side for different reasons. I like that." Condor smiled warmly and his eyes softened.

"Why are you really here. Certainly didn't come all this way to blow your cover."

"Remember that slight problem with obsession I told you about?"

"Yes." Kate's sideways glance had returned.

"Well, I had several unresolved issues that only finding you could solve. At some point I suspected you might be working for American intelligence. Once the raid happened and I noticed Americans on site I was pretty certain you were either part of the Intel community or you were in trouble. Either way, I felt compelled to find out."

"And how did you do that?"

"I just asked my people to ask your people. Told them I thought you might be in trouble and wanted to know if they knew where you were."

"And they told you?"

"Not in so many words, but I knew you had gone to Moscow. When I turned up here I was visited by MI6 and told to stand down until I heard otherwise. So I waited. Once news broke of the Admiral's shooting I was visited by your Agency. Some very stern looking men asked why I was looking for you. I shared our history and told them what questions I had for you. They agreed to get us together."

"I see. So what did you want to ask me?"

"Did you find the Luminiferon? What did Alfie want it for?"

"Yes, I found it. Stealing it was his call for help. He wanted to be found. Is that all?"

"No, one more thing. Would you like to have dinner with me sometime? Just one dinner and you never have to see me again if you don't want to."

Kate tilted her head at Condor. He was not the man she had first met, that man she would have had dinner with in a heartbeat. Now he was someone different. Condor was yet another person in her line of work who would come and go and maybe one day betray and deceive Kate for a higher calling. But it was just dinner, right?

Throwing caution to the wind Kate replied, "Dinner? How about now?"

"Perfect, let's go."

Condor offered his arm and they launched together into the cool Moscow evening.

51
WASHINGTON, DC

The first thing Kate noticed as she stood below the marble, square-toed shoe of Abraham Lincoln was the lack of birds. On her first trip to the memorial, some fifteen years earlier, the statue had been awash in the droppings of a rather persistent flock of birds. These same birds dive-bombed and pecked the heads of visitors who perceivably threatened their valuable cache of spiders. The National Park Service's strategy of waiting until later in the evening to turn on the memorial's lights to discourage the congregation of insects, which fed the spiders, and in turn allured the birds, seemed to be working.

A young girl of about three was next to Kate wearing a long purple shirt over pink leggings, a tutu encircled her waist. The girl was twirling around on her Crocs performing an adorable dance for the late

President.

"Watch me!" the girl squealed as she attempted a grand jeté, but failed to stick the landing. Undeterred, the girl rolled across the marble floor in a series of recumbent pirouettes before leaping to her feet and offering a grand bow.

"Well done!" Kate applauded as the young girl's mother took the girl by the hand and led her away.

It was then that Kate's phone signaled a text message: *We need you to come back.*

Kate boarded the Metro and wound her way underground back to the NSA owned building she had left an hour and a half earlier. The exfiltration from Russia of Kate, Joe, and Elliot had been accomplished without incident three days earlier. Since then, the trio had individually been subjected to 48-hours of debriefing. The remainder of the day was down time before Kate was to return home. Being asked to return to a debriefing site was rarely a good sign. Kate turned the last 48-hours over in her mind and could find no obvious reason she would be recalled.

As was expected of her, Kate had disclosed her role up to and including the order from the President to shoot Admiral Reynolds if he resisted. The President had apparently not denied making the request and all agreed Kate was within the limits of the law when she performed the execution. Her debrief report, however, would be sealed for at least seventy-five years and would likely never be declassified. No one outside of her debriefers and high-level intelligence executives would ever know exactly who brought down Admiral Reynolds.

Pushing through the throng of people at her destination Metro station, Joe pulled up beside her, "You too, huh?"

"Yes, I wonder what's up."

"I don't know, but these things frequently end badly."

"I'd already considered that, but thanks for the confirmation."

"Any time." Joe elbowed Kate in the ribs and tried to get her to smile.

The security guards were expecting Kate and Joe when they arrived and handed them both visitor's badges.

"You two know the way, right?"

"Yes, I think we can manage," Kate answered.

When they entered the suite of offices, Elliot was milling around with a cup of coffee in his hand. He appeared relieved to see them.

"So, they recalled the two of you. That makes me feel a little better."

Before Elliot could return to his pacing, PDD Lanser emerged from deeper within the suite of offices.

"This way," Lanser beckoned as he gestured with his hand.

The trio was led to a conference room with eight chairs sitting around an oblong table. CIA Director Nancy Wolf sat at the head of the table facing the door. Lanser closed the door, flipped a switch, and a red light came on above it. The room's soundproofing created a deathly silence until Director Wolf spoke, "Have a seat."

Joe and Kate sat next to one another, while obligation of balance drove Elliot to the opposite side of the table next to Lanser.

Director Wolf began, "Our debriefing sessions with Mr. Alfie Brand have brought to light some issues we need to discuss. What is said in this room must never leave. Is that understood?"

All present answered in the affirmative.

"The reason I've called you here is because you are already familiar with the case and the circle on this needs to be extremely small. Now, I realize when Admiral Reynolds talked about keeping the circle small his motives were nefarious, but when you hear what I have to say, I think you'll understand my motives."

Director Wolf leaned back in her chair and placed her hands flat on the table, "While Admiral Reynolds was a point of contact from which Alfie took direction, he was not the man who hired Alfie."

"Then who did?" Kate knitted her brows and rested her forearms on the table as if to brace herself for the answer.

"This man." Director Wolf slid a composite sketch across the table toward Kate.

Kate squinted at the artist's rendering, "He looks vaguely familiar." She handed the sketch to Joe who in turn passed it to Elliot.

"We thought so too. So, we distributed it to our friends around the world looking for an ID, although we didn't tell them why we were asking. We also ran it through our database of government employees and came up with some possible matches."

The director pulled out a stack of six employee badge photos enlarged to
8 ½ x 11 glossies and laid them across the table. The

grouping was of Caucasian men in their late thirties to early forties with dark, short hair, brown eyes, moustache and goatee.

"We put these photos in front of Alfie and without hesitation, he selected this one." The director held up one of the photos by a corner. "Unconvinced, we took Alfie to an area where this man would likely move in and out of a crowded corridor. Alfie positively identified the same man in the wild. This, along with Alfie's detailed descriptions about the man's voice, speech patterns, and bearing, has left us convinced this is the man who hired him."

"Who is he?"

"The Vice President's Chief of Staff, Andrew Scott Holler."

52
WASHINGTON, DC

It was as though a bolt of lightning had struck the center of the conference room table. Those around it sat dazed, counting the seconds until the next thunder strike in the growing storm. Lanser and Wolf allowed the stunned silence to hang in the room as each pair of the summoned trio's eyes darted around in thought.

Kate was the first to recover her voice, "Does the President know?"

"We have not discussed this issue with the President."

"Let me get this straight," Joe had finally recovered. "The Vice President's Chief of Staff hired Alfie to release U.S. secrets. What was the connection with Admiral Reynolds?"

"According to Alfie, Andrew Scott Holler hired him to infiltrate the computer systems of our allies, not to release information. He told Alfie the 'Five Eyes' agreement had broken down and they needed access to determine what information our allies had on the U.S."

"What's 'Five Eyes'?" Kate inquired.

"It's a Cold War-era alliance in which the U.S., Britain, Canada, Australia, and New Zealand all share signals intelligence with each other. It's a way to spy on your own country's citizens as well as allies and their citizens without doing so directly. For example, the U.S. can legally spy on British citizens, the British on Canada, Canada on the Australians and so on. When they find something that might be of domestic interest to the foreign country they're engaging in surveillance on, they share it."

"So where does Admiral Reynolds come in?" Kate redirected to Joe's original question.

"Admiral Reynolds was either assigned as Alfie's overseer, or was part of Holler's original plan, we don't know. Regardless, Reynolds was the one in direct contact with Alfie once he was hired. It was Admiral Reynolds who broadened the scope of Alfie's work and had him begin releasing foreign intelligence on the U.S. as well as internal information and communications. According to Alfie, Holler had just asked him to do a quick smash and grab to get as much information as he could off the British, German, Canadian, and Australian systems as quickly as he could without getting caught and to provide it to him. Once that was complete, it was Reynolds who asked Alfie to get back in and continue a slow trickle of information. Reynolds also provided the internal information and communications posted by Alfie."

"So," Kate wondered, "it is possible that the motives of Holler and Reynolds were quite different?"

"Yes. Reynolds' motives at this point are a little better known. He discussed with Alfie his paranoia that the Department of Defense was trying to marginalize the intelligence community and that the President supported those efforts. His motives seemed to be to discredit both the Department of Defense and the President and to a lesser degree the CIA."

"If Holler ordered the foreign data breach and Reynolds coordinated the online data releases and provided additional internal information, where did the false information come from?"

"It appears this is when Holler lost complete control of the situation. Reynolds made a deal with Russia. In exchange for keeping Alfie safe and at Reynolds' disposal, he would allow the Russians to release any intelligence they had that would also help Reynolds discredit the President, the Department of Defense, or the CIA via Alfie's website. Reynolds wanted Alphie's site to become a global source of data release, like Wikileaks, but one he alone could control. We don't think he realized the information provided by Russia was false. At least not at first."

"To what end?"

"We think his aim was to consolidate more power within the NSA."

"Yet, none of this tells us why Holler hired Alfie. Does the VP's Chief of Staff hire someone to do these types of things without the consent of the Vice President?"

"The Chief of Staff could have acted independently,

but we don't know if he did or not in this case. That's what I need you to find out. I'll start by using Five Eyes to contact the Directors at our allies' agencies and see what they know. I'm giving the three of you an office in this building to analyze the information to try to determine a motive for Holler."

President Darin Cooper strolled the rose garden, his hands buried deep in his pockets. The fingers of his right hand moved restlessly in search of the coins they used to fidget with when he was deep in thought. Now as president, the coins were gone yet his thoughts were deeper, the consequences of any actions he took ever more serious. He knew what he had to do, but the exact path to implementation remained elusive.

The President returned to the Oval Office. While his personal Secret Service detail accompanied him inside, they immediately dispersed to take up positions outside the adjacent private dining room. The remainder of the staff had been sent away for lunch, an unprecedented move, but one that assured optimal privacy. President Cooper walked across the Oval Office and entered the President's personal dining room where he found the Vice President already present, sitting on a sofa watching a news channel on the small television set atop a buffet table.

Beside the television, a light buffet lunch had been laid out. The steward offered President Cooper wine. He refused and asked for iced tea instead.

"Leave the carafe too and seconds of whatever the Vice President is drinking. Then leave us in privacy please."

"What's troubling you Darin? You look as though you've seen a ghost."

"Fix your plate, then we'll talk." President Cooper wanted a few more minutes of life as it still was at this moment in time. There was no need to rush.

The two men rose from their seats and filled their plates with chicken, salmon, rice, asparagus salad, and tropical fruit. The Vice President talked about baseball and President Cooper pretended to listen, already distancing himself from his longtime friend.

They had met at Yale Law School where they first rose to power in student government and as co-editors of the *Yale Law Journal*. The pair had been a political force to reckon with ever since. But today all of that would change.

Returning to their seats the Vice President became more insistent, "All right Darin, let's have it. What's on your mind?"

"We have a very serious problem, you and I," he pointed at the VP and then himself.

53
WASHINGTON, DC

It wasn't the sort of thing any of them had in mind when they agreed to work for the country's intelligence services. Slowly and deliberately unseating dictators who slaughtered their own people with nerve gas and treated women like dogs was one thing, but seeking motives for the actions of a Vice President's Chief of Staff was awkward at best. How does one quietly investigate such a man? Your own countryman, a man ordinarily outside the bounds of your touch. There was no clear beginning and no ending that didn't involve controversy and the obnoxious din of politicians on the warpath, the crude weapons of politics raised above their heads, screeching about how their party, office, branch of government, and/or reputation had been slighted, blindly attacked, and illegally investigated. Yes, once the forces of politics got wind of what they were doing, statistics would be pulled out of thin air describing the irreparable harms done to law abiding, patriotic Americans by the intelligence community. Both the job and the task remained thankless.

"Where shall we begin?" Joe looked at Kate.

"Since we have the data from Alfie's computer, let's start by separating the smash and grab data ordered by Holler from the stuff supplied by Reynolds."

"Won't that be difficult to do?" Elliot asked.

"No, because we have a strategic asset in all of this."

A low buzzer sounded and Kate went to the control panel. The external camera's feed showed what she was waiting for. She buzzed the door open.

Two stern, gym-muscled men with closely cropped hair accompanied Alfie into the room.

"Thank you, gentlemen. You may wait outside."

Kate introduced Alfie to the team. Alfie limply shook each of their hands as he scratched his forearm through the sleeve of his t-shirt. His eyes were glassy and his cheeks sunken, he had aged ten years since Kate had first laid eyes upon him.

"How may I help?" Alfie asked sheepishly.

"You can start by showing us which of your files contain the data from the smash and grab you were originally hired to perform."

Alfie sat down at his computer as Kate turned on the projector and a recording device. A moment later Alfie's computer lit up on the room's large screen.

"Please talk through what you're doing as you do it in case we need to recreate it later."

Alfie walked them through the path to his files

including his passwords at various access points.

"Let's begin with some qualitative analysis of the stolen information. We need to classify it by subject, origin, people involved, and who/what the information might possibly harm. Alfie, was there any specific instructions about what info you were supposed to grab?"

"No, just U.S. data. That was all."

"Thank you Alfie, you may wait outside until we need you again. Elliot, please copy this data to our internal servers."

They worked for three weeks, while Alfie waited with his American overseers just outside the secured conference room door. The stolen material covered a wide range of issues, but slowly what the VP's Chief of Staff might have been looking for began to emerge. It began with a single telephone recording with a thickly accented man.

Andrew, it is so good of you to return my call so quickly.

President Assad, how are things in Damascus?

Well, I am above ground so that makes it a good day for me. However, there appears to be movement on the ground and I am beginning to feel a bit pinched. What do you plan to do about it?

Well, Mr. President, I'm working with a member of the intelligence community and a couple of Democrats on The Hill to see if we can get you some support. Our actions have to be covert so that slows us down a great deal. But I'm confident we will get the funding put into the budget, then the rest will be up to the intelligence operations leg. We've already pumped up the number of

HOLLY A. BELL

U.S. weapons on the black market so there will be plenty available to move in your direction.

Wasn't Charlie Wilson a Democrat? Be sure these Congressmen know not to fund the mujahidin this time. Wilson put those jihadists into power; you need to get them out of power.

Yes sir, I'll admit, I miss Sadaam Hussein. Like you, he understood the only way to keep stability in the region was to brutally keep the mujahidin locked away. Will you be reopening Mezzeh prison to maintain order in the future?

No, Mr. Holler, that will not be necessary. With your support, the mujahidin will all be dead.

54
WASHINGTON, DC

No one said anything as they waited impatiently, the sullen air recirculating through the room. Joe lightly drummed his fingers on the table. Elliot sat stone still, staring intently at his hands folded casually in his lap. Kate nervously rubbed her hands on her thighs, stopping only when the friction on her pant leg caused her palms to burn.

What seemed like an eternity later, there was a beep and the door of the conference room hissed open; fresh air rushed in along with PDD Lanser and Director Wolf. They did not appear to have good news.

"We've spoken with our colleagues at a number of foreign agencies about our suspicions that someone within the administration may have Syrian sympathies and may be offering them military aid. At first, no one claimed to know anything."

"Are you saying that changed?" Kate put her hands on the table in anticipation.

"The Chief at MI6 called back a few hours later and told us to talk to President Cooper."

"The President knows?" Kate was alarmed. "Is the President working behind the scenes to supply the Syrian military with arms?"

"I don't know. Why don't you ask him? We're all meeting with him at five o'clock under cover of a briefing on a major national security event."

Joe and Kate decided to spend the next two hours walking around the city and testing the worthiness of several park benches. Extended time alone with Joe had become a rarity and they talked easily as they strolled.

"So, tell me about Condor. Are you two an item now?

Kate smiled warmly, "Condor and I had a nice dinner, but agreed any sort of long distance cross-country inter-intelligence agency relationship was doomed to failure. We've parted as friends."

"And potential assets?"

Kate shrugged, "Isn't everyone a potential asset?" Joe smiled. Kate pulled back her sleeve and looked at her watch, "It's about time to head back."

The team rode together to the White House in silence as a second car carrying Lanser and Wolf trailed behind. They cleared security and were ushered into the Oval Office.

"The President is running about ten minutes behind schedule, may I offer you some coffee, tea, or water?"

"Nothing for me," Director Wolf responded, "Anyone else?" Her query was greeted by shaking heads and a chorus of muttered 'No, thank you'. The secretary excused herself.

The group milled around the Oval Office too nervous to sit down. Several vain attempts were made to admire the room's artwork, but they all had too much on their minds. Tomorrow, they likely wouldn't remember anything they saw in the room anyway.

The tension was broken when the President burst through a side door and offered his characteristically warm greetings to everyone in the room.

"So sorry I'm running late. It's the curse of being the last appointment of the day. I'd like to introduce you formally to a few members of my staff."

The President proceeded to introduce his Chief of Staff, the Deputy Chief of Staff, and the President's Chief Strategist. The members of the team introduced themselves to the President and his staff members.

"We were all just in a staff briefing, I thought I'd bring them along to hear what you have to say."

Director Wolf stood straight and tall while looking the President straight in the eyes, "I think it might be best if we began this conversation alone. Once I tell you what we wish to speak with you about, feel free to bring your staff back in if you believe it is appropriate."

For a moment, Kate thought she saw the President's smile falter before quickly relighting, "Well, if you insist. Gentlemen, why don't you wait outside and I'll call you in if it becomes necessary." He escorted the men from the room.

"Please have a seat." The President gestured toward the two sofas surrounding the coffee table in the middle of the room. He remained standing, but leaned against the *Resolute* desk and folded his arms in front of him, his brow furrowed. "What can I do for you?"

Director Wolf leaned toward the President, "Mr. President, it has come to our attention that what happened in Moscow may not be exactly as it seems. Is there anything you would like to share on that front?"

"Whatever do you mean?"

"Are you supplying arms to the Syrians, sir?"

"Of course not. You know my policy is too stay as far away from that mess as possible."

"Are you aware of which member of the White House staff has Syrian sympathies and is working to supply arms to Syrian government? We are and so, apparently, is MI6. We'd like to know more about your role in all of this."

55
THE OVAL OFFICE

The President unfurled his arms, walked to the door and opened it. He flashed a brilliant smile, "Gentlemen, it looks like I won't be needing you. Head on home, we'll talk in the morning." As the door clicked closed, the smile disappeared as quickly as it had materialized.

President Cooper slumped into his desk chair, reached for the pitcher of water on his desk and poured a glass. He raised his eyebrows as he motioned the pitcher toward his guests. They waved him off.

Just get on with it, Kate thought while at the same time knowing what might come next could not be rushed. As a flush began to wash over his face, the President brought the glass to his lips and drew in half the glass.

"The Vice President and I have been close friends for a very long time." He paused and took another pull from the glass. "To the best of my knowledge, neither he, nor I, have ever been involved in providing aid to Syria. You can imagine my surprise when the Chief of MI6 called me directly to inform me that they believed a member of the Vice President's staff and my Director of the National Security Agency were working to provide weapons to Syria."

Director Wolf moved to the edge of her seat, "Why didn't you come to me with this information?"

"I didn't know whom to trust. There was no way to know who Holler and Reynolds were working with inside the intelligence community and how many people were involved. MI6 didn't even know. It's why they called me directly." President Cooper paused to study his hands sorrowfully. "My heart was broken. What was the Vice President doing to me? I'll never really know, I suppose.

"The Vice President claims to have had no knowledge of the actions of Holler or Admiral Reynolds. I want to believe him, but it's not easy. The scenario I keep seeing in my mind is a conspiracy to make it look as though I was covertly supplying arms to the Syrians via the intelligence community while preaching a hands-off approach. Once that information came out, impeachment wouldn't be far behind. I'd be forced to resign and the Vice President would move into the Oval Office, perhaps bringing along Admiral Reynolds as his VP."

"Is it possible Holler was acting on his own?"

"I suppose, but why? What would he get out of it? The only reason to arm the Syrians and release the data is to weaken my presidency and increase their own relative power."

Kate turned sideways on the sofa, "So your motive for having Admiral Reynolds killed was not to ensure he didn't escape or do additional harm, it was to protect the Vice President. Reynolds was the only one who had something to gain by outing the involvement of the Office of the Vice President."

"I repeatedly told myself I didn't give the order just to protect the Vice President. That I would have done the same thing even if he didn't need protecting, but I'm not sure I would have."

Kate continued, "It was also the reason Reynolds needed to protect Alfie, wasn't it? He was the only one who could vouch for Holler being the one who hired Alfie.

The President nodded in the affirmative. "I just don't understand why Holler hired Alfie to infiltrate our allies' databases."

Lanser chimed in, "It's likely that Holler wanted to discover what was known about his operation and then have Alfie remove anything incriminating. We regularly monitor President Assad's phone lines, so we should have picked up the same phone conversation between Holler and Assad that MI6 recorded. But when we checked, we found that it had been scrubbed from the tape, most likely by Reynolds."

"Mmmm," was all President Cooper could manage.

Director Wolf stood and walked toward the President's desk, "We need to talk about next steps, Mr. President."

"I think the next steps are under control. Mr.

Holler and his Congressional co-conspirators have been put on notice that the jig is up. In exchange for my silence and now yours, they have agreed to cease their efforts and submit to round the clock surveillance. They will sign whatever waivers are required for the FBI to keep a close eye on their actions. The Congressmen will not seek re-election and Mr. Holler's tenure will end shortly.

"Next week, the Vice President's wife will become ill with a chronic, unspecified illness. The press will be chasing their tails trying to figure out exactly what malady she's been stricken with. That distraction will be beneficial to us. Two weeks later, the Vice President will be stricken with a case of strong family commitment and will chose to step down to care for his ailing wife. Mr. Holler will resign quietly at the same time.

"When asked about what we talked about today, I will be telling my staff it was the national security concerns associated with a personal issue involving a member of this staff and that they will know about it next week. That issue will be the health of the VP's wife. Are we clear?"

"Crystal, sir. I am sorry you had to carry this burden alone."

"It is imperative that this scandal never comes to light. The chaos that would follow is certain to inflict immeasurable damage to the country. Our entire system of government would be at risk."

"I can't say I disagree. We do have a few loose ends to tie up though."

"Such as."

"We're quite certain Reynolds had Faulkner killed. Reynolds believed Faulkner was the most likely person to be able to catch him, so he brought him inside and put him in charge of the internal investigation to keep him close. With the Joint Task Force tripping over themselves trying to pin the breach on each other's agencies, Reynolds figured there wouldn't be any danger of exposure coming from them.

"Reynolds received twice daily updates from Faulkner and when Faulkner began to move down the proper trail, Reynolds had him killed. It was then that Reynolds decided to personally hurry the process along in hopes of meeting his goals. Once his power position was improved, he could pin the breach on whomever he wanted and the information would stop, thereby looking like the perpetrator had been neutralized."

"What do you suggest we do about those who helped Reynolds."

"We need to make Faulkner's death appear completely unrelated to this case. Nothing more than a crime of opportunity in the middle of the night near a 24-hour deli in a high crime neighborhood. The Agency would be happy to help you with that."

"I'll leave that to you then. Thank you all for coming and for informing me that the Vice President's wife is ill and that there are no significant security threats associated with that revelation."

With that, the team filed out of the room each building a false memory of the evening in their minds.

56
PALMER, ALASKA

The day was bittersweet, as so many more seemed to be at this stage of Kate's life. It was her day of retirement from academic life, an early retirement, but a retirement nonetheless filled with the regrets and longings endings bring. There would be a mourning period, followed by being busier than ever in her more active role in her late husband's software company and as an Emeritus Professor quietly helping the intelligence community. With Zoe devotedly by her side, Kate took the last box of her belongings to the car before making their way to the campus cafeteria where the celebration of her retirement was already underway.

"There she is! We thought you were going to skip out on your own party." Kate's colleague hugged her fervently. "We're going to miss you so much. Speech?" The room erupted in applause and calls of

'Speech! Speech!'.

"I don't really know what to say. I'm going to miss this place terribly, maybe not the students with failing grades who ask for extra credit even after the semester has ended," her colleagues murmured agreement about such students, "but certainly all of you."

"After my husband Max was killed and I went through my kidnapping ordeal, you all provided a foundation for me, a sense of routine and normalcy that I desperately needed during and after that time. You've each in your own way made me stronger, more resilient and able to move forward with my life and toward new goals. For that, I thank all of you."

The assembled burst into applause and lined up for hugs. Tears streamed down Kate's face as Zoe lovingly leaned against Kate's leg in a supportive embrace. The hugging complete, Kate dried her eyes as cake was served. With her first bite of buttercream frosted chocolate cake she started her life anew.

Events from the previous years of her life were pushed farther away and acceptance of more recent adventures washed over her. She didn't necessarily agree with the way the President had handled the situation, but she empathized. Even a President can be a pawn in someone else's game. Kate was learning to do what any seasoned intelligence officer would do, keep your head down, perform your role to the best of your ability, and then preserve the secrets whether you like it or not.

57
WASHINGTON, DC

Thirty years later.

"This is recording 87, day 3, of the CIA's History Center Classified Dark Web Oral History Project. Please state your name and affiliation at the time of employment."

"My name is Dr. Olivia Ivanov and I was a Senior Psychologist for the Central Intelligence Agency."

"Thank you, Dr. Ivanov. You've told us the story of Dr. Kate Adam's Dark Web Mission, as you know it. What exactly was your role in the project?"

"I was responsible for the post mission counseling of Dr. Adams. It was in those sessions that I was told the mission story I shared with you earlier."

"And why was counseling ordered for Dr. Adams?"

"It is routine after an agent has their first Agency mission kill, that we ask them to dialogue about the experience with an Agency counselor."

"Tell me more about your roll after a first kill situation."

"Since we have a diverse group of agents, we have a wide range of reactions to a first kill. My job is to make sure they're moving through the coping process in a healthy way."

"What is that coping process?"

"It's different based on the individual. Some go through a classic mourning process and exhibit the five stages of grief: denial, anger, bargaining, depression, and acceptance. Others have more of a post-traumatic stress response and we have to work with them to develop the tools to cope with nightmares, insomnia, flashbacks, anxiety, and triggering situations in a healthy way to minimize symptoms before they become longer-term problems."

"But Dr. Adam's situation was somewhat unique. Can you tell us about that."

"Yes, Dr. Adam's had been kidnapped during a previous mission. In an attempt to avoid being taken, Dr. Adams had killed one of her abductors in a very intimate manner."

"She killed him with a hatchet to the head, correct?"

"She did. That was a very up close and personal kill, but because it was self-defense and not an ordered kill, she was never given any formal, what we call, 'out-kill therapy'."

"Yet, she had some unofficial help, didn't she?"

"Yes, my husband Joe Bell, who was a field-based Agency psychologist, had been assigned to the same Alaska mission that Dr. Adams was unintentionally involved in. It was that mission which had led to her kidnapping. Joe always felt a strong bond of friendship with and responsibility for Dr. Adams after their shared experience. Afterwards, he unofficially kept an eye on her emotional well-being and worked with her closely on other missions."

"And you and your husband had talked about Dr. Adams before she was sent to you, is that correct?"

"Joe only discussed her in generic terms and he never shared her name, but we had talked about her anonymously."

"Did Dr. Adams have any idea you were Joe's wife?"

"No, Dr. Adams chose not to know about Joe's personal life. I think she had some sense that she was always one of his projects, official or not." Dr. Ivanov laughed lightly, "In fact, after Blackpool I think she assumed Joe was gay after seeing him with Elliot Poe. But Elliot alone was gay. Joe just always felt very comfortable with Elliot and they worked together a lot, so it's natural that she might suspect they were a couple."

"Did Joe have any concerns about Dr. Adams?"

"Yes, he believed she had suffered some untreated post-traumatic stress from her kidnapping, but she still seemed to be functioning through her anxiety. He'd observed that she had formed a propensity to isolate, avoid relationships, and reported nightmares. There were also panic attacks, especially when she felt out of control of a situation, but they seemed short-lived when they occurred and Dr. Adams had developed some of her own coping techniques to deal with them. He described her as having 'rational anxiety'.

"Meaning what?"

"Meaning that she was never completely out of control of herself. When Dr. Adams would have a panic attack, for example, she always knew what was happening to herself and began a conscious series of steps to relieve her anxiety. Really, that's what we would have taught her to do anyway. Yet, Joe always believed she hadn't quite found the way to set it all aside and get on with her life."

"When did you finally realize he was talking about Dr. Adams?"

"After Dr. Adams was sent to me for counseling, she told me about her history with the Agency and I was able to put two and two together."

"Did your husband ever know you worked with her?"

"No, I had to maintain confidentiality. I never told him or even hinted that I had met and worked with her. Yet, it worked out well because Joe continued to give me updates on his anonymous Agency friend, which always gave me some insight into how she was doing."

"How was Dr. Adams coping over the time you worked with her?"

Dr. Ivanov smiled at the memory, "At first I thought she was doing too well."

"That's good news, isn't it?"

"Not usually. Lack of symptoms after such an event is usually a sign of serious psychological trouble, but not in this case."

"How many times did you meet with her, and what did you discuss?"

"We met eight times. During the first meeting, we talked about her experience with the Agency and I knew right away who she was, but when I asked about symptoms like panic attacks, which I know she's had in the past, she said they had gone away."

"Isn't that unusual? Wouldn't you expect her anxiety to be more pronounced after the Dark Web Mission?"

"Usually, but in this case the mission and her ordered assassination of Admiral Reynolds actually returned her sense of control."

"In what way?"

"Dr. Adams admitted she was suffering from trauma after her kidnapping, but she regained her confidence and sense of control over her own destiny during the Dark Web Mission. She had been unable to take out the perpetrators during her last mission, which weighed on her psyche. Being able to do so this time, helped give her the closure she needed. Granted, it hardened her a bit, but that's a process most in this business go through. Except..." Dr. Ivonov's voice trailed off.

"Except what?"

"Though Dr. Adams never articulated it, I realized that if she was ever going to have a healthy relationship with anyone again and fully move forward, she was going to have to resolve her feelings about Operations Officer Bradman Owen Oakley and the betrayal she felt following her kidnapping in Alaska."

ABOUT THE AUTHOR

Holly A. Bell was born and raised in Beaver Dam, WI. She moved across several states during her 17-year career in business administration before settling in the Mat-Su Valley of Alaska where she became a professor and administrator at the University of Alaska Anchorage. Her writing has appeared in the Wall Street Journal, New York Times, CNBC, American Banker, The Journal of Investing, and notable academic publications. With degrees in economics, foreign policy, and business administration, Dr. Bell enjoys writing novels that reside at the intersection of these disciplines. You may follow her on Twitter @HollyBell8 or on facebook.com/AuthorHollyABell

CPSIA information can be obtained
at www.ICGtesting.com
Printed in the USA
BVHW031831280222
630257BV00005B/36